Bendy ... His
father ... a living
by copy... yet he was
apprentic... ...master printer,
whom he ... k he admired. His
brothers wo... ...g to stop books being
printed in hun... ...endy knew they were plot-
ting to keep the ... of Unicorn water-marked paper
from the printers.

What should he do? Who was in the right in this
quarrel? These were questions Bendy had to work out
for himself.

At the same time there came a long and dangerous
search for the remainder of a manuscript of wonderful
stories about King Arthur and his distant days of
chivalry, which had been written by a knight called
Thomas Malory as he lay disgraced in prison.

The special value of this book, apart from the excitement of the story, is that the author is showing us life in
London exactly as it was lived in the fifteenth century.
She makes it vivid and interesting, and every intelligent
boy and girl of eleven or over will enjoy it.

Cynthia Harnett studied at the Chelsea School of Art
and intended to be a painter, but her brother encour-
aged her to write and she began by writing short
stories. Then after the war she started writing historical
novels, and won the Carnegie Medal for *The Wool-
Pack*. Her artistic training was not wasted, for she did
her own illustrations. She died in 1981.

They were visible only for a few seconds

* * *

Other books by Cynthia Harnett

THE GREAT HOUSE
THE WOOL-PACK

THE
LOAD OF UNICORN

WRITTEN AND ILLUSTRATED BY

CYNTHIA HARNETT

PUFFIN BOOKS

Puffin Books, Penguin Books Ltd, Harmondsworth, Middlesex, England
Viking Penguin Inc., 40 West 23rd Street, New York, New York 10010, U.S.A.
Penguin Books Australia Ltd, Ringwood, Victoria, Australia
Penguin Books Canada Limited, 2801 John Street, Markham, Ontario, Canada L3R 1B4
Penguin Books (N.Z.) Ltd, 182–190 Wairau Road, Auckland 10, New Zealand

—

First published by Methuen 1959
Published in Puffin Books 1966
Reprinted 1971, 1976, 1978, 1986

—

—

Printed and bound in Great Britain by
Cox & Wyman Ltd, Reading
Set in Monotype Bembo

Contents

1	The Scrivener's Shop	7
2	'Master Gaston'	17
3	The Table in Paul's	30
4	Money from the Coffer	41
5	Ten Groats Each	52
6	Westminster	64
7	The Long-Boat by the South Bank	83
8	The Honest Pirate	98
9	A Box on The Ear	109
10	Meet Me in the Cloister	125
11	The Printing House	134
12	The Valiant Soldier	152
13	By All Means Let Him Go	166
14	A Small Town on the Avon	175
15	Newbold Revel	192
16	Open to the Sky	205
17	The Black Abbot	216
18	Challenge to the Crowing Cock	226
	Postscript	242

CHAPTER I

The Scrivener's Shop

THE rain was coming down in torrents when Bendy reached the back door. He could hear voices inside and he paused on the step to reckon his chances of getting upstairs unnoticed. Contrary to orders he had gone off to school without the cloak or galoshes he was supposed to wear in bad weather. Cloaks and galoshes were silly considering that he had such a short way to go – just along Paternoster Row, under the arch into Paul's Alley, and then straight through the cathedral itself to St Paul's Grammar School, less than a bowshot away.

Though the overhanging houses gave some shelter, the cobbled street was a swirling river of London muck, and he had to admit that he was soaked to the knees with filth. He would get a scolding from old Mother Collin and possibly a threat of the rolling-pin. But Mother Collin was fat and slow-moving. It was his half-brother Matthew whom he feared. If Matthew caught him before he had stripped off his stinking hose it would probably mean a beating.

He set his ear to the crack of the door and listened. That was Matthew's voice for certain, but whom was he talking to? If only it was his father there might be a chance of getting off lightly. But he knew that his father was still in the cathedral; he had seen him just now, busily writing at his table.

Cautiously he opened the door a bare inch. The room inside was half kitchen, half living-room. At one end old Mother Collin stood by the fire, lifting a cauldron on to a pot-hook. He could slip past her; she was as deaf as a post. But at the other end Matthew, tall and gaunt with greying hair, was standing close to the bottom of the stairs. He was deep in talk with Tom Twist, the pedlar, a thin, sharp-nosed fellow who often appeared in Paternoster Row. They were probably talking business, for Tom Twist was useful. Not only did he travel round the fairs and markets of the country with a pack full of cheap little books, written out by hand upstairs in the scribes' room by Matthew's copyist, but he often brought a load of paper, for which Matthew paid him immediately. There was something funny about the paper; Bendy had a shrewd suspicion that it was concerned with the King's Customs. But none of that mattered now. The one important question was whether or not to make a dash for the stairs? Though Matthew's back was turned, Tom Twist would be bound to see him. Tom Twist had a merry chuckle, but was he to be trusted?

Bendy hesitated. Should he go round to the front and slip in by the shop door in Paternoster Row, under the hanging signboard of the Crowing Cock? It was possible that Cornelius, his second half-brother, might have closed the shutters because of the storm and gone upstairs to the scribes' room; in that case the coast would be clear, and he could reach the stairs round the far side of the big dining-table, with his legs well hidden. But on the whole it was hardly worth the risk. He was so wet that he was shivering. He might as well get it over.

He pushed the door open just enough to squeeze through and, keeping back against the wall, began to work his way round the edge of the room. Matthew was intent upon Tom Twist. With any luck he might slip past unnoticed.

They were talking in low voices; even Tom Twist's Cockney twang was muffled, though Bendy caught the words 'a load of *Unicorn* on the *Madalena*'. So it *was* about paper. '*Unicorn*' was paper with a Unicorn water-mark. Lots of it came to the Crowing Cock.

A Unicorn water mark

Matthew did not hear so clearly. 'A load of *what*?' he whispered back. 'You can speak up, man; there's none to hear.'

The pedlar raised his voice, jabbing at Matthew with a sharp finger to drive home his point. 'A load of *Unicorn*. 'Tis on the *Madalena* and she's a-mucking. 'Tis yours on the usual terms.'

'The place is weighed down with *Unicorn*,' growled Matthew. 'It is soft paper; the quill splutters on it.'

Twist shrugged his shoulders. 'As you will. Maybe it would serve in a press. The Red Pale might favour it.'

Matthew swore under his breath. 'A pest on you, man; aren't I a good customer? Well, bring it if you must. I care not what becomes of it so long as the Red Pale gets it not.'

9

He half turned away and Bendy edged a few steps nearer. He too had an interest in this paper business. Already the loft where he slept was full to the rafters with stocks of paper, and Cornelius had said in his hearing that the timbers would not stand much more.

The pedlar became affable again. 'Maybe I can store it for you. There's a barn at – you know where. So long as I have your money, sir. The *Madalena* must be cleared.'

Matthew began to fumble in his gown. This was Bendy's chance. With three swift steps he had almost reached the bottom of the stairs when to his dismay he heard footsteps coming down. His heart sank. If it was Cornelius then all was over with him, for though Cornelius was less of a tyrant than Matthew, the two always worked together.

Then, to his relief, he saw that it was not Cornelius but Humphrey, a boy near his own age who worked in the scribes' room, serving out ink and paper, collecting the written sheets, and fetching and carrying at Matthew's will. He and Humphrey had been together in the Song School at Paul's, but when Bendy's voice broke his father sent him on to the Grammar School, greatly to the annoyance of his half-brothers, who would have found him useful at the Crowing Cock. So Humphrey got the job and did well out of it, for his widowed mother had very blue eyes and an appealing way of looking at Matthew. Bendy had little use for Humphrey; he was sly and smug; but at least Humphrey would not give him away.

Humphrey carried a load of slim paper books for the pedlar's pack. He stopped dead on the bottom step, grinning at Bendy and making a grimace, as though the stink were overwhelming. Bendy grimaced back. Surely the fool could see that he was blocking the way. Exasperated, he crept close and gave him a sharp pinch.

Humphrey let out a yell. 'Bendy, you clown!' he cried. 'O-oh, you are dirty. *Just look at your legs.*'

He had almost reached the bottom of the stairs

It was deliberate and Bendy could have killed him. But that would have to wait. He shoved Humphrey aside and made a dive for the stairs. He was only two steps up when Matthew halted him.

'Benedict!'

When Matthew used his full name it was serious. Groaning to himself, Bendy went down again.

His half-brother was scowling. 'Why aren't you at school?'

That was easy. ''Tis my respite hour, sir. I read the Lesson.'

'What lesson? What are you doing here, skulking about eavesdropping?'

Bendy ignored the last part. ' 'Twas my turn to read the Lesson at Vespers, sir. Then I came straight home.' Surely even Matthew must know that the boy who read a Lesson at Vespers in the Cathedral was entitled to the rest of the day for himself. It was splendid that he should be attacked where he was on such sure ground. But his triumph was short-lived. Matthew saw his legs.

'And so you come in dripping like a cess-pit. Upon my soul if I did not fear to soil my hands I'd beat you here and now. Strip off your hose, boy. Go on! Strip them at once.'

Bendy hesitated; but as Matthew still glared he did as he was bid, fumbling with cold fingers at the points that tied up his hose, while Humphrey, safely shielded by Matthew and the pedlar, grinned and made faces at him.

Matthew threw him a towel from the kitchen line. 'Here's a clout to gird yourself. Now get you to the pump.'

Angry and humiliated Bendy wrapped the towel round his bare legs. The pump was out in the cold yard. He brushed past Humphrey hissing savagely, 'Mark you well, I'll *flay* you for this.'

When he got back, his teeth chattering, Matthew and Tom Twist were counting the little books. Old Mother Collin ladled a mugful of broth from the cauldron and held it out to him, but he shook his head. All he wanted was to get away to his own loft.

The tiny stairs were steep and twisting. He dragged himself up wearily and emerged into the parlour, the best room of the house, reserved for company. The only sign of use was a table by the window with Cornelius' writing things on it, and a half-finished page of parchment, beautifully penned. Bendy

She ladled a mugful of broth

stopped to look at the first line – '*In the name of God and on this first day of June in the year of our Lord* 1482 –'. So it was actually written today. Cornelius, plump and easy-going, loved fine work; he took after his father. But he was under Matthew's thumb and gave most of his time to Matthew's scheme of producing quantities of small books to sell at a cheap price.

At the far end of the parlour a door led into the great chamber, a bedroom with a window overlooking Paternoster Row. On a sudden impulse Bendy pattered across and stood in the doorway. This had been his mother's room and he had hardly set foot in it since she died. Now he stood looking round with a sort of ache at the base of his throat. The big bed was there just the same; so was the coffer at the foot of it where the money was kept. But the hooks where her gowns used to hang were empty. Only his father's old furred bed-robe lay flung across the foot of the bed. Seeing it lying there in this empty room, Bendy suddenly understood why his father chose to stay out of the house all day.

When his mother was alive it had been a happy home. His father was master, but it was his mother who ruled, a rule of smiles and kind words. Even Matthew and Cornelius seemed different then. Though she had been younger than her stepsons

they called her 'madam' and served her and their father willingly. Now everything was changed. The Masters Matthew and Cornelius Goodrich were the scriveners of the Crowing Cock. Their father spent his days in the Cathedral at one of the tables set up in the nave by the Dean and Chapter where picked members of the Scriveners' Guild sat to help citizens who could neither read nor write.

As he turned to go, he noticed something blue hanging behind the door. It was his mother's old blue woollen cloak, the one she had worn every winter day. He caught his breath; he had often been wrapped in it when he was small. On a sudden impulse he unhooked it and threw it round him. He was so cold that he hugged himself, carefully holding up the ends as he mounted the next set of stairs.

The second floor was the scribes' room – the 'scriptorium' as Matthew liked to call it. The stairway, which emerged at one corner, was screened off with a heavy curtain to keep out the draught. Bendy paused on the top step and peeped through a chink into the busy room.

At long trestle desks sat the scribes, more than a score of them. For the most part they were old men or feeble creatures, half crippled. The only qualification was that they could write. Matthew paid them little and bullied them with his constant demand that they should 'hasten'. They could not refuse, for they had no chance of work elsewhere.

At the far end, near the window, sat Cornelius, dictating from a book open on a lectern, while Humphrey sorted loose paper on the floor. This was the way they worked in the scriptorium of a monastery, Matthew declared, with one monk dictating and the rest writing it down. Bendy had his doubts about it. At Paul's he saw plenty of great books which had been penned by monks; they were without errors and showed no signs of haste.

Cornelius was reading slowly and carefully – very different, so Bendy thought, from Matthew's impatient way. The book was the story of Chanticleer from the *Canterbury Tales*. Bendy was certain that every scribe in the room must know it by heart. As soon as it was finished they would take fresh paper and begin all over again. Twenty copies at a time five times over would make a hundred copies, and a hundred copies of Chanticleer made good money at country markets.

As he peeped Bendy stifled a sigh. He loved books and read every one he could lay hands on, provided it was in English. But to copy them, day after day, till hands ached and the lines danced on the page – He hoped above everything that he would not have to become a scrivener.

Suddenly he heard a footstep on the stairs. That would be Matthew, coming up to take over the master copy from Cornelius. He liked to do the dictating himself. Cornelius, he said, was too slow.

The scribes heard it too. There was an uneasy stir along the benches. Bendy did not wait for more. In a corner a steep ladder led up to a trapdoor in the roof. He gathered the blue cloak tightly round him and was up it in a couple of seconds. With the skill of long practice he closed the trapdoor noiselessly behind him and sank back thankfully on the floor of his loft.

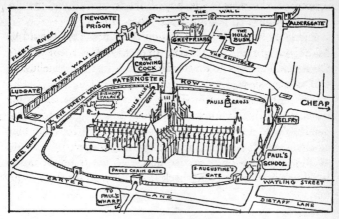

St Paul's Cathedral

CHAPTER 2

'Master Gaston'

THOUGH there was nothing overhead except rafters and tiles, to Bendy the loft was a cosy place. The steep roof made it almost like a cave, the walls formed by bales of paper packed along the sides. The main chimney of the house ran up through it and on a cold night he could drag his bed close to the warm bricks. But above all he loved it because he shared it with nobody. Out of all the household, only he and his father had rooms to themselves.

The window was in the gable end, closed only by a hinged lattice of wooden slats. Bendy enjoyed sticking his head out and finding himself suspended almost half-way across Paternoster Row, with the attic window of the house opposite so near that he could toss apples backwards and forwards with the boy who lived there.

He went to the window now and looked down. It was still raining and the street was deserted. Then he heard the clatter of a horse slipping about on wet cobbles. He could not see it, for it was underneath him, hidden by the jutting house; but he guessed that Tom Twist was departing. Presently, with the curve of the road, he emerged into view, leading his old white pack-horse with a couple of casks lashed to its back – that was how Matthew packed his books. The pedlar wore his tattered Lion cloak. Tom Twist was known everywhere by his cloak.

A lion rampant still showed

It had once been the surcoat of a knight and in spite of a dip in dyers' dregs a fine lion rampant with two tails still showed clearly through the muddy brown.

Bendy wondered idly where they were going and what was afoot. It was plain that Matthew's rage downstairs was largely because he thought that his conversation with Tom Twist had been overheard. Only afterwards had he noticed Bendy's hose. What *had* they been saying? Something about the *Madalena*;

the *Madalena* was obviously a ship carrying paper. The *Madalena* was 'a-mucking'; what that meant he had not the faintest idea. But the puzzling part was why Matthew wanted so much paper. There was enough up here in the loft to last the twenty scribes for years. And why should it all be so secret?

He remained staring at the rain long after Twist had vanished. The boys who read the Lessons at Vespers really earned their reward. It took days and days to become word perfect in the Latin. Then they had first to read it over in private to the Chancellor himself, and finally to stand up publicly in the Cathedral, knowing that for one single mistake they could get seven strokes of the cane. And now, having got through it safely, here he was, on a soaking wet afternoon, virtually shut up by himself.

He looked across at the opposite window, hoping that his friend Peterkin might have come home. Peterkin did not stay late at Paul's. He was only a poor Almonry boy in the Song School, who received his keep and a few simple lessons in return for singing in the choir.

As there was no sign of life across the way Bendy whistled. Nobody answered but he saw a shadow move and an old woman came to the window. It was Peterkin's grandmother. She was blind.

'Has Peterkin come from school yet?' he called.

'From school? Why, long since, young master. He's gone down to the river. He's working nowadays for a waterman below Bridge. Didn't you know?'

Forgetting that she could not see him Bendy shook his head. 'Will he be long?'

'I've no notion, master. He comes and goes at all hours, as oft as not in the middle of the night. But, praise be to God, he earns money, and 'tis well, for my beads do not bring in enough to keep us. Shall he call you if he comes?'

Bendy thanked her. He always felt a little ashamed with Peterkin and his grandmother because he was well off and they were so very poor. They lived in the attic by the charity of the man who owned the shop below. He was a maker of Paternoster beads – some people called them rosaries. In his workshop was a small lathe where all sorts of beads were shaped and polished, and the old blind woman sat all day threading them into strings, always the right number of beads and always neatly spaced and knotted.

He watched the rain for another minute after she had gone.

Paternoster beads

On the whole he envied Peterkin. Life on the river was much more exciting than a scrivener's shop in Paternoster Row. Boys at school brought all sorts of stories. A French ship had been raided in the night and casks of wine thrown overboard to float down on the tide; but by the morning they had all vanished. Ships came into port telling how they had been boarded by pirates in the Channel. And, of course, though King Edward the Fourth was adored by the people of London, it wasn't much more than ten years since the Wars of the

Roses, and there were whispers that the Lancastrian cause wasn't dead yet. There was still a Lancastrian prince, Henry Tudor, over in Brittany.

He shivered. He'd forgotten his bare legs. He turned away from the window and knelt by the old wooden chest where his clothes were kept. From deep down at the bottom he unearthed his two most secret treasures, and with them he made a dive for his bed, wriggling under the old sheepskin that covered it. There was still enough fleece on it to warm his cold legs. With the blue cloak round his shoulders he settled down to enjoy himself.

The first treasure was a small book bound in vellum. It was a Prymer, a prayer-book, in Latin, containing the Little Office of Our Lady, the penitential psalms, and all the other usual things. What made it so precious was that it was *printed*. To possess a printed Prymer was a feather in his cap at school. His father had given it to him on St Benedict's day, the feast of his name saint, his patron. With it he had received a whispered warning that he had better not show it to his brothers. Bendy did not need the warning. The very mention of the word *printing* threw Matthew into a rage. Bendy could still remember the storm there had been a year or two back when Caxton, the Westminster printer, had produced printed copies of the *Canterbury Tales*.

He soon laid the Prymer aside and took up the second treasure, a roll of papers, tied round with a tagged leather lace. There were many sheets covered with handwriting, but they were all sizes and few of them seemed to match. The roll was a collection of stories of King Arthur and his Knights of the Round Table, and Bendy knew them almost by heart. True that many had no beginning or no ending and some were no more than an odd page or two. But he did not mind; he filled in the missing bits out of his head. He loved stories and devoured all the ones that were written in the Crowing Cock, particularly any about adventure and romance. But these of King Arthur were the best of all.

The last story was actually complete -- the one that told about the death of Arthur, and how his great sword Excalibur was thrown into the mere, and how a barge rowed by three queens came to carry him away. On the last page of all there was a message from the knight who wrote the stories. He said his name was Sir Thomas Malory and he asked everyone who read the book to pray for his 'good deliverance'. It sounded as if he was a prisoner, and Bendy took the message quite seriously. He added the name of Sir Thomas Malory to his night prayers, and sometimes, in Paul's, he remembered to light a taper for him.

He wished that he could show the roll to his father, but he would be asked where he got it and he dared not say; for the truth was that he had won it at dice, gambling in an alehouse. He had been persuaded once to go home with Will Soper, a boy at school whose father kept the HOLLY BUSH near Newgate. They had diced in the yard at the back and there had been plenty of strong drink. Bendy could not remember all that had happened, but he had come away lacking the pence from his pocket but with this roll tucked under his arm.

Though all this had to be kept secret for fear of a beating, it did not prevent him from revelling in the stories, and he settled down under the sheepskin to read how Sir Lancelot smote down more than thirty knights at the great tournament that King Arthur held at Winchester.

He was deep in it when he heard a whistle across the street. He threw back his cover and pattered to the window.

Peterkin was leaning out of the attic opposite, his red hair standing out from under the kerchief knotted round his head.

'Gammer said you called. How comes it that you're home at this hour?'

'I read the Lesson,' said Bendy briefly. 'I thought we might go down to the river; there are the water sports on Saturday. But of course I didn't know of your new work. You've been precious mum about it.'

Peterkin looked sheepish. 'I was told to keep my mouth shut. I get paid for going where I'm wanted whatever time it is. You see, my voice is breaking. I'll soon be out of the choir and I've got to earn money because of –' He tossed his head backward in the direction of his grandmother.

Bendy nodded. 'She said the beads weren't enough. You're lucky to get with a waterman. Can I come with you sometimes?'

'No,' said Peterkin forcefully, and looked down into the street as though to change the subject. 'What's afoot with you? Your shop is shuttered.'

One of the advantages of this hob-nobbing was that Peterkin could see the front of the Crowing Cock, and sometimes even report what was going on in the scribes' room.

'It's just the rain, I think. It was soaking when I came in and there was a to-do about my hose. I was outlawed up here.'

'There's someone knocking at the door.' Peterkin leaned farther out. 'I can't see who it is. He looks like a fine gentleman. Ah! Mother Collin has opened to him. *They* are both in the scribes' room.'

Bendy wasn't really interested. It was only someone to see Matthew. He wanted to hear more about the river; Peterkin's secrecy whetted his appetite. He had put one or two direct questions without getting much by way of an answer when Matthew's voice bawled at him from downstairs.

'Bendy, where are you? Come down at once.'

Afraid lest his half-brother should mount the ladder, Bendy lifted the trap-door and peered down.

'Why are you wasting your time up there? Some gentleman or other below stairs is asking for my father. Dress yourself quickly and take him to Paul's.'

Muttering to himself Bendy pulled on a pair of hose. It made him angry when Matthew spoke of '*my* father' as if he were not Bendy's father too. Hurriedly he bundled Sir Thomas Malory and the Prymer and the blue cloak all together into the coffer and banged down the lid.

Matthew was waiting at the foot of the ladder. 'Are you clean, boy? The gentleman is in the shop. Goodwife Collin says his name is Gaston and he is a mercer. Praise be to Heaven it is my father he wants, not me; I am busy.' As he brushed through the curtain into the scribes' room he looked back – 'and mind you take your cloak and galoshes this time.'

Glad to get away at any cost Bendy hurried down the stairs, pausing only in the kitchen to take the cloak and the wooden-soled clogs with leather tops which Mother Collin had ready for him.

He found the visitor alone in the shop examining a fine

The visitor alone in the shop

Psalter penned by his father years ago – one which had capital letters painted by the limner who used to do the illuminating for the Crowing Cock. Bendy stared. All the stranger's clothes were rich, though they were clearly far from new and somehow looked a little odd. His high boots of soft leather were heavily embroidered. No one in London wore embroidered boots. Perhaps he wasn't English. Gaston might easily be a foreign name.

The stranger glanced round. He was an elderly man but his eyes looked young and bright.

'Your pardon,' he said with an English voice. 'I was so relishing this fine work that I did not see you. You are to lead me to Master Goodrich? I think the rain has ceased.'

As Bendy closed the shop door behind them he heard a soft whistle overhead. Thinking it must be Peterkin he stepped out into the street to look up and saw not Peterkin but Humphrey hanging out of the window, a silly grin on his face.

'*Don't forget your cloak and galoshes,*' he chanted mockingly.

Bendy snorted angrily. The sly dog was making game of him. Master Gaston glanced round smiling.

''Tis wise to have cloak and galoshes,' he said pleasantly. 'I doubt if the storm is finished yet. You are Master Goodrich's apprentice?'

Swallowing his wrath, Bendy said that he was Master Goodrich's son. Master Gaston looked surprised.

'I was told that he had sons but I thought they were much older. It was my good friend Robert Tate, the mercer, who sent me to your father.'

Bendy looked at him curiously. Master Tate was a very great man, a sheriff of the City. This Master Gaston must be a person of importance.

'You are a mercer, sir,' he ventured.

'Yes, I'm of the Mercers' Company, and a Merchant Venturer, though I do not trade nowadays.'

A Merchant Venturer. Bendy looked at him with awe. Merchant Venturers did business with distant lands. Perhaps he had sailed the seas. He decided to ask him.

Master Gaston laughed. 'I've crossed the Channel, if that is good enough. Most of my life has been spent in Bruges, at the Domus Anglorum – you've heard of the English House in Bruges? It is a sort of college where all the English merchants live together – very much as the German merchants of the Hanseatic League live in the Steelyard here in London.'

Bendy nodded. Though he'd never heard of the Domus Anglorum everyone knew the Steelyard, down on the river. The Hanse merchants claimed special privileges for their ships and got themselves so well hated for it that sometimes they were almost besieged behind their high walls.

'What did you do there, sir?'

'Do? Why, we traded; bought and sold almost anything that could be carried on a ship. I went there when I was but just finished with my apprenticeship and for the last years I was Governor of the Domus Anglorum; so you see I've had a life-time of it.' As a sudden flash of lightning lit up the dark clouds behind Paul's spire he pulled his cloak round him. 'I said we

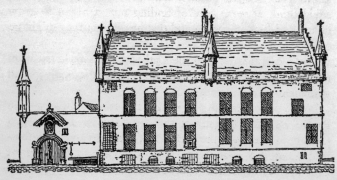

The Domus Anglorum

had not finished with the storm. Here comes the rain. Quick, boy! Run!'

They were only a few yards from the stone gatehouse at the entrance to Paul's Alley. As the rain teemed down both of them ran, and flung themselves into the shelter of the archway, the older man puffing breathlessly. It was pitch dark until another flash of lightning lit up everything. Master Gaston hastily crossed himself.

'God send that Paul's spire doesn't catch light again. It did, you know, when I was young. A priest from St Mary-le-Bow climbed up and dowsed the flames with vinegar – a valiant fellow; he should have been dubbed knight for it, though 'tis not done to knight a priest. It was just after I went to Bruges; I was not much more than your age.'

'Did you never come back to England, sir?'

'Come back? Of course I came back. Bruges is not the Indies. It was my task to arrange treaties for the King's Grace with the Duke of Burgundy, so I was back and forth many times.'

Bendy stared through the darkness. The King; the Duke of Burgundy; Master Gaston *was* a great man. He longed to know what was the business with his father, but before he could think of some way of finding out, it began to grow lighter and his companion said that he thought they might go on.

Paul's Alley, leading to the Cathedral, was sheltered from the rain. Master Gaston pottered along slowly, looking around with an air of enjoyment.

'We Londoners do not realize the treasure we have in Paul's,' he said, stopping at the corner of the little Pardon Cloister to peer up at the network of pinnacles and flying buttresses outlined against the sky. 'I have seen many great churches but none that is finer. Did you know that it is the longest cathedral in the world?'

Bendy, who spent every day at Paul's, had never stopped to think about it. The longest in the world! That was something to be proud of. As they pushed open the north door, he looked at the great majestic Norman nave with new eyes.

As usual it was full of people: country folks with bundles and babies sitting on the floor to rest before starting their tramp home; and Londoners meeting each other to walk up and down and talk business, or engaging servants who waited by a certain pillar to be hired, or consulting lawyers by another pillar, or, as Bendy himself did every day, just using it as a short cut. There was a steady hum of voices all round him, but he noticed how the sound was carried up and lost in the high vaulted roof.

As they threaded their way through the crowds he halted and looked from end to end. *The longest cathedral in the world.* It was, he supposed, because of the great length that the noise of all this bustle scarcely penetrated to the choir and sanctuary, like another church beyond the rood-screen, where all the masses and prayers were said.

At the bottom of the nave stood the row of tables where the scribes sat. Bendy caught a glimpse of his father's silvery head beneath a signboard which read JOHN GOODRICH, SCRIVENER. Feeling pleasantly important he led the way.

His father was copying a letter for an old woman in a widow's wimple who sat on a stool beside him. Bendy dutifully waited for him to look up.

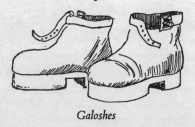

Galoshes

'Sir,' he began; 'Matthew bade me bring this gentleman to you. His name is Master Gaston and he is a mercer.'

John Goodrich peered over his spectacles. 'Gaston?' he said as though it meant nothing to him. 'Master *Gaston*?'

The mercer stepped forward with a smile.

'Not *Gaston*, sir,' he said. 'Your son has heard wrongly. It is *Caxton*, by your leave: William Caxton of Westminster.'

CHAPTER 3

The Table in Paul's

BENDY could hardly believe his ears. Surely this could not be
Caxton the printer; the man whose very name threw Matthew
into a storm of rage? Why, it was Matthew himself who had
sent Bendy to take charge of him. *This* Caxton was a mercer.
In all the talk about Bruges and the Merchant Venturers, and
the tasks for the King, there had not been a single word about
printing. How could it possibly fit in?

He watched his father shake hands warmly while Master
Caxton explained again that he had been sent by Master Tate,
the sheriff, because he needed advice and help.

'I am honoured, sir,' cried John Goodrich. 'Come sit down
and tell me what I can do for you.' He suddenly remembered

the poor widow. 'Ah, mistress, your pardon; I have your letter to finish. Stay! Here is my son; he can copy it for you. He writes a good court hand and I can look it over to see that he has made no mistakes. Would that suit you? – You say you live in Distaff Lane? Very well, then; he shall finish it now under my eye and if it would please you to go home, he shall bring it to you before curfew.'

Bendy stood quaking while the widow woman fumbled for

The desk

her purse. It was the first time he had ever done any of his father's work.

'Nay, mistress; no payment. Stop and say a prayer for me on your way out and I shall be in *your* debt. Come, Bendy; let us see what you can do.' He cleared a place at the desk and handed the quill to Bendy. 'Copy it exactly, boy; 'tis just a letter of agreement leasing her backyard to the wheelwright next door. Now, worshipful sir, I am very truly at your service.'

Bendy's hand shook as he wrote the first few words. He must do his very best, and yet he wanted to hear what was said.

The two men settled down at the other side of the desk.

'It is good of you to meet me with such courtesy,' Caxton began. 'I am not always so well received by scriveners. One cannot blame them. I suppose they fear that I will spoil their trade.'

'No, one cannot blame them. But it is always fruitless to stand up against progress. For myself I am all agog to hear about your printing press.'

Then it was true! Bendy had all he could do to keep quiet.

'I shall be proud to show it to you, sir, if you will honour me at the Red Pale. It brings its own problems, you know. I can print a hundred books in the time it takes a scribe to copy one. But a hundred books use a hundred times the paper, and paper has to be brought across the sea. There are paper-mills in Flanders, where I learned my printing; but none is made in England and the few reams stocked by grocers are soon swallowed up. Nowadays my press is idle half the time.'

John Goodrich fingered his white beard thoughtfully.

'Yes, it is a problem; and one that hasn't arisen before. Monks and lawyers still use parchment and so do scriveners for their more important work; so until recently the paper handled by the Grocers Company has been ample for everybody. Now, I believe, some scriveners import paper direct. They make their own arrangements with the shipmasters. Could you not do likewise? For a mercer of your standing it should be easy.'

Caxton shook his head. 'I assure you it is anything but easy. I place my orders but the paper does not arrive, and when I inquire, no one has ever heard of it. I have been so long in Bruges that I am almost a stranger in London. That is why I went to Robert Tate; I knew his father in my youth. He said that you of the Crowing Cock issued more books than any other firm of scriveners, and he advised me to come and beg your guidance.'

'Master Tate does me great honour. But I have retired, you know. The Crowing Cock now belongs to my sons; and I grieve to say that you are unlikely to get help from them.'

'Retired?' Caxton seemed surprised. 'Surely you have not bowed to young men already? Wisdom is not so easily replaced.'

'They are not young men. I was twice married and Benedict here is the son of my old age. Matthew and Cornelius have spent most of their lives in my service and they have earned their independence. So a twelve-month back, when my second wife died, I handed over the keys of the coffer. They are good sons to me and if their work is not always to my taste' – he shrugged his shoulders – 'well, I have had my day. I am old-fashioned; I admit it. I like a book to be a treasure that a man may hoard for life. They employ a score of scribes and churn out little tales that go by pecks and bushels in a pedlar's pack. I suppose they fill a need. A book within reach of a yeoman's purse is good company on a winter's night.'

Caxton nodded thoughtfully. 'The best of company. I too have set myself to bring out stories of valour and romance. Small wonder that your sons do not look on me with favour, since I must presently outstrip them. It is a pity.' Sighing he got up to go.

John Goodrich pressed him back. 'Not so fast, Master Caxton. Have you actually ordered shipments of paper to be sent direct to you?'

'Indeed I have. I sent orders to the mills in Flanders as soon as I settled here, and at first it travelled safely. They unloaded the ship below Bridge and brought the paper up to Westminster by barge. But the loads began to dwindle; much of it arrived damaged, so that I could not use it, and finally it stopped altogether. I have been to the King's Customs; they shrug their shoulders; and I have written to the merchants in Bruges, who vow that they sent it on this ship or on that.' He fumbled in his pouch. 'Why, I have here a letter declaring that a consignment was sent a month ago aboard the *Madalena*, but not a sheet has come. It was a load of Unicorn, an excellent paper for printing. I would willingly pay a big price for that paper.'

Bendy's left hand, in which he held the ink-well, suddenly shook. The quill made an ugly blot on the parchment. His father heard him exclaim and jumped up.

'You young fool, what are you at? Give it to me before you make it worse.'

He held the inkwell

It took several minutes with pumice stone, a shell of cuttle-fish, and an ivory burnisher to repair the damage. His father handed it back to him with a stern injunction to be more care-ful, and Bendy, chastened, gave his full attention to the copy-ing while the two men talked of dull matters like the war in Scotland and how much money the King was borrowing from the City merchants to pay for it. He had reached the last line when he heard his own name.

'What have you in mind for Benedict? Is he to be a scrivener too?'

Bendy's father lowered his voice, but it was still clear. 'I think not, though he writes well enough. Maybe I will appren-tice him to a notary and let him turn towards the law, but certainly I shall not put him to the Crowing Cock. His half-brothers have no patience with him. They say that his mind is full of nothing but jousts and tournaments and vain dreams of chivalry. They are for ever bidding him wake up; those things are all of the past.'

'More's the pity,' cried Caxton quickly. '*My* sympathies are with the boy. This modern spirit is an accursed one, empty of all that gives grace to life. Drive out chivalry and what will you get? – naught but self-seeking and the worship of money. If I had my way I would petition our Lord the King to declare jousts two or three times a year, so that every knight should have horse and armour and come to the lists to tourney against each other.' He sighed as he pushed back his stool. 'Now truly I must go. Master Goodrich, you have received me generously. I beg that you will crown it by coming to visit me at Westminster.'

'There is nothing I should like better. Your workshop is just outside the south door of the church, I'm told – up against the Chapter House; a good station, direct in the path between the Abbey and the Palace of Westminster.'

'A wonderful station; when Parliament is sitting we are so busy that I have to rent an extra shop. You will recall that the Lords meet in the Palace and the Commons in the Abbey Chapter House, so you may guess the comings and goings that brush against us. But, mark you, the space is much too small, and lately the Lord Abbot has kindly granted me another holding, in the Almonry – the sign of the Red Pale. There I have a good house for my wife and daughter, and a loft over the Almonry gate which makes a fine workshop for the press.' He dived into his gown and produced a sheet of paper which he unfolded. Bendy saw that it had lines of printing on one side. 'This will help you to remember, sir. It is to direct people who might like to buy the new list that I have lately made – a list giving the order of commemoration of certain feasts.' He smiled a little. 'It kills two birds with one stone, for it is, at the same time, a sample of the manner of printing.'

'A good notion,' said John Goodrich, running his eye over it. 'Surely this must be the first time that printing has been used for such a purpose – as it were to send round the town crier. A merchant could well proclaim his goods this way.'

He laid the sheet down where, by craning his neck, Bendy could read it. There were only about half a dozen lines.

'If it please any man spiritual or temporal to buy any pyes of two or three commemorations of Salisbury use, enprinted after the form of this present letter, which we well and truly correct, let him come to Westminster into the Almonry at the Red Pale and he shall have them good cheap.'

John Goodrich saw his guest off from the Cathedral door, and returned briskly to his table.

'Well, my son, that was a meeting to remember. Master Caxton is obviously a man of rare quality – a man after my own heart. Mark you, I would not have you think that I am turning my back upon my own craft. A book well written in a fair hand is a work to rejoice in and offer to God. But times are changing. One cannot halt them; and books are not only things of outward beauty, they are food for a man's mind, and if these new ways supply that food as we cannot, then we must treat them with due honour.' He caught sight of Bendy's face and smiled. 'Look not so scared, boy. I do but think aloud. Now – let me see your copy. Yes, it is fair enough and the blot doesn't show. Take it at once to Distaff Lane, the house at the corner of Friday Street. I will go straight home. – And, Bendy, say not a word about our visitor. I will tell the news at my own good time.'

Bendy set off at once up the nave and out through the south transept, the way he usually went to school. He was hugging himself at the thought of sharing so important a secret with his father.

But he was also worried. Something fishy was going on about paper. He had suspected it when he overheard Matthew and Tom Twist whispering about the *Madalena* and the load of Unicorn. Caxton's paper should have come on the *Madalena*; and Matthew had said, '*I care not what becomes of it so long as the Red Pale gets it not.*' At the time the words *Red Pale* meant nothing to him. Now it was only too clear. They were trying to keep the paper from Caxton.

The question was what ought he to do? The obvious answer was tell his father. But the more he thought of it the more difficult it seemed. His father never permitted him to say a word against Matthew or Cornelius, and the moment he began he would be bidden to hold his tongue. As for accusing Matthew of something as shady as this, his father would merely go red in the face and shout him down. Matthew would deny it; there would be a beating, and that would be the end of it. Certainly his father would never believe it; he could hardly believe it himself. It was one thing to buy paper cheap, even if it were smuggled as he had long suspected; but a knavish trick like this –

The rain had stopped and inside the walls of Paul's Churchyard the stationers were reopening their stalls after the storm.

The stationers' stalls

They occupied *stations* allotted to them by the Dean and Chapter, and sold pens and ink and parchment and all the oddments needed for writing; and often books as well.

He left the Churchyard by St Augustine's Gate and crossed Old Change into Distaff Lane. Obviously the widow was watching for him through a gap in the horn window-pane, for she came to the door at once and he had difficulty in cutting short her thanks.

But he got away at last, and on his way home he lingered in Paul's to think it out. Instead of going straight down the nave, as he had come, he turned to the right under the carved stone rood-screen into that further half of the Cathedral, which was still called the *New* Work, although nobody living remembered it being built. Here tall slender arches soared up and up; light filtered through windows of richly painted glass. The busy hum of the nave seemed no more than a distant murmur. Everything was dim and quiet. A few people knelt at their prayers and a couple of clerks moved from one side chapel to another, setting the altar candles for tomorrow's Masses.

Bendy tiptoed along the full length of the ambulatory, the long aisle which ran right round the outside of the choir and the sanctuary, till he reached the Shrine of St Erkenwald, Paul's first bishop. Beyond it was the Lady Chapel with its great Rose window – the far east end of the Cathedral. The Rose window was the glory of Paul's. He stood for a moment watching the tiny pinpoints of light on the gold and jewels of the shrine lying securely behind its painted wrought-iron screen. He did not say any particular prayer. He did not even think. And yet suddenly he found that his mind was made up. He would not deliberately tell his father about Matthew. But if Caxton's visit was mentioned at supper, he would watch for a chance to bring in the *Madalena* and the load of Unicorn, and watch the effect.

By the time he reached Paternoster Row the evening sun

was slanting from the west through the gaps between the houses. One shaft struck the paternoster-maker's shop, opposite the Crowing Cock. It lighted on a patch of white – the wimple and the white apron of Peterkin's grandmother, sitting in the doorway, her tray of beads upon her lap, with her old blind face turned upwards to enjoy the moment of warmth.

At the sight of her an idea shot into Bendy's head. Caxton had said, '*I would willingly pay a good price for that paper.*' There might be something for Peterkin in this.

With one kick

He was so struck by the thought that he slowed down. Suddenly he saw Humphrey emerge from the Crowing Cock, his cap stuck at a jaunty angle, a grin upon his face.

Humphrey's home lay in the opposite direction, so Bendy waited for him to go. He did not want a meeting just now. There was a reckoning to be settled between them but he was in no hurry.

Suddenly Humphrey skipped nimbly across the kennel, the deep gutter in the middle of the street. With one swift kick he tossed the blind woman's tray of beads into the air, hovered for a moment to watch the effect, and then took to his heels.

In a flash Bendy was after him. He caught him before he rounded the corner and dragged him back by the neck of his tunic. He was too angry to know just how he did it, but he pushed Humphrey down and held him there until he had collected the scattered beads out of the muck. Then for good measure, and in payment of his own account, he rolled him over into the flowing kennel and left him spluttering. That done, he gave the old woman her tray and tried to rub the beads clean. When he looked round again Humphrey had vanished.

Matthew sprang to his feet

CHAPTER 4

Money from the Coffer

FEELING suddenly cheerful Bendy retired to the pump. By the time that he was clean supper was ready. The table was set and his father was already waiting. Matthew was there too, and as Bendy slipped into his place, Cornelius came downstairs, peering shortsightedly and asking pardon. When his father had said Grace, Bendy joined Goodwife Collin, who was ladling broth into bowls. It was his business to serve his elders, but he kept his ear cocked; he did not want to miss anything.

After the soup came a pudding made of pork mixed with eggs and crumbled bread, and flavoured with sage and saffron and currant syrup. It was a favourite of Bendy's and he hurried

41

to fill the mugs with ale and his father's cup with wine, so that he could sit down to it.

They were talking about the King's hunting party in Epping Forest, to which the Mayor and members of all the City companies had been invited, and gifts of venison sent for their ladies to have a feast on their own.

"Tis but currying favour to make them forget the money he owes,' grumbled Matthew. 'He must know that if he pleases them not, there is young Henry Tudor ready and waiting in Brittany. You notice that only the richest companies were invited, the Grocers and the Vintners and the Fishmongers, and of course the Mercers. That reminds me, sir; there was a mercer called upon you an hour or so ago. I sent Bendy to lead him to you. Did he find you? Truth to tell, I looked out as they were going towards Paul's; he looked like a man of some substance.'

Bendy paused with a morsel of pudding in his fingers. John Goodrich inclined his head. 'Yes, I saw him. I am sorry that you did not meet him too. Did you hear his name?'

'It did not strike my memory. Something like *Gaston*, I think.'

'Something like Gaston, maybe, but *not* Gaston. His name is Caxton; William Caxton of Westminster.'

Matthew looked dumbfounded. 'Caxton? Caxton the printer? He actually came here in the guise of a mercer? Before heaven, if I had known –'

'And if you *had* known? I trust you would not have shamed your father's house. And he was not "in the guise of a mercer"; he *is* a mercer. He was for years Governor of the Domus Anglorum at Bruges.'

'That but makes it worse; a rich man who has earned a fortune and spends it in killing our trade. He doesn't set up in the City, mark you, where the Mayor's court and the Guilds can protect the craftsmen. Oh, no! He lies snug at Westminster, under the wing of the Abbey and the Palace.'

John Goodrich sat calmly twisting his silver wine-cup by the stem.

'Not so fast,' he said. 'You talk as though Caxton had *invented* printing. There have been printing presses for years in Germany and other lands. He did but bring it to England, and already German printers have followed him. There are a German and a Fleming set up by All Hallows Church; and another German, Theodoric Rood, in Oxford. Did Caxton not see to it that there are English printed books, you would wake up one morning to find the book trade in the hands of foreigners.'

'Ah! But they print different matter. They do not touch our business as this man does, with his stories of Troy and his *Canterbury Tales*. It amazes me, sir, that you can bring yourself to play the Judas. Go out into Paternoster Row or Creed Lane, or Ave Maria Lane, or to the stationers at their stalls in Paul's Churchyard. What will you find there but books and more books, every page of them writ by hand? What will become of the scribes that do the copying, most of them old men or poor, weedy fellows? What will be *their* fate when books spawn like fishes?'

Bendy looked from one to the other and held his breath. Matthew had actually called his father a Judas! He waited for the storm to break. But with an obvious effort John Goodrich controlled himself.

'For a clever man you are something of a fool, my son,' he said quietly. 'Like it or not, this printing has come to stay, and nothing you can do will stop it. All honour to you for your thought for your scribes; but, mark you, it will be many years before the printer steps into the shoes of the scrivener. By that time your aged men will have gone and the young ones will learn new ways. If books spawn like fishes, as you call it, more people will learn to read. It will turn the craft of books upside down; it may well turn the world upside down. If you were wise you would make a friend of this printer; you would bring him into the Craft, make him a member of the Guild of Stationers, and a Scrivener of the Writers of Court Hand. Then the Guild might keep its hold. As it is you are heading for disaster.'

Matthew was silent. After a moment Cornelius said, 'You have not told us what Caxton wanted.'

'He wanted advice about the best means of getting paper. ... He explained his trouble; he cannot get enough. 'Tis obvious that if a printer produces ten times the books, he needs ten times the paper; and there is none made in England.'

Matthew sprang to his feet; his voice shook with anger. 'And so he would like us to provide him. No doubt he would be glad for us to strip the Crowing Cock so that he might profit by it.'

'He did not ask for paper, though from what I see of your stocks it would scarce hurt you to tide him over a difficulty. Of course the work of this house has changed since my day. It may be that you need all that you have got. But I know that you import your supplies. He is having trouble about shipping. Surely you might offer him the succour of your experience.'

Matthew banged his fist upon the table. 'So I am to cut my own throat to oblige Master Caxton! Saving your grace, sir, you ask too much. Let his mercers and his merchant venturers help him. They are all birds of a feather.'

'To lose your temper profits nothing,' said his father coolly. 'He will get his paper anyway sooner or later. 'Tis just that some ship he counted on has not arrived.'

Bendy caught his breath. This was his chance. He spoke up as clearly as he could. 'The *Madalena*, sir. He said the *Madalena* with a load of Unicorn.'

It was like a thunderbolt from on high. Matthew glared at Bendy. Cornelius cried, 'Tchut, tchut, tchut!' as though he were silencing a child. Even John Goodrich looked astonished.

Beardless boys at table with their elders spoke only when they were spoken to.

Bendy clenched and unclenched his hands. Should he go on? The question was decided for him. At that moment the door flew open and a woman burst in. It was the Widow Pratt, Humphrey's mother, breathless and wide-eyed. Her gown was hitched and a confusion of flaxen curls peeped from beneath her wimple. She pushed Humphrey in front of her. He was bandaged and whimpering.

Bendy was certain that Matthew welcomed the interruption. He left the table hastily.

'What ails you, mistress?' he exclaimed, full of solicitude. 'Is the boy ill?'

Bendy groaned to himself. Humphrey was always his undoing.

She raised troubled eyes to Matthew before she remembered to bob to his father. 'He has been set on, sir; Benedict attacked him savagely and threw him in the kennel. When he came in you never saw his like. I had to heat water and fill the tub.'

Everybody looked at Bendy. His father called him. 'What is this?' he demanded. 'What have you to say for yourself?'

'He baited the blind woman,' said Bendy glumly, knowing that he was doomed. 'He kicked her tray when he thought that no one was looking. The beads all went in the muck and I made him pick them up.'

'But his head is cut,' declared Mistress Pratt, lifting the bandage; 'his arm and knee too; and he was soaked with filth from top to toe. Picking up beads could not have done that. He says that Benedict had his knife into him. Benedict had vowed that he would flay him.'

'That is true,' Matthew interposed. 'I heard him say it. Benedict came in like a scavenger this afternoon. He was trying to sneak upstairs behind my back, and Humphrey was in his way. He plagued Humphrey then till the boy cried out. I dare

45

She raised troubled eyes to Matthew

swear that he threw him in the kennel deliberately because *he* had been caught covered with filth.'

Bendy's heart sank. Everything added up against him. How could he know that Humphrey would cut his head on the cobbles?

John Goodrich was frowning. ''Tis all a mess of tittle-tattle,' he complained. 'Boy – you – Humphrey; did you touch the blind woman's tray?'

Humphrey looked frightened. 'I knocked against it. It was a mishap, I swear it was. And before I could start to pick it up –'

'That's a lie,' cried Bendy in a rage. 'You kicked it and ran away, you snivelling little rat.'

His father turned upon him. 'Hold your peace,' he roared. 'Would you wrangle in front of your father? Now – did you throw Humphrey in the kennel or did you not?'

Bendy looked at him desperately. 'Yes, sir; but only because –'

'No *only's* to me. Did you threaten that you would flay him?'

'Yes, sir – but –'

'That will do. You have answered me. Get you to your bed and study how to keep your temper. I will not have you brawling like an alehouse clown. I should beat you soundly were I sure that there was no provocation; so begone quickly before I change my mind.'

Bendy dragged himself upstairs. It was dark and he had no taper, but he could feel his way. He respected his father's justice, for he had enjoyed punishing Humphrey, though Humphrey had well and truly earned it, the little lick-spittle. But his chief concern was that he had lost the chance of hearing what more was said about the *Madalena*. Probably Matthew would see to it that the subject was dropped; and his own problem, of whether to tell his father or not, was as far as ever from being solved.

He flung himself on to his bed without undressing. The full moon was rising. Paul's spire stood out, black and silver, against the blue night sky. The room was as light as day. He could not go to sleep. Perhaps he could read.

He got up and opened the chest to find his King Arthur stories. On the top lay the blue cloak. He had forgotten all about it. His father would miss it when he came to bed, and he did not want to say why he had taken it. Probably they were all still downstairs. If he hurried he could put it back.

Compared with his loft the deserted scribes' room was dark, and the parlour, on the lower floor, darker still. But there was

Black and silver against the sky

a light inside the great chamber, his father's room. To his dismay he saw Matthew standing there beside the open money coffer, a taper stuck in a taper-holder flickering on a stool beside him. As Bendy watched he lifted out a fat money bag, untied it and counted out golden angels, one at a time, until he had a handful. The light glinted on the coins as he slipped them into his pouch. Bendy's eyes widened. He had never seen so much money out of the coffer before.

Matthew stooped to replace the bag and Bendy crept back to the stairs, trusting that the creak of the coffer would drown any sound. Luckily Matthew went down instead of coming up. The glow of the taper faded and the door at the bottom closed. It took Bendy less than a minute to hang up the cloak and scurry back to the loft.

This time he undressed and got into bed. He had been there only a little while when he heard a low whistle. He was at the window in a trice. Peterkin's face was clear in the moonlight.

'Gammer says you had a fight,' he said in a hoarse whisper. 'What happened?'

Glad to pour it all out, Bendy leaned across as far as he dared. Curfew had rung some time ago; there was no one in the street, and Peterkin shared his views about Humphrey. At the end of a few minutes he felt better. He noticed that Peterkin was still dressed.

'Where have you been?' he inquired curiously.

'On the river,' said Peterkin curtly. It was plain that he was saying no more. But it jogged Bendy's memory.

'Peterkin,' he said softly. 'D'you know a ship called the *Madalena*?'

Peterkin grunted as though taken aback. It might have been Yes, but it certainly wasn't No. 'Then listen,' said Bendy. 'I've got a bellyful to tell you.'

He began with what he had heard between Twist and Matthew. Then he went on to explain about Caxton, and rounded it off with his own idea that Matthew was holding up the paper.

'It's Twist,' said Peterkin shortly. 'He does it.'

'Does what?'

'Gets the paper, of course. 'Tis a paying game. Oh, there's a deal goes on down the river if I durst tell you. But they said they'd kill me if I opened my mouth.'

This was impressive. He looked at Peterkin with respect. 'Listen,' he whispered urgently. 'Caxton said he would pay a big price for that paper. And *you* said this afternoon that you've got to earn money.'

There was a long pause. 'The ship's the *Madalena*,' said Peterkin at last. 'Is there anything else?'

Bendy racked his brain. 'The paper is called Unicorn; that's all. And, oh yes, there was something else; a word I didn't understand; *a-mucking*; the *Madalena* was a-mucking. Does that help?'

Peterkin woke up. 'A-MUCKING! Holy saints! Does it *help*? I'll wager it does.'

'What does it *mean*?' urged Bendy.

But Peterkin held up his finger for silence. He was peering down into the dark street. Bendy could see nothing, but he heard a muffled thudding sound almost underneath him. He knew what it was: a horse with its feet stuffed into bags of straw. For a second or two a patch of light appeared on the wall of the house opposite, as though a door in the Crowing Cock had been opened and closed again. Peterkin hissed softly. He barely caught the word: '*Twist!*'

They stayed quiet for so long that Bendy began to shiver. Why should Tom Twist come at this time of night and with such secrecy?

Then the dull thudding began again. It moved away and grew gradually fainter. Twist had taken his departure.

Bendy fixed his eyes on the curve in Paternoster Row where the street became visible from his window. By good fortune a shaft of moonlight cut across it. Sure enough the old white pack-horse plodded into the beam and out again with a cloaked and hooded figure walking beside it. They carried no light, as honest men were bound by law to do, and they were visible only for a few seconds; but Bendy noticed that there were no casks on the horse's back, as there had been before.

'They've brought a load,' said Peterkin softly.

Bendy nodded. He knew now why Matthew had wanted

money from the coffer. It was when he was back in bed that he did some calculation. The full load that the pack-horse could carry would not cost a quarter of that. Why was Matthew paying Tom Twist all that gold?

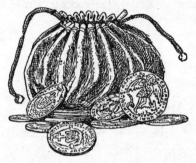

All that gold

CHAPTER 5

Ten Groats Each

HE woke in the morning with a sense of being late. Though the
sun was still behind the houses he rolled out of bed, dressed and
scrambled down the steep stairs to the pump.

As he hurried along Paternoster Row apprentices were
opening shutters and sluicing the cobbles in front of their shops
so that the kennel once more became a dirty river. All the
shops, except the paternoster-bead makers, had something to
do with books; they were scriveners, or bookbinders, or
limners who did the illuminations, or stationers who sold ink

and quills and parchment as well as trading in the finished books. Some of the apprentices hailed Bendy, but he did not stop. The last part of his turn of duty, which had begun with the Lesson at Vespers, consisted in serving the Chancellor's Mass at six o'clock – directly after prime. The Chancellor had arranged to say it at the altar of St Thomas of Canterbury. Bendy was glad about that. It helped him to remember Sir Thomas Malory.

Mass over he crossed to the Grammar School, a huddle of ancient buildings at the east end of Paul's Churchyard. The scholars' breakfast of bread and ale had already been served out; but he went to the school buttery and was rewarded by a specially large mug and a hunk of pasty. These he took to a bench in the sun. He would just have time to enjoy them before lessons began at seven.

The storm had gone and already it was hot. The Cathedral towered over him like a cliff in the morning light, its pinnacles picked out in silver against the blue sky. He craned his neck right back to see up to the top of the spire. The ball and cross looked tiny, yet he'd been told that the cross itself was fifteen feet high and the ball a great sphere of solid gold containing a relic of the True Cross.

He sat munching his pasty contentedly. Yesterday's problems had vanished with the storm. Why should he worry about what Matthew and Cornelius did? He had best keep out of it. He was back at school, and this was a normal day.

He glanced round at some boys kicking a ball about in the playground. One of them was Will Soper, a sallow, pock-marked fellow from the Holly Bush, the alehouse where he had won his manuscript of Malory's stories. He didn't like remembering that business and he loathed Will Soper; so he shifted on the bench to face the other way.

That put him in full view of the Cathedral, and for a few minutes he watched people passing in and out – the devout on the way to Mass, the worldly hurrying about their business. His eye lighted suddenly on a boy with a bandaged head. It was Humphrey and he was coming towards him.

Bendy cursed under his breath with a good schoolboy oath. Humphrey was the last person he wanted to see, but he wasn't going to pay him the compliment of running away from him. So he dived into his pouch, pulled out his Cicero, and bent studiously over the passage for today.

He expected at any moment to hear Humphrey's footsteps beside him but none came. He waited some minutes and then peeped round. To his astonishment he saw Humphrey standing in the playground deep in conversation with Will Soper. What on earth were they talking about? Will was one of the older boys at the Grammar School, while Humphrey had never been more than a Song School brat and now had nothing to do with Paul's. And how came he to be free at this time in the morning? He should be cleaning out the Scribes' room. Bendy snorted out loud. Of course he was trading on his broken head. He had got his mother to make a fuss about it, and Matthew was always ready to oblige her.

Anyhow, Humphrey seemed to be in no hurry. He was acting in front of Will Soper like a mountebank, swaggering about and lunging out with his fists, so that Will was convulsed with laughter and stood clapping and crying, 'Well done! Oh, bravely done!'

It was a full minute before it dawned on Bendy that Humphrey was giving his own version of last night in Paternoster Row. It was all he could do not to rush in there and then and teach the little toad a lesson which he would never forget.

But just then the school bell rang and he pulled himself together. He'd been in enough hot water about Humphrey. To knock him about for the second time would mean real trouble with his father. Luckily neither Humphrey nor Will Soper appeared to have noticed him, so, controlling his rage, he slipped quietly away, put on the gown that he had to wear in class, and went into the schoolhouse.

But he couldn't get the incident out of his mind. The first lesson of the day was RULES, a dreary recitation of Latin rhymes which were supposed to teach good manners as well as good grammar. He knew them all by heart and was able to think over what he had seen. There was no doubt at all that Humphrey had been making a mock of him, and to Will Soper, of all people; his blood fairly boiled at the remembrance of it.

They all sat round the master

But RULES was followed by EPISTLES, which was simply a lesson in letter-writing, and as his father's son he enjoyed it. They all sat round the master, a lanky, hawk-faced tyrant known as the Falcon from his habit of swooping without warning, and turn by turn translated letters out of Latin into English. Next they were set to write original Latin letters on subjects that the Falcon picked for them. Bendy had to compose a letter about an order for silk. That suited him nicely. He settled down to his wax tablets, sucking his stylus thoughtfully. Humphrey and Will Soper were forgotten. He would write a letter from a mercer in London to a merchant adventurer living at the Domus Anglorum in Bruges.

He had not quite finished when the bell rang for a break, so he lingered before he too went out into the playground. To his astonishment he found Will Soper waiting for him just outside the door, a grin upon his ugly face.

'By my soul, Bendy, you're a glutton for work today. Have a sugar-plum; the tavern wench made them.' As Bendy shook his head he went on quickly. 'I've been wanting a word with you. Have you still got that roll of stories you had from me at dice?'

Bendy was instantly on his guard. 'Maybe, maybe not. What do you want with it? I won it fairly.'

'*Won* it!' Will Soper threw back his head and guffawed. 'You *bought* it, my son, with two groats out of your purse. The truth is you were so sotted you knew not what you did. But that's no matter now. I've come to say I'll buy it back from you. I'll give you four groats. That's double price.'

'You won't,' said Bendy stoutly. 'I'll not sell it.'

'Then you *have* got it. That's good; we can strike a fair bargain with it. I can sell it for twenty groats, and as you're so close-fisted I'll share with you – ten groats apiece.'

Bendy shook his head. There was something fishy about all this, and not for a purseful of gold would he part with the manuscript.

Will Soper changed to a wheedling tone. 'Harken, Bendy; you wouldn't get me into trouble, would you? If I don't bring that roll back, my father will tan the skin off me.'

Just for a second or two Bendy hesitated. This might put a different face on matters. But he looked up suddenly and caught Will's beady eyes watching him narrowly. A picture rose in his mind of Humphrey showing off and Will crying, 'Bravely done!' He hardened.

'Spare your breath to cool your broth,' he said defiantly and turned away.

''Tis *your* broth that will want the cooling,' Will cried after him. 'How will your high-and-mighty brother take it that you were besotted at the Holly Bush, or your fine father with his table in Paul's? Suppose *my* father goes to the Crowing Cock to demand his roll of writing? What will you say then? – that you were so drunk that you knew not what you carried off?'

Bendy's only answer was to go inside and slam the school-room door. The Falcon promptly gave him a stroke on each hand and he retired glumly into the corner to nurse his tingling palms and think about his problem. He did not believe that Will or his father would really go to the Crowing Cock, but if they did the fat would be truly in the fire. The whole thing was mysterious. Will had changed his story half a dozen times. What did he want with the roll? Who would pay twenty groats for a few bits of stories, none of them even complete?

He puzzled over it all the morning and barely escaped another caning for letting his wits go wool-gathering; but at the end he was no nearer solving it.

After dinner he was moodily kicking a stone round the play-ground when he suddenly saw his father coming towards him. His heart jumped into his throat. Had they been making trouble already?

But John Goodrich was smiling.

'Well met, my son; I had come to look for you. I hope you have worked well today, for I would beg you off school this afternoon. Master Caxton has come to take me to West-minster, and he particularly desires that you may come too.'

Bendy was struck dumb with relief. His father looked at him with astonishment.

'Come, boy; you've not been invited to a dirge. 'Tis a great honour, and I shall tell your master so. Go and offer your duty to Master Caxton. He's waiting in Paul's by John o' Gaunt's tomb. I'll come as soon as I've made your peace.'

Quite dazed by the turn in his fortune Bendy went into the Cathedral. Not only was he to miss school and escape from Will Soper, but also he was actually to see the wonderful invention that made books without the trouble of writing. To reach John o' Gaunt's tomb at the north side of the Choir he walked right round the ambulatory, stopping for a minute at the Lady Chapel to say a quick prayer that Will's father might *not* go to the Crowing Cock. It struck him suddenly

France Ancient   *France Modern*

that perhaps it was scarcely fitting to bring a matter of dicing and drinking to the Mother of God; but he consoled himself with the thought that if his own mother had been alive she would certainly have done her best to get him out of a scrape.

As soon as he turned into the north aisle he saw Caxton attentively examining the coats of arms on the great carved tomb. He looked round as Bendy came up.

'Well met, young Master Benedict; so you have got out of school. Then let us see how much you know of herald's lore. Can you tell me, for instance, why the royal arms of France are shown here *azure semée de lys*, not as the King bears them today with three fleurs-de-lis, two and one?'

Slightly ashamed of himself, Bendy shook his head. He re-

cognized the arms of France, of course. They were quartered
with the English leopards as the royal arms of England. He had
often noticed on these old tombs that the fleurs-de-lis were
powdered all over the shield, but though he knew as much
heraldry as most other boys, he'd never stopped to ask why.

Caxton smiled as though he were glad of the chance to tell
his little tale. 'Well, I will enlighten you. When John o'
Gaunt's father, King Edward the Third, claimed the throne of
France he bade his heralds quarter the lilies of France with the
leopards of England on his shield. But the king of France was
so wrath that there and then he altered the arms of France; for
the future, instead of *azure semée de lys* – France Ancient as we
call it – it should be blazoned as *azure three fleurs-de-lis or*. Of
course it helped him not a jot, for the English heralds soon
copied it, and now both kingdoms use France Modern. Ah,
here comes your father. Now we shall know whether you are
allowed to come to Westminster.'

Bendy looked round quickly. But his father was still smiling.
'You are excused your lessons, boy. But upon my word I am

Paul's Wharf

sorry I did not send you home to change your gown. You put shame upon us in your shabbiness.'

'He is going to a workshop, not to a great lord's hall,' said Caxton with a laugh. 'If I know anything of boys he'll be covered in printing ink before the day is out. Now, sir, are you ready? I have a boat waiting for us at Paul's Wharf.'

Feeling that he had found an ally, Bendy followed the two men out of the churchyard through Paul's Chain Gate and down the sharp incline to the river.

Beating sheets in the river

Paul's Wharf, one of the City's main landing-places, was clean and free of the smell of fish which pervaded most of the other wharves. Caxton's boat was a wherry, with two watermen who sprang forward attentively to help their master and his guests aboard. Then without further ado they unshipped their oars and pulled away from the side, putting their backs into it so that the boat shot ahead.

As the tide was ebbing they kept close to the bank to avoid the current midstream. Two men unloading a barge of fresh-cut floor-rushes shouted abuse as the wash from the wherry's bows all but flooded them. Some laundresses beating sheets in the river scolded shrilly and got back gibes as good as they gave. The waves slapped up against the walls of Baynard's Castle, and at that moment somebody emptied a slop-bucket from one of the towers, narrowly missing Caxton's head. John Goodrich said hotly that he would report it to the sheriffs; there were strict rules against throwing garbage into the river. But Bendy had all he could do to suppress his laughter. Really, the day that had started so badly was turning out exceedingly well.

Once they were past the mouth of the Fleet River the watermen swung out across the stream to take advantage of the curve of the south bank. Small boats dotted about the water had to scuttle out of their way and a torrent of good Thamesside oaths floated after them.

Caxton caught Bendy's eye and smiled. 'A good exchange for your Latin verses, eh?' he said into the wind that carried his voice away from the rowing men. ''Tis the mother tongue of London river. But 'pon my soul, I'd rather have their rough curses than the smoothness of the mariners in foreign ports. It was my task once to enlist crews for the King's invasion of France. I carried orders from the Council round all the shipyards of Flanders. They feasted me everywhere, but not a man would go on board until he had a month's pay in his pocket, and then they made trouble at every turn. Luckily the King made peace with France and the invasion was discarded. I can promise you that I slept the more soundly for it.'

John Goodrich nodded. 'That I can well believe. But tell me, sir, when you were excelling as a merchant and had all these important duties thrust upon you by the King, how did you ever come to take up printing?'

Caxton trailed his fingers in the water, picked out a floating rush, and tied it into knots. 'It started as a hobby,' he said thoughtfully. 'A busy man needs a hobby-horse to play with in his spare time, so I took to translating old romances from French into English. One of them was the *Recuyell of the Histories of Troyes*, a book of stories of the Greek and Trojan wars and the total destruction of the noble city of Troy, which has never been rebuilded to this day. It shows how dreadful and how rash it is to begin a war; and I made it into English because Englishmen have been at war either abroad or among themselves for more than a hundred years. But I stray from your question, sir. Before I had finished my translation I married. But wives are not permitted at the Domus Anglorum, so I gave up the Governorship and was honoured with a post at the Court of the Duchess of Burgundy; as doubtless you know, she is the Lady Margaret, own sister to our King. One day she chanced to see my *Recuyell*; she liked it so well that she graciously bade me finish it for her.'

'A singular honour,' nodded John Goodrich. 'But the *printing*, Master Caxton?'

He laughed. 'I am coming to that, though my story twists like a leopard's tail. I had so many requests for copies of the *Recuyell* that my hand grew weary; so when my lord the King sent me to Cologne on a mission concerned with trade, I set myself to learn the new art of printing. There had been printers in Cologne for some years, you know. I returned to Bruges all aglow and joined with a Fleming named Colard Mansion, who worked in the great library of the Duke of Burgundy. I bought a press and two founts of type, and we printed in a room over the porch of the church of St Donatus.

There were no troubles about paper *there*. Ah! That reminds me; I forgot to tell you that good Master Tate is sending me some paper – not a great deal, but enough to keep the press fed for a short while at least. Maybe it has arrived at Westminster by now. And speaking of Westminster, here we are. Look, Bendy! The Royal Standard is flying from the mast; that means that the King is actually at the Palace with his court.'

The Palace of Westminster

CHAPTER 6

Westminster

THE time had passed so quickly that Bendy looked round surprised. The wherry was gliding swiftly towards the landing-stage known as Westminster Bridge, though to Bendy's eye it was not at all like a bridge, except that it was built out into the water. The air seemed fresh after the stuffy smells of London. There were trees overhanging the walls of the King's Palace and above them appeared the carved turrets of the royal chapel of St Stephen's.

This was not his first visit to Westminster. Once in his Choir School days he had come with a party from Paul's to join the Palace singing-boys at the High Mass of Easter. Then they had landed at Westminster Bridge, trooped under the archway into New Palace Yard and through a network of courtyards

64

and cloisters to St Stephen's, a small but lovely church, full of delicate carving and glowing colour that matched the gorgeous dresses of the King and the Queen and the courtiers.

But today the watermen did not pull in to the landing-stage. They continued to row up-stream, along the river-front of the Palace.

'I have bidden them take us to the little wharf by the mill,' said Caxton. 'It is a pleasant walk that way to the Almonry outside the walls of the Abbey – more to my liking than the bustle of New Palace Yard. And the boy can get a good view of the Palace from the river. See, Bendy, that is Westminster Hall at the back; look at the length of its roof, how it dwarfs everything. And this church, with the four turrets at the corners, is St Stephen's, the royal chapel. It is most beautiful within.'

Bendy was tempted to say that he knew it, but his father might be down on him for boasting, so he only gazed and said nothing. The Palace itself was like a small town of stone roofs and castellated walls.

But it ended at last in a stretch of orchards and green water-meadows. Bendy took a deep breath of air laden with the scent of meadowsweet. Farther up-stream a wagon with two horses was actually being punted across the river by a couple of men with great poles. He stared. He had never seen that done before.

'Ah! The horse ferry,' said Caxton, following the line of his eye. 'It crosses to Lambeth, and 'tis a great short cut if you would take carts over the river; else you must go right down to London Bridge. But come along, boy, stir yourself; none of us can move till you do.'

The boat had come to rest alongside a small stone wharf where a mill stream opened out into the river. The steps were steep and slippery, but Bendy scrambled safely ashore and helped to pull his father and Caxton up after him.

From the wharf a pathway ran inland. It was wide and well trodden, and it ran between the mill stream fringed with pollard willows, and a high stone wall, far too high for him to see over it. The wall was broken by two gateways. As they passed, he peeped through the first and saw a courtyard where men-at-arms were drilling with long, shining halberds. This was obviously the back entrance to the Palace and he longed to stay and watch; but Caxton and his father had gone on and were waiting outside the second gate – a large stone archway, with a figure in a niche above it of St Peter with his keys.

'The south gate of the Abbey,' he heard Caxton say as he caught up. 'It leads to the farm and the granary, and it's the way they bring the corn in from the Abbey lands across the river – by the horse ferry you saw just now. Bendy, peep inside; the building on the right is the new schoolhouse for the Grammar School. Till lately we suffered it in the Almonry, but my Lord Abbot took pity and moved it. We still have the Choir School, but that at least is a nest of singing-birds. The Grammar School was more like a gathering of young screech owls.' He caught Bendy's eye and chuckled. 'Your pardon, boy! Doubtless all the lads at Paul's coo like turtle-doves.'

'This is in truth a most engaging path,' exclaimed John Goodrich. 'I had no idea you were so countrified.' He paused at the corner where the wall turned sharply at a right angle, and looked across the expanse of green water-meadows. The stream also turned, dividing into two, round a little island, one branch continued along the new line of the wall, while the other meandered away through beds of osier willows.

Caxton looked pleased. 'I am happy to have brought you this way. It reminds one that Westminster is built upon an island. The mill-stream is just one of the many mouths of the Tyburn brook which run into the Thames with one spit of firm land between them. In the old days it was called Thorney Island. We've got the water channelled into ditches now, but it is still an island for all that. This channel here is known as the Long Ditch. It is lost among houses in a moment, but you will meet it again, for the Red Pale almost overhangs it.'

'What made you choose Westminster for your press?' inquired John Goodrich. 'Surely London would have been more central for you.'

'Everything pointed to Westminster. To begin with, my old father was living here – he died but a couple of years ago. Then I have a kinsman among the monks who helped to put me on the right side of my Lord Abbot. And I will confess, sir, that I was not so modest as to hide myself from the King after I had already made my mark in his service.'

Bendy's father laughed, remarking that Caxton was very

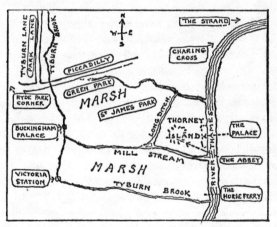

Westminster is built upon an island

wise; Bendy himself suddenly remembered Matthew: '*He lies snug in the shadow of the Abbey and the Palace.*' He began to see where the shoe might pinch.

They had turned the corner and were still following the wall. Ahead of them, instead of water-meadows, lay a jumble of roofs and chimneys, with the tower of a great stone gate-house rising from their midst.

'There is the great west gate of the Abbey; facing down Tothill Street,' remarked Caxton. 'It is a prison, you know; and, strangely, the King's prison, not the Abbot's; which means that the prisoners have to be brought to it from the *outside*; if they set foot inside they could claim sanctuary. They come by way of that dark alley beyond the gatehouse – Thieving Lane; I can promise you it is a regular rookery of scoundrels. Thank Heaven we have our own small postern into the Almonry, so that we avoid the gatehouse. I should know no peace if my wife and daughter were to set foot in Thieving Lane.'

'Surely we must be close to the Almonry?' Bendy's father halted. 'Upon my word, I have completely lost my bearings.'

'We are very close,' smiled Caxton. 'See you, sir; here is our little postern. Look inside and you will soon learn where you are.'

He pointed to a small open door in the Abbey wall. Bendy peeped inside. A path that led towards the great west gate skirted a closely fenced garden – the Lord Abbot's garden, said Caxton. Beyond the garden rose the grey stone buildings of the Monastery with the Abbey church towering over them.

'Ah!' said John Goodrich, from his greater height. 'That is the Abbot's dwelling, I see, and the entry to the cloister beyond it. But I am still lost for the Almonry.'

'Small wonder! Look *behind* you, sir. It lies outside the wall, remember; this postern leads to it from within. I have confused you by bringing you the back way.' He took John Goodrich by the elbow and gently turned him round. 'See! There is the gateway into the Almonry, with my printing-loft. My house lies on the left of it.'

Bendy swung round too. He saw a cobbled way, little more than a passage, leading to a stone archway with a beamed loft above it. Through the archway he got a glimpse of a sunny enclosure. His keen eye spotted a signboard hanging from a door; the sign of the Red Pale.

'Come,' said Caxton hospitably. 'You must be tired, sir. We will have some wine and then I will show you the press. Hold a minute, though! It looks as if I have visitors already.'

Bendy could see a group of people gathered in the shadow of the gateway. There seemed to be a pack-horse in their midst. Suddenly one figure detached itself and came racing towards them. It was a girl, a mere child, with no coif on her head and her long hair streaming out behind her.

With an exclamation Caxton stopped dead as the child, scarcely pausing to bob a curtsy, almost flung herself against him.

'Sir, they've done it again. They made a sally in Thieving Lane and threw it in the mud. Wynken says 'tis all spoiled.'

Caxton held her at arm's length. 'You impudent hussy, can't you see that I have guests? Make your obedience quickly, or this gentleman will think I have a hoyden for a daughter.' As the child bobbed hastily to Bendy and his father, he swung her round to face him again. 'Now what is it all about? What has been thrown in the mud? Do you mean the paper?'

She nodded breathlessly. 'The paper from Master Tate. The porters were cudgelled in Thieving Lane and the whole pack went into the kennel.'

Caxton spread his hands with a despairing sigh. He looked at John Goodrich. 'Did I not tell you, sir? Not a sheet is allowed to reach me. Forgive me if I hurry.'

He started almost at a trot down the Almonry Lane, with the girl running beside him and his guests at his heels. They plunged under the loft and emerged beside a group of men all staring at a mud-spattered pack-horse. One of the men came forward. He wore an apron smeared with black ink.

'Sir, this is bad news. The porters were set on. Cloaks were

A girl came racing towards them

thrown over their heads so that they could see nothing, and when they got free there was no one in sight. All the paper was scattered in the kennel. The girths had been cut and the covers slit with knives.'

'Before Heaven this is too much,' cried Caxton angrily. 'Bring me the porters, good Wynken; let me speak with them.' He looked round, remembering his guests. 'Your pardon, Master Goodrich. I have lost my wits, I think. This is Wynken de Worde, my master printer. Let me take you to my wife. She will give you some wine while I talk to these fools.'

Bendy waited, uncertain whether to follow or to stay behind. The house with the sign of the Red Pale was a large one; it stood on a corner, with a stream running in a deep gully beside it. The path crossed the stream by a little bridge and continued into the Almonry. The stream must be the Long Ditch, he supposed. He looked again at the men and the packhorse, but nobody took any notice of him, so he plucked up his courage and followed his father indoors.

He found himself in a deserted room containing a large trestle table, some benches and stools, a livery cupboard for food with drinking-cups standing on it, and nothing more. It was just an ordinary family hall-room, and he felt faintly disappointed. A door opened on to a set of stairs. He paused at the bottom, then heard his father's voice above and decided to go up.

He emerged into a comfortable parlour, with lots of bright cushions, an embroidery frame on a stand, and a round gilt mirror that reflected the whole room at once. In it he saw his father talking to a lady and the girl who had met them outside. A sudden shyness seized him, and he would have turned tail down the stairs had not Caxton himself suddenly spotted him.

'Hola! boy, where have you got to? Tell me not you are too timid to make your bow.'

He gripped Bendy by the shoulder and pushed him forward, presenting him first to Mistress Caxton, a gentle, smiling lady with pale gold hair, and then, with a chuckle, to the girl, as if they had not met before.

'Daughter, here is a playmate for you. His name is Benedict. I dare say there is not too much difference between you in age; but if he is too grand to play with you, then he can be a gallant and hold your silks. You may talk with him if your mother allows.'

Bendy bowed, wishing that the ground would swallow him. He knew no girls and he was annoyed at being taken for the same age as this silly child. He remained with his head bowed, staring at the floor. A minute passed. He heard her titter.

'You may stand up straight if you want to, Master. You're much taller than me, and much older too. I was eleven last birthday. How old are you?'

Bendy glanced at her. She looked a merry little maid, but he was determined not to tell his age. Quite unabashed she said, 'Benedict's a nice name. There's a chapel to St Benedict in the Abbey. I'm Elizabeth. Are you at school or are you apprenticed? Do you make books? Are you going to work in the printing house?'

He didn't know which question to answer first, so he said simply that he was at Paul's Grammar School. She began again:

'I wish I were a boy, so that I could work with my father in the printing house. He reads his books to me; he reads them in French before he makes them into English. Do you read books in French?' When he shook his head she asked with a touch of scorn. 'What do you read in, then? Only in English?'

Stung, he replied sharply that he read in Latin.

'My mother can read in Latin, *or* in French, *or* Italian. Can your mother read in French or Italian?'

He said gruffly that his mother was dead. He heard her gasp.

'Oh-oh, I am sorry. God rest her. It must be woeful to have no mother.' There was a pause. She started again as cheerfully as ever: 'Do you live in Westminster or in London? I've lived in Salisbury for nigh on a year. My mother's sister has her house in Salisbury. I was in waiting on her, learning manners. Have you been to a great house to learn manners?'

He was speechless again, and rather angry. He longed to say that what she had learned had not done her much good, but he managed to keep his temper.

Suddenly she leaned towards him and whispered confidentially, 'Have you seen the pack-horse and the paper? Who do you think can have done it? My mother said that it must be somebody with a grudge against my father. Who *could* have a grudge against him? I'd give a king's ransom to find out.'

Bendy's heart suddenly missed a beat. *He* could tell her of someone who had a grudge against her father. But it could not possibly be true. Matthew and Cornelius would never descend to such villainy as this.

At that moment he heard his name called and saw that his father was going downstairs, so he hastily made his bow. To his astonishment she dropped him a curtsy. No one had ever curtsied to him before. In his panic he almost forgot to bow to her mother, who smiled at him indulgently. Feeling a fool, he smiled back; then he bolted after his father.

Caxton was waiting for them below. 'Those rogues have done their work with a will,' he declared ruefully. 'Wynken and the others are going to wash the paper in the Long Ditch, but I doubt that any of it will be usable.'

'I wonder that you do not seek justice in Westminster Hall,' said Bendy's father. 'You have friends at Court. Why not make use of them?'

'The Exchequer moves like a snail. I should be in my grave before I got redress. Master Tate sent a message bidding me see him again. Maybe he has something up his sleeve. After all, I care not where the paper comes from so long as I get it. But you must be tired of waiting. Come and see the press.'

He led them out of the house, across the Almonry path, and into an empty stable on the other side. From this a stair ran up to the printing loft. As Bendy waited his turn he suddenly thought of Peterkin. Maybe there were others besides Master Tate who had something up their sleeve.

The printing house was light. There was a window at each side, one facing down the passage to the Abbey postern, the other looking across the little bridge towards the sunny courtyard which Caxton said was the Almonry. He pointed out the building which had been till lately the Grammar School and now housed the Song School, and beyond it to the Hospice with its chapel, where lived some of the old people who were supported by the alms of the Abbey.

But Bendy was not interested. It was the printing that he wanted to see. The workshop was empty. Caxton said ruefully that everyone was busy washing paper.

In the middle of the workshop stood the press, a great wooden erection secured between two upright posts that ran from floor to ceiling. Bendy gazed at it, full of awe. He had seen a press before; the binder who bound books for the Crowing Cock had one of the same shape – with a heavy board that was moved up and down by a big vertical screw. But the binder's press was tiny. This was a monster.

'Of course the press is no new thing,' said Caxton. 'It is the *type* which is new. The old way of pressing paper on to a carved block is useless for books; you need a new block for every page. Now we have all the letters of the alphabet cast in metal, each letter separate, and we build up a page word by word and letter by letter. When we have printed enough copies we pull the type to pieces again ready to set up for another page. Come and see for yourselves.'

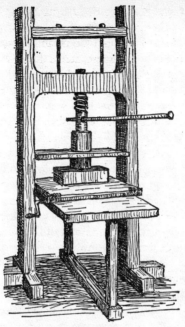

The press

Though the loft was large, the press took up so much room that the remaining space seemed crowded with benches and tables.

'However large a workshop is, one always wishes it larger,' sighed Caxton. 'It is impossible to think how I ever printed in my old shop by the Chapter House. Can you find your way, sir? Wynken de Worde does most of the "composing" – that is the word we use for setting up the type. He has built himself into his corner as though it were a fortress. Can you see? The type is in these two cases. They are sloping so that it is easier to pick out the letters quickly.'

Bendy clambered over a bench to get a better view. The

cases proved to be two large, shallow boxes divided into many compartments. Each compartment held a number of neat little pieces of metal. Caxton selected several and laid them in the palm of Bendy's hand.

'Notice how the letters are raised to take the ink,' he said. 'Can you recognize these that I have given you?'

Bendy stared at them. One was a capital *S*, but somehow it did not look right. But he was sure about a small *d*. Caxton laughed and shook his head.

'No; it is *b*. You see, they are all backwards, or they would come out the wrong way round. You have to compose backwards too, with the words running from right to left instead of from left to right. Let me show you.'

He pointed to a flat tray lying on a bench in which the little type letters were arranged in words and in lines and clamped into place to look oddly like the page of a book.

'Here is the closing of the *Chronicle of England* which I first printed two years ago. All the copies were sold, so I set it up afresh this year, but it has come to a full stop for lack of paper. Try to read it, Bendy. Remember; it is all backwards.'

Bendy stared at it; but before he had even succeeded with the first few words his father began to read it out, slowly but quite steadily.

'"*Thus endeth this present book of the Chronicles of England enprinted by me William Caxton in the abbey of Westminster –*"'

'Worthily done!' cried Caxton. 'You read it more easily than I do. A trained compositor reads backwards almost as fast as he reads forwards, but I am still a babe at the game. Most of my time is spent translating, or writing prologues and epilogues for the books we print. You must watch Wynken de

Worde compose a page of type. His fingers fly over the letters like a skilled lute-player's flying over the strings.'

'How do you decide what to print?' asked Bendy's father.

Caxton fingered his chin thoughtfully. 'A printer, like any other man, must live. I make it my business to print a book pleasing to some great lord, or maybe to a wealthy merchant who will bespeak a number of copies for the satisfaction of having his name printed as patron. The first book I printed here in Westminster, for instance, was the *Dictes and Sayings of the Philosophers* translated from the French by my lord Rivers, the Queen's brother. He was pleased to accept it and, what was more, to offer a gift of it to the King and Queen, which was of great benefit to me. Then last year I printed this' – he lifted from a shelf a pile of loose pages folded in parchment – 'the *History of Godfrey of Bologne, or the Conquest of Jerusalem.* This was produced under the patronage of the King himself. It tells how Christian knights fought in the Holy Land, and my hope was that it might inspire him to call a new crusade and win back Jerusalem from the infidels.'

'A new crusade,' repeated John Goodrich thoughtfully. 'Surely this modern realm has grown away from crusades.'

'To its own undoing!' Caxton waved his hands. This was obviously a subject near to his heart. 'There was a time when the noble deeds of English knights were renowned throughout the world. Think of Richard Coeur de Lion, or Sir Robert Knolles, or Sir John Chandos, or the victorious Harry the Fifth. Think of King Arthur, with all the noble knights of the Round Table. What do the knights of England now but play at dice?'

His voice was withering, and Bendy felt himself turn turkey red. '*Play at dice!*' What would they say if they knew about the Holly Bush?

John Goodrich turned back to the tray of letters. 'When the type is all set, what next, sir?'

Caxton awoke from his dream. He laughed. 'I am an old fool; you do well to recall me. Let me see, I was explaining how we set up a page of type. It is composed line by line; as each line is finished it goes into an iron framework, a *forme* we call it; the blank spaces are filled in and it is all clamped firmly together, ready for the press.' Quite suddenly he peeled off his gown and pulled up his sleeves. 'Come, we will take a pull of these last pages of the *Chronicle* to show you how it is done. Nay, sir; do not try to lift the forme. It is far too heavy. I will call one of the men.' He went to the window and cried, 'Wynken; Pynson; one of you; come hither quickly.'

Bendy, agog with excitement, took up his position beside the press. As he did so the head and shoulders of a lanky youth appeared up the ladder. He was so tall that there seemed to be no end to him.

'This is Dick Pynson, my eldest apprentice,' said Caxton, with a nod. 'You may believe that he finds our change of workshop a boon. When we were squeezed in by the Chapter House he could scarcely unbend at all. Dick, lift over this forme and ink the type. I would show these good masters how we print.'

To be called a 'good master' was flattering, for Bendy judged that the tall boy was considerably his elder. He had a turned-up nose spattered with freckles, and when he grinned at Caxton's jest his face seemed to be all mouth. Though he looked weedy his long arms gathered up the heavy forme without difficulty. He placed it carefully on the bench in front of the press, turning back the hinged top of a wooden frame to make room for it. Bendy looked at the frame, wondering what it was for; the lid was doubly hinged, so that it opened twice.

The forme safely in position, Dick Pynson fetched what looked like two large mushrooms, smeared with something black and greasy.

'The ink,' said Caxton briefly. 'Go to it, Dick. Show how it is.'

Bendy watched enviously as Dick dabbed the face of the type with the two mushrooms; *he* would enjoy doing that. Dick set about it with a flourish that looked most professional. Obviously he was delighted to show his skill. When he had finished Caxton came forward with a clean sheet of paper, which he laid in the open frame alongside the inky forme.

'Now you see why one needs two pairs of hands for printing,' he observed lightly, folding down the rim of the frame to keep the paper flat. 'You may imagine that the fellow who inks cannot touch the paper.'

Peeping at the forme to make sure that the inking was to his liking, he turned the frame over so that the paper rested on the type. At a sign from his master Dick worked a handle in the side of the press and the whole bench-top moved slowly into the jaws of the monster. Then he reached up and grasped the lever of the great wooden screw. Creaking and groaning, the heavy board came slowly down.

'Enough,' cried Caxton. 'Unscrew, and let us see it.'

Bendy bent forward eagerly as Caxton spread out the printed sheet. It was easy enough to read now:

Thus endeth this present book of the Cronycles of Englonde/
Enpryntede by me William Caxton in thabbey of Westmestreby

the letters were the right way round. Suddenly Caxton snatched at his arm.

'Keep off the type,' he cried, and roared with laughter as Bendy held up a hand smeared with black ink. 'Did I not say he would be covered before the day was out? Don't rub it, boy. You'll get it on the other one too. It will wear off in time. I'll give you a piece of pumice-stone to take home.'

As Bendy stared ruefully at his hand, he heard a little snigger behind him. The child Elizabeth! Why must the wench appear just when he had made a fool of himself? But Elizabeth quickly looked away. She bobbed a curtsy to her father.

'If it pleases you, sir,' she said, with an air of importance. 'My mother asks if you will beg Master Goodrich to stay and sup with us.'

'Sup?' cried John Goodrich. 'Is it near to supper? The time has passed so quickly. Indeed, sir, I must go. It would be night before we reached home, and I should not relish the hazards of the river in the dark.'

Caxton, finding argument useless, said that he would walk with them part of the way. Elizabeth insisted on coming too; so, much to his indignation, Bendy found himself following his father and Caxton, with Elizabeth on one side of him, and on the other Elizabeth's Flemish nurse, an old woman with a face like a withered apple under a coif of the most outlandish shape.

This time they went through the postern into the Abbey, and skirting the boundary of the Abbot's garden, came out on to the green close near the main doors of the church.

'As you see, they are still at work on the tracery of the west window,' said Caxton, pointing up at the forest of scaffolding. 'This nave has been nigh on a hundred years in the making and it is not finished yet.'

He led the way across a stretch of open ground which he said was called Broad Sanctuary. Elizabeth, pattering along between Bendy and her nurse, caught the word 'sanctuary' and pointed to a cluster of little houses huddled inside the Abbey wall.

'Look! That's where all the thieves and vagabonds lodge when they claim sanctuary,' she said in an awestruck whisper. 'My father can't imagine why the Lord Abbot puts up with them, except that it always has been so. If the King's men break bounds to try and take them, they bar themselves in that tower; do you see it, standing among the houses? It's supposed to be a belfry, but it is so strong that it would stand a siege. And look' – she shifted the direction of her hand – 'there's St

Margaret's, where we go to Mass. It's the parish church, and my father's very important there; he keeps accounts of their money.'

Bendy merely grunted. The child was like a hurdy-gurdy. He wanted to look about him as they passed under the north gate of the Abbey into King Street, the road to London. But she hadn't done with him yet.

'Look, here's the beginning of Thieving Lane. It goes right round the outside of Sanctuary and comes out by the west gate.' She crept close and hissed into his ear, 'That's where they spilled the paper.'

The Sign of the Red Pale

Bendy glanced round quickly this time. The dark alley running off to the left looked an unsavoury spot and he had no desire to explore it. A few yards farther on they turned under a large, imposing gatehouse and found themselves in New Palace Yard. This was familiar ground. In that far corner lay the wharf where they had landed when he came with the choir.

It was crowded and noisy after the quiet of the Abbey. But Elizabeth's shrill voice still rang in his ear:

'Oh, look at all the people. That's a bishop; the page is carrying his mitre. And look at those swaddled babies; they must be twins. Oh, and there's the spice man; he's wearing his lion cloak.'

Bendy turned sharply. 'Lion cloak? Where?'

'Over there by the well. He seems to be everywhere.'

Bendy looked where she pointed. Lounging against the timbers of the well-head in the middle of the Yard was Tom Twist.

'*What* did you call him?' he demanded.

'The spice man. He goes round selling spices. My mother buys from him. She says he goes all over England with his old white horse. *I* saw him selling spices in Salisbury when I was there.'

Bendy suddenly awoke to the fact that Caxton and his father were just turning down to the river. He told Elizabeth to come quickly, and hurried after them. Only when he was sitting with his father in the boat did he have time to wonder if it was mere chance that Tom Twist was at Westminster, so close to Thieving Lane, where the paper had been attacked.

The long-boat was heavy

CHAPTER 7

The Long-Boat by the South Bank

THE sun had gone down before they reached Paul's Wharf. All the way from Westminster, Bendy had dabbled his hands in the water and rubbed them with his piece of pumice till they were quite sore; but the ink-stains would not move. His father looked with raised eyebrows and laughed. Not a word was said, which made Bendy feel pleasantly like a conspirator. To feel like a conspirator with his father was new, and he enjoyed it.

As they approached the Crowing Cock the door opened suddenly, throwing a beam of light across the darkening street. A woman came skipping out, laughing merrily. She almost collided with Master Goodrich, then recovered herself, bobbed a curtsy, and fled. Bendy stared in astonishment. It was the widow Pratt, Humphrey's mother, but he had certainly never seen her look young and merry before.

John Goodrich glanced after her; then, without comment,

he went indoors, while Bendy hurried to the pump. But pump water was no better than river water for removing stains and there seemed nothing for it but to go in to supper and hope for the best.

His father and his brothers were already seated at the table. Matthew seemed in a rare good temper. He was telling a story about a rogue dressed up as a monk who had been caught collecting alms for lepers. He was clapped in the stocks with the collecting bag round his neck, and what the passers-by put into it was ill-fitted to be told at supper.

Bendy shouted with laughter, all his fears forgotten. Without thinking, he reached out for a slice of brawn from the dish and Cornelius saw him.

'Bendy, for shame! Your hands! Have you forgotten your way to the pump?'

Matthew looked round. 'Did he ever know it? Why, boy, they are black. Tar, I suppose. You've been down to the river.'

Bendy grinned. Tar would do very well. But his father did not accept it. 'Not tar,' he said quietly. 'Just ink.'

'Ink? Then he has *not* washed himself. There is no ink on *my* hands.'

'This is different. It won't come out without much pains, I fear. It is printing ink.'

Matthew frowned. 'Is this a joke, sir?'

'No joke, my son. Bendy came with me to Westminster at the invitation of Master Caxton.'

The colour mounted in Matthew's face. He stared at his father as though unbelieving. 'To *Westminster*?'

'Yes; why not? It is full of interest, I assure you.'

For a moment there was silence. Matthew's rage could find no words.

'I – I'll not have it,' he exploded. 'I'll have no traffic between this house and that. You know full well, sir, how I abominate this damnable false craft. 'Tis naught but a work of the devil to cheat honest men of their livelihood by aping true handwriting. Yet you, who call yourself a scrivener of repute, actually keep company with it.'

John Goodrich remained calm. 'We have discussed this before, and I see no reason to grow heated. There was a king once who tried to stop the sea. He achieved nothing but to wet his feet; but since his day we've learned to make the tides grind our corn. Profit from that story, my good Matthew. Where you cannot stay a torrent, study how to harness it.'

'Harness the devil!' cried Matthew roughly. 'If you are set on playing traitor to your own craft, I suppose I cannot stop you. But before Heaven you shall not take the boy. I am master of the Crowing Cock now; Benedict is my brother, and I'll not have it.'

His father stiffened. He was angry at last. 'Curb your tongue, sir. How dare you speak me thus! You are so stiff-necked with pride and jealousy that you cannot turn your head to face facts. Your brother is my son; it is for me to decide what is rightful for him. If you are master of the Crowing Cock it is because I made you so, and now you rule it in your own way, telling me nothing. Why, then, should I consult you? But I am your father as well as the boy's, and by God's law I am entitled to your courtesy.'

Matthew stood up. 'Sir, if I have lacked courtesy I ask your pardon. You say I tell you nothing. That must be set right. This is not the moment I should have chosen for my announcement, but I will delay no longer. I have to ask your blessing on my marriage. I am shortly to wed the Widow Pratt.'

There was dead silence. Bendy's mouth dropped open. The Widow Pratt! *Humphrey's mother*. It came like a stab of lightning out of a stormy sky. They had been disputing about Caxton, and now suddenly *this*. He looked at his father; but John Goodrich was once more completely calm.

'So far as you desire my blessing it is yours,' he said. 'It is long overdue that you should wed. I pray that you may be very happy.'

Matthew softened. 'I thank you, sir. I would assure you that Mistress Pratt is in earnest about her duty. I believe that you will gain a daughter and Benedict a new mother.'

A new mother! It was the last straw. Bendy clenched his hands until they hurt. He saw the muscles stiffen round his father's mouth. But Matthew, apparently satisfied, continued without pause:

'Benedict in truth will profit greatly from the change. He gains also a brother. I will ask you, sir, to order his compliance that he may behave to Humphrey as a good brother should.'

'He will behave, I doubt not, as I would have him to do,' said Master Goodrich quietly. 'Bendy, fetch the wine. We must drink a toast.'

Thankful to turn his back, Bendy collected his father's silver cup and the latten ones which served the rest of the family. The mugs of ale were pushed aside, and, standing, John Goodrich drank to his eldest son. Bendy, waiting miserably at his elbow, was comforted by a sip from his father's cup and thankful when immediately afterwards his father bade him go to bed.

At the top of the stairs, in the parlour, he almost bumped into old Mother Collin. She was folding sheets in the linen-press by the light of a single taper. His first thought was that she had been listening, but that was unlikely; she was too deaf. Only when she gripped his arm did he realize that she was waiting for him.

'Hist! Master Bendy,' she whispered. 'The old blind dame across the road made me vow that I would give you a message, word for word.' She leaned nearer. 'Go to the morrow Mass at St Benet Hithe.'

'Was that all?' he asked, puzzled.

'Just as she said it. Have you got it clear, master?'

'Quite clear. I am to be at St Benet Hithe at dawn for the morrow Mass.'

She gave him a little pat and returned to the half-folded sheet, while he continued on his way.

Up in the loft he sat on his bed and stared into the darkness. The day, for all its fun, had been full of worries: Will Soper and his threats; the suspicions about Caxton's paper; Tom Twist hanging about Westminster; the rumpus downstairs; and, worst of all, Matthew's marriage, which meant Humphrey – Humphrey always there, Humphrey smug and self-righteous and making trouble, Humphrey as a *brother*. It all felt like a big bruise and deep down inside him was a spot that he dared not even touch – Humphrey's mother where *his* mother should have been.

He roused himself at last. The morrow Mass was at daybreak. If he did not go to bed he would never wake. He knelt down to say his night prayers, partly from habit, partly hoping that he would feel better. But presently he found himself kneeling, without knowing whether he had said them or not. So he crossed himself carefully, as a sort of excuse, undressed quickly, and pushed in between the coarse-woven sheets. He lay turning and tossing while the moon crept round the room. A watchman passed again and again calling the hour. Bendy listened, afraid to sleep lest he should oversleep. It was still moonlight when he fumbled his way into his clothes and crept downstairs.

He planned to go out by the shop door because the back door was heavily barred. But as he reached the bottom step, to his dismay he saw a light in the shop. Who could be up so early? If it were Matthew there was no hope for him.

He tiptoed forward and peeped. To his relief he saw his father at the desk, writing by candlelight. Anxious not to startle him, Bendy said softly, 'Sir, it's me.'

John Goodrich looked round over his spectacles, then took them off and smiled.

'Why, Bendy, what are you doing at this hour?'

'By your leave, sir; the morrow Mass.'

His father nodded gently, 'Good boy,' and Bendy felt a hypocrite. Clearly his father thought he was going out of piety. In the flickering light John Goodrich looked old and weary. On a sudden impulse Bendy took a step forward and knelt for his father's blessing, as his mother had taught him when he was quite a little boy. He felt his father's hand linger gently on his head. As he got up he said, 'God keep you, sir,' and quickly unlocked the door.

Behind the houses the sky was already light. He must hurry.

St Benet Hithe was a small ancient church in Thames Street, not far from Paul's Wharf, where they had embarked yesterday. He made his way to it by little back streets without going near St Paul's. He still had nearly three hours before he was due at school.

By the time he arrived Mass had begun, but the church was still pitch dark. The only light came from the two candles on the altar and it was impossible to recognize any of the kneeling figures dotted about. He settled himself near the door so that no one could go in or out without his seeing, and suddenly felt secure. He was too far off to hear the priest at the altar but he could see his movements, and it was all so familiar and so safe that the nightmares of the past hours slipped away.

Of course it was Peterkin that he was looking for. The message could mean nothing else, but he began to feel uneasy when the church emptied with no sign of him. He decided to wait outside and had just popped his cap back on to his head when Peterkin appeared breathless round the corner.

'You're late,' cried Bendy. 'I thought I'd got the message wrong.'

'We had trouble at the Bridge. We could only just make the rapids. We've got a heavy load.'

'A heavy load? What of?'

Peterkin grinned. 'Use your wits, Tom Fool!'

Bendy's spirits rose like a hawk. 'Paper! Where is it?'

'In the long-boat across by the south bank. Come on; hurry!'

A slippery gully by Baynard's Castle

He led the way along Thames Street and suddenly dived down a slippery gully beside the stone wall of Baynard's Castle. At the bottom a small skiff was tied to a ring in the wall.

'Get in,' said Peterkin briefly. 'I'll row you across.'

The river was cold and misty. Bendy, sitting in the stern, tried to collect his thoughts. He had guessed that Peterkin had some news about paper, but here, apparently, was the paper itself, and he supposed that they were going to take it to Westminster.

'How did you get it?' he inquired when they were in mid-stream.

'Wish that you may know,' returned Peterkin crisply. 'Maybe there's more to come if no questions are asked.'

He was rowing at a slant across the river and soon through the mist Bendy saw the bank of reeds that fringed the shallows. Peterkin nosed the boat gently along until they almost touched the side of a slim, flat-bottomed barge lying well concealed. It was loaded with bales, but there was no sign of life about it, and Bendy was just about to inquire how they were to work it by themselves, when the head of a man appeared from behind the bales. He was a huge, swarthy man and he grinned at the boys, revealing broken fangs of teeth and a great empty cavity of a mouth. He made strange noises in his throat that seemed to be an attempt at speech. Bendy stared aghast; it was like an animal.

'He's dumb,' said Peterkin. 'His tongue was cut out by pirates. But he's strong as an ox and he's asking where we're to take the load. I told him that you would know.'

With an effort Bendy pulled himself together and thought of the little wharf by the mill bank where Caxton had landed with them only yesterday.

The huge man nodded.

'You see! Black Jack knows it,' remarked Peterkin triumphantly. 'Get aboard while I hide the skiff in the reeds.'

Bendy found the journey very different from the last one. The long-boat was heavy, and though the tide was flowing up-stream it took the combined efforts of the huge man and the two boys to move it through the water. By the time that the church bells rang out the hour of six they had got no farther than Temple Stairs, and Bendy realized that he could not possibly be at school by seven. Worse still, it was the day of the water sports. If he arrived late he would certainly be kept in all the afternoon. However, missing the water sports was a small matter compared with the adventure of taking a load of paper to Caxton.

With aching arms he laboured at his pole, too tired even to glance at the Palace of Westminster as they slid by it. At the mill wharf Peterkin took charge, calling to the miller that they had a load for Master Caxton and wanted to pull in.

'Do you go and look for him,' he instructed Bendy. 'Find out where he would have us carry it. I will beg a barrow from the miller. Oh – and Bendy, bid him bring his purse. We durst not go back without the money.'

Bendy set off by the path along the stream. He was even too tired to resent being treated like Peterkin's apprentice. Before turning down into the Almonry he stopped by the postern in the wall to smooth his tousled hair and wipe his face on his sleeve. Suddenly he heard a woman's voice behind him.

'Pray move, good fellow; you are blocking the gate.'

He swung round to see Mistress Caxton herself standing in the postern. She held Elizabeth by the hand and they both carried prayer-book slings. Clearly they were returning from Mass. Elizabeth recognized him at once.

'Why, madam, it is Benedict: the boy who came yesterday.'

Bendy, conscious of his bedraggled state, hastily made his bow.

'You are betimes this morning,' said Mistress Caxton kindly. 'If you want my husband, he is still in church. Nay – here he comes. Wait for him if you wish.'

Smiling at him, she passed, with Elizabeth, into the Almonry passage. At that moment Caxton himself emerged from the postern. At the sight of Bendy he looked surprised.

'Why, boy, what brings *you* so early? There's naught amiss with your father, I hope?'

Bendy drew a deep breath. 'I have brought you a load of paper, sir. It is in the barge-boat down by the mill.'

'Paper!' cried Caxton; 'and a boatload of it. What news!

I suppose your father sent it. I trust I am not robbing the Crowing Cock?'

Bendy almost laughed. Robbing the Crowing Cock! 'My father knows naught of it,' he said. 'I have a friend who works on the river. I told him your trouble, and he sent word that he had procured a load for you. But' – he hesitated – '*I* don't know where it comes from, sir, and I am pledged that you won't ask questions.'

Caxton whistled. 'Bendy, you are too young for this sort of game. How came you to be mixed up in it?'

'I know nothing, sir,' cried Bendy, afraid lest the plan should miscarry, after all. 'I did but mention it to Peterkin and then show him where to bring it. 'Tis not dishonest, sir; they want to be paid for it.'

'I'll warrant that they do! Well, if you give me your word that you have no part in it, I'll say no more. 'Tis all a battle of wits. Till now I have been on the losing side, and if the wind has changed, who am I to quarrel with it? I must have paper if I am to live, so lead on, boy; I'll play fair with your friends if they play fair with me.'

The business was quickly done. When they reached the wharf the barge was already turned and facing down-river. Black Jack stood in the stern, pole in hand, ready to push off at the first sign of trouble. Peterkin was watching for them, and when Bendy signalled that all was well, he came forward, bringing with him a piece of paper as a sample. He actually waved Bendy away while Caxton examined it and they conducted their bargain. Bendy stood kicking his heels on the wharf, uncertain whether to be more angry or astonished. He knew Peterkin only as a Song School boy, far below himself in class and learning, and yet here he was accepting Peterkin's orders without a murmur.

In a few minutes Peterkin was back, grinning broadly. The miller's barrows were trundled out, and while Black Jack unloaded the boat, the two boys went backwards and forwards, dumping the bales beside the doorway of the Red Pale.

When it was all finished and Peterkin joined Black Jack in the barge, Caxton held Bendy back.

'Have you broken your fast, boy? – Why, you must be famished. Here – give this to your shipmates to spend at the tavern and do you come home with me. I'll send you back to London later.'

Now that he thought of it, Bendy realized that part of his weariness was sheer hunger, and he followed Caxton gladly. On the table in the hall-room at the Red Pale stood a loaf and some cheese with a covered ale-mug.

'You see, my breakfast awaits me,' smiled his host. 'But we'll do better than that for you.' He clapped his hands loudly, and Elizabeth came running in. 'Here is a young man who is starving. Go to the kitchen like a good wench and fetch something tasty. He has done me a service and earned better than bread and cheese.'

Elizabeth stared at Bendy as though she would learn what service he had done, but, as her father grunted at her, she disappeared and returned quickly, carrying a dish of roasted capon and a bowl of ripe strawberries.

'That's better,' said Caxton. 'Now fall to, boy. Get the edge off your appetite before I ask you any more questions.'

Bendy needed no more telling. The capon was luscious and dripping with jellied gravy. Elizabeth watched him, obviously hoping for an invitation to join the feast; but her father bade her go, so she curtsied, then helped herself to two large strawberries, and withdrew.

Caxton cut a slice of bread and cheese. 'You know,' he said slowly, 'that was a good stroke of business. Of course there is not enough paper to finish the *Chronicle of England*, but your friend Peterkin thinks he can bring more. The strange part is that it is Unicorn, the self-same make that I ordered from Flanders – one of the best for printing.'

Bendy looked down at his food, hoping that his face did not betray him. This was getting dangerous. Supposing the paper really *was* part of the load of Unicorn that Tom Twist had spoken of to Matthew? How much did Caxton guess, and what awkward questions was he going to ask?

But Caxton did not mention paper again. His questions were about Peterkin. Peterkin seemed a bright lad; where did he live? How did Bendy know him? Greatly relieved, Bendy explained about Peterkin at Paul's Song School and told how he had now gone to work on the river to earn money for his old blind grandmother.

Caxton nodded approvingly. 'I said he was a good lad, though he may well have got into the hands of rogues. London river is alive with rogues. But talking of Paul's School, how comes it that you are abroad at this hour of day? Is it a holiday, or is your exeat of yesterday a little overstretched?'

Bendy bit his lip. He did not like to be reminded of school, for it was now so late that his punishment could be nothing less than a beating.

Caxton saw his face and laughed. 'You must not have to pay too heavily for bringing me a load of paper,' he said. 'Hark you; I have a thought. I am pledged to go to London myself this afternoon. I am to see Master Robert Tate again – the same who directed me to your father, and who sent the paper that reached us in such a sorry state. If you would like, you shall come with me. Your schoolmaster cannot pluck you from the sanctuary of a sheriff's house, and on the way back I will call upon your father and beg him to put matters right for you. What say you? – Then go to the workshop and wait for me there. Doubtless you will find plenty to occupy you.'

Thanks to the arrival of the paper, everyone in the workshop was busy. Wynken de Worde, Dick Pynson the lanky apprentice, and a couple of small boys were all stripping the canvas from the bales, smoothing the sheets, and then laying them in neat piles with heavy boards to flatten them. Bendy quickly pulled off his doublet, and in shirt and hose joined in the work. He had often helped with paper at the Crowing Cock. Wynken de Worde watched him for a moment, then, seeing that he knew what he was doing, went back to his composing at the far end of the workshop.

Left alone with the boys, Bendy picked up a sheet and held it up to the light to see the water-mark. Yes, it was a Unicorn. He looked round and found Dick Pynson grinning at him. He turned red. Probably they thought he was showing off. Pynson opened his mouth to say something but not a sound came and his mouth seemed stuck. Bendy stared. He had never seen any-one stutter before. With a supreme effort the youth grimaced and got out the word 'You-you-you-U-nicorn'.

Simultaneously they sighed with relief and then both laughed. The youth said, 'You're a scr-scr-scrivener, aren't you? You know about p-paper. My name's Dick P-Pynson. What's yours?'

Bendy gave his name. He felt pleased. 'My father's a scri-vener,' he said. 'Unicorn's soft paper; the quill sticks on it.' He was quoting Matthew, but it sounded well.

'It's good for p-printing, though, to my mind, not so good

Bull's Head Water-mark

Hand and Flower Water-mark

as *Bull's Head* or *Hand and Flower*; and there's not enough of it. Every c-copy of the *Chronicle of England* t-takes nigh on a hundred sheets. The d-d-devil's at work in this paper business.'

Bendy ran his eye over the paper, now nearly all sorted. A hundred sheets; there would not be very many copies printed from this lot. He thought of the paper stacked in his loft and felt ashamed.

With the last sheet safely flattened, the apprentices gathered

A composing stick

up the canvas and began to sweep the floor. Bendy tiptoed down the workshop and stood quietly behind Wynken de Worde, who was setting up a page of type. Caxton had said that Wynken's fingers were like the fingers of a lute-player, and he watched him fascinated. A page of copy was stuck up in front of him; in his left hand he grasped a stick with a long groove down the middle, and into the groove he popped the letters, one after the other, as he picked them from the sloping case. His hand flew backwards and forwards with hardly a pause except when he finished a line and slid it unbroken from the stick into the framework which Caxton had called the forme.

Bendy was so engrossed that he scarcely noticed when Caxton himself appeared to take stock of the morning's work, and he did not move until he felt a tap upon the shoulder.

'We must be away, or Master Tate will think that I have forsaken him.'

The sun was high by the time they left the Almonry. It had been cool enough in the early morning, and Bendy was astonished to find it so hot. Instead of crossing Broad Sanctuary in the blazing sunshine, Caxton kept to the shade along the

Houses huddled between the buttresses

north side of the Abbey Church. Bendy looked curiously at the houses built close up against the great walls – some of them actually huddled between buttresses, cutting off half the light from the windows. They had nothing of that sort at Paul's.

'Geoffrey Chaucer ended his days here,' remarked Caxton pointing to one between the Abbey and St Margaret's Church. 'I often think how he would marvel to see his *Canterbury Tales* imprinted hundreds of times within a bowshot of his own door. Doubtless he would be glad, because his fame is bound to grow more and more with all the copies of his stories. He was Comptroller of the King's Customs in his day. Did you know that, boy?' He suddenly laughed. '*He* would have been the person to help us about paper!'

Bendy laughed too, their voices sounding hollow as they dived into a tunnel between overhanging houses. But another thought had just sprung into his mind. If printing could add so much to a man's fame, how about Sir Thomas Malory?

Mucking Creek

CHAPTER 8

The Honest Pirate

WELL fed and reassured that things would be put right for him at school, Bendy settled down beside Caxton in a double-oar wherry, feeling as important as the Mayor of London. True that he would probably miss the water sports, but what were water sports compared with going to visit Master Robert Tate, the Sheriff? To add to his pride, they disembarked not at Paul's Wharf, but farther down towards the Bridge, at the Three Cranes, which was the landing stage used by the Mayor and the great men of the City.

From the river they went up the hill past the Tower Royal, across Budge Row, and out into the busy, noisy turmoil of Cheap, near where it merged with the Poultry mart. Cheap on a Saturday morning was as good as a fair, with all the house-wives out marketing for the Sunday dinner; the poultry-sellers yelling at one end 'Chickens and fat capons', 'Young ducks and goslings at your fancy', 'Buy, buy, buy', and at the other end the shrill voices of apprentices crying, 'Buttons and laces', 'Ribbons and coifs', 'What d'you lack? What d'you lack?'

Bendy would have liked to linger, but it was difficult enough not to lose Caxton in the crowd. They were parted once when Bendy was tempted by a gingerbread man, and he was looking round for him when he felt somebody pinch his arm. A voice said near his ear, 'Hey! young master, I see you keep good company.' He turned quickly, and was just in time to catch a glimpse of a cloak with a faded lion. A pest on the fellow! Now the story would go straight back to Matthew.

He found Caxton at last and followed him round the corner into a street with the sign 'Old Jewry'. Half-way along they stopped in front of an ancient stone house with a great studded door and little slits of windows. Could this be where Master Tate lived?

Caxton shook his head. 'Nay; Master Tate has a fine new house out on Moorfields. *This* is where I was apprentice many years ago. I like to look at it when I pass. My master, Robert Large, had a big family round my own age. They were good days and merry ones.'

'It looks old,' said Bendy, staring at it.

'It *is* old. They say it was a synagogue of the Jews before they were cast out; then it was a house of begging friars, and then the hall of the Lord Fitzwalters. Those are the Fitzwalter arms above the door. Robert Large, my master, was one of the greatest mercers of his day. He was Mayor while we were in that house. 'Tis no small matter to be prentice to the Mayor, I promise you. I can remember my master himself saying that; *he* was prentice when Dick Whittington was Mayor.'

'The Mayor who had a cat?' cried Bendy, suddenly alert.

Caxton looked down at him and laughed. 'Yes, the Mayor who had a cat. He did more for the City than any man before or since; but I suppose that he is lucky to have a cat to be remembered by. Look not so puzzled, boy. My poor wit is not worth the explaining. Come on now; we've lingered long enough.'

They went out of the City through a small gate in the Wall and crossed the moat by a wooden footbridge. To Bendy, Moorfields was familiar ground. The boys of Paul's played football there and in the winter it was flooded and everybody skated. But *this* end of Moorfields was different. Streets of new houses were springing up and Caxton said testily that the town was swallowing the country.

Master Tate's house was a large one, its timber frame filled in with bright new bricks instead of white-washed plaster. Caxton exclaimed at its ugliness, but Bendy secretly thought it very fine.

A neat apprentice met them at the door and led them upstairs to a big room handsomely panelled in creamy oak. An open window looked out to distant wooded hills.

At a richly carpeted table sat a stout, middle-aged man. His gown was thrown open and his double chins overlapped the edges of a fine lawn shirt. He rose to his feet as they entered.

'God greet you, Master Caxton. I had begun to fear you weren't coming. You must be dead with heat. I have wine cooling in the well for you.' He signed to a young man standing behind him. 'This is my kinsman, young Jack Tate. Jack, I prithee fetch the wine; the lads would surely bring the wrong flagon. – Did you ride, sir? Has someone taken your horse?'

'Nay, we came by river. I had a fancy to walk up Old Jewry, past Robert Large's house, where I was prentice many years ago.'

Tate nodded sympathetically. His small eyes, though shrewd, were bright as a robin's. 'I know the house. Are you acquainted with Hugh Clopton, who lives there now? He's from Stratford-upon-Avon, in Warwickshire, my own county; another mercer, and a pleasant person. You should call on him. He would be honoured to receive a visit from so illustrious a member of our Guild. But sit you down, sir; sit you down. To walk from the river in this heat is no jest.' He placed for Caxton a carved chair with a cushion on it. Then he glanced at Bendy. 'The boy here, is he your apprentice? Shall he join the lad downstairs, or would you prefer that he should stay?'

'If you are agreeable let him stay. He is not my apprentice, but he has just done me a service at risk to himself of a sound beating. May I tell you the story? You may find it entertaining.' He began forthwith a light-hearted account of the arrival of the long-boat with the dumb man and the two boys.

Master Tate tucked in his double chins and chuckled almost silently. A fine gold chain lying on his chest bobbed up and down. 'That is a good story, though 'tis galling to think that these boys succeeded in getting paper to you where I failed. Seriously, sir, I was perturbed to get your letter about the trouble in Thieving Lane. It looks perilously to me as if you had an enemy at work. Is there any with a grudge against you?'

'None that I know of. True I have always been a White Rose man, but we have a White Rose King. The Red Rose is dead. Young Henry Tudor in Brittany is of small account.'

'The evils of London river go back much farther than the Wars of the Roses,' Tate reminded him. 'My grandfather used to say that he could not count on bringing a single cargo up the Thames without some knave taking toll of it. If it escaped the pirates and smugglers it was pillaged by the Customs men. Ah! Here comes the wine.'

As the young man entered, the older one reached up to a row of silver cups on a shelf.

'Pour it out for Master Caxton without delay, Jack. And how about the boy? What will he drink? Wine? Ale? – or our water here is notably sweet. We fetch it every morning from the conduit by Cripplegate – the one set up by Dick Whittington. My wife makes orange syrup, and the children enjoy a dash of it in the water; how would that suit you?'

Flattered by so much attention, Bendy decided for orange. It was delicious, and he sat on a joint stool sipping it while Jack Tate filled and re-filled the wine-cups and the men discussed the problem of paper.

'I wonder that there is no paper made in England,' said Jack Tate, breaking in upon his elders. 'That would solve the whole matter. Tell me, sir, does it contain such rare substances that no one has tried it?'

'Naught but cloth rags beaten to pulp in running water. In Flanders they are rich both in cloth and water.'

'But we are cloth-weavers too, and we have plenty of rivers.'

Caxton smiled at the young man's eagerness. 'True enough. Then here is your chance, young master. Build a paper-mill, and when scriveners throw away their pens and take to printing your fortune will be made.' He turned back to Robert Tate. 'What you say of London river is bad hearing, sir. In Flanders the ports are well kept. How comes it that England lags so far behind?'

'Ah, but Flanders is easy to guard; their harbours lie near together. Think of the English coast from Newcastle right round to Bristol. There are too many shores with easy landing and only twelve ports to oversee it all. And across the Channel lies Brittany, honeycombed with little rocky bays where pirates can have their hiding-holes.'

'But the King's Customs? There are Customs officers at every port.'

Robert Tate snapped his fingers in the air. '*That* for the King's Customs! We know better than to trust the Customs. Consider! At each of the twelve ports there are a couple of Customs officers and a handful of Searchers to board the ships, with miles and miles of coast to guard. And here's the rub: the Searchers have no wages. They get nothing except a share from the contraband they seize. Their pockets can be better lined if they turn a blind eye on smuggling, or even make common cause with it.'

Caxton frowned. 'But if things are as bad as that, how can business go on at all? After all, a merchant lives by the goods that are shipped to him. If he is robbed every time a cargo comes up London river how does he survive?' He glanced round the room at its oak wainscot, its costly hangings, the little painted panel of the Blessed Virgin gleaming with gold leaf, the ivory casket standing on the table, and he smiled mischievously. '– and I must confess me, sir, I see no signs of penury.'

Master Tate chuckled again, enjoying the joke. 'Praise be to God, we survive.' He leaned forward confidentially. 'I beg you, sir, to remember that I speak not as Sheriff, but as plain Robin Tate, the mercer, in private counsel with his fellow of the Guild. The King and his Customs cannot protect us, so we must need help ourselves. There is an old saying about set a thief to catch a thief. It is sage advice and many of us follow it. Do you grasp my meaning?'

'You mean, I suppose, that you employ some fellow who knows the ropes to pilot your goods.'

'Precisely; and so long as we receive good service we do not inquire too deeply. Now you would benefit from such a fellow, and, truth to tell, I have one in mind for you. So far as I know him, he is an honest knave, true to his word. He knows the river and all its creeks as you know your own hand' – he cocked an eyebrow – 'and if he also knows the coasts of Brittany, that is no business of ours. But tell me, do I shock you?'

'I am too old to be easily shocked,' said Caxton, 'so long as there is no cheating in it. If I were still governor of the Domus Anglorum it might be different. But I am now but a poor printer in need of paper for my trade. What is the fellow's name and how may I get in touch with him?'

'His name is John Stern; he is a shipmaster from Bristol and he owns a privateer – the *Katharine*. Truth to tell, he is waiting in my warehouse. I thought we might have need of him. Jack, I pray you go and bring him here.'

Bendy sat as quiet as a mouse, in case Master Tate had forgotten him. He did not want to be sent away just now. From what he had heard there seemed no doubt that this John Stern was a pirate – an honest pirate, perhaps, but a pirate all the same. Some of the boys at school talked boastfully about pirates, but he couldn't remember anybody who had actually met one.

He was hugging himself at the thought when the door opened and Jack Tate ushered in the strangest figure he had ever seen. The shipmaster was a dark man, broad-shouldered, with a big nose and a walk that was half a swagger, half a roll. He wore parti-coloured hose, yellow and black, tucked into water-stained boots, elaborately fringed and thonged. His leather doublet was old and greasy, but over it, instead of a gown, he wore a flowing scarlet cloak of cloth so fine and silky that even Bendy, who was no mercer, stared at it. As he swept a bow it billowed out, revealing a belt with jewels in it and an analace in a sheath richly enamelled. On his head was perched a velvet cap of emerald green, set off by a long feather.

Invited by Master Tate to sit down, John Stern glanced round, then he seized the joint stool from which Bendy had

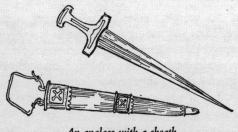

An analace with a sheath

risen at his entrance and straddled it, the analace clanking and the scarlet cloak draping the floor. Bendy gazed at him, trying to memorize every detail to describe to Peterkin later. It was only when the word *Madalena* caught his ear that he realized he had not been listening. He could have kicked himself. How much had he missed?

'She was bound straight for London,' Caxton was saying. 'And, mark you, this is not by a long chalk the first cargo I have lost.'

'The *Madalena*,' said the pirate thoughtfully. 'Ay, I know

The Madalena

the vessel. She bears a maiden's head upon her mainsail. Her master is of Sluys and her crew a mongrel lot. I wonder what else she carried. I'd stake my life that there were spices.'

'Spices would be worth the robbing,' commented Master Tate. 'But why should anyone want paper? 'Tis bulky and of no great value.'

John Stern grinned. 'As like as not they have a market for it. These fellows burrow underground like conies. A merchant as far away as Oxford or Northampton might want paper – or for that matter any other goods. If he is prepared to pay through the nose he will get it. Of course wine and spices are the most favoured contraband – easy to sell and hard to trace; but there's little that they cannot market somewhere.'

'At the Customs office they told me that the King's Grace himself was taking action,' said Caxton. 'By his order there was to be a new fleet with the special task of guarding vessels entering the Thames. *Convoyers*, or *wafters*, they called them, I believe.'

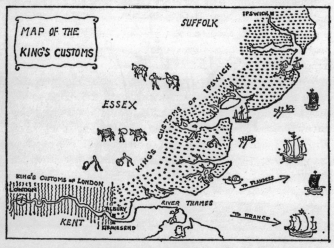

A hundred miles of the busiest waterway

Stern threw back his head. 'The *Customs*,' he laughed. 'Did you know, sir, that London Customs have charge only for a few miles down the river? Beyond Gravesend it is the duty of Sandwich. And likewise on the north bank, from Tilbury onwards it belongs to Ipswich. Ipswich! I ask you! A noble little port full of worthy burgesses, but a hundred miles away along the foreshore – a hundred miles of the busiest waterway in the world. Have you ever sailed the coast of Essex, my masters? The inlets are like weevil runs in a cheese – from Pennyhole Bay right round to Mucking Creek.'

Mucking Creek! Bendy gasped so loudly that they all looked round. Suddenly inspired, he pretended that something had stung him, and rubbed the back of his neck. The discussion turned to practical matters; could John Stern succeed in bringing paper from Flanders, and how much should he be paid for it?

Bendy scarcely knew whether he was on his head or his heels. When Tom Twist had said to Matthew 'She's a-mucking' it had never occurred to him that Mucking might be a *place*. And now here was everyone discussing what could have happened to the *Madalena*, and *he knew*.

What should he do? Say so? Tell Caxton? He must have more time to think. Peterkin had known the name, which meant that Peterkin was in it, and he would never give Peterkin away. And Matthew? Disgrace for Matthew would break his father's heart. He must find out more. He did not even know where Mucking Creek was, except that it was in the direction of Ipswich. He must see Peterkin. Now that he knew so much, surely Peterkin could not refuse to tell him more.

He was still befogged with it all when John Stern took his leave. Caxton rose too, but Master Tate insisted that they must stay to dinner. Moreover, afterwards Caxton must ride home to Westminster. He had a mare which would serve the purpose excellently. And as Jack Tate was all agog to see the press, he could accompany their guest and bring the horses back.

For a moment Bendy was panic-stricken. Had Caxton forgotten his promise to put things right about school? But Caxton had not forgotten.

'I thank you for your kindness,' he said to Master Tate.

'But I have an undertaking to call at Paul's as I pass. My errand will not take much more than a paternoster while, and if Master Jack would kindly hold the horses outside the Cathedral, I would gladly accept your offer.' He smiled at Bendy. 'Then the boy can find his own way home.'

The arms of Tate

They stared at one another

CHAPTER 9

A Box on the Ear

AFTER a dinner of roasted beef, with puddings and preserves and sauce served with it, Bendy felt heavy with sleep. He had been awake most of the night, and got up before dawn. The one thing he longed for now was his bed. He waited to see Caxton mount a beautiful chestnut belonging to Master Tate and then he started off to follow on foot to Paul's. Doubtless Caxton would make his peace for him with his father, but all the same he must go and ask pardon for playing truant.

He set off across Moorfields with the afternoon sun in his eyes. On an ordinary Saturday Paul's boys would have been playing there, but today everybody was at the water sports. He was sorry about missing them, but it had the advantage that he could cross Moorfields without running into half the school.

He entered the City at Aldersgate and made his way to Paul's by short cuts well known to him, carefully avoiding the neighbourhood of the Holly Bush, the alehouse where he had diced with Will Soper.

The nave of the Cathedral was as busy as ever, but his father seemed to be alone at his table. Bendy had a moment of fear. Supposing Caxton had not arrived. He hung back a little, but his father looked round, so there was nothing for it but to go on, drop on his knees, and hope for the best.

To his great relief he heard his father laugh. 'Get up, you young fool. You look as smug as a cat lapping cream. Truant all day and *I* am to see that you are not beaten for it! I thought you were at the water sports. Master Caxton says you brought him a load of paper. Where in Heaven's name did you get it? I trust you've not been robbing your brothers?'

Bendy scrambled to his feet. He was bubbling to tell his father the whole story, but it was too dangerous. So he said only that Peterkin had got hold of the paper; he was working for a waterman.

'Peterkin? Oh, the boy opposite with the blind grandmother. How came he to know of the matter?'

'I told him, sir, after Master Caxton first came to you.' He hesitated and then decided that a measure of the truth could do no harm. 'It helped him, sir, because they are in desperate need of money.'

John Goodrich looked mildly astonished. 'And so you matched need to need, with benefit to both. 'Pon my word, I think I had best make a merchant of you. I may tell you that Master Caxton was so pleased with you over this day's work that he came to ask if I would let him have you as apprentice.'

Bendy caught his breath. Apprentice to Caxton! It was as though the sun had suddenly blazed out. But it clouded again at once.

'Of course I had to say No,' his father continued evenly,

turning over some papers on his desk. ''Tis out of the question. It would be too rude a blow to your brothers. But I am glad he asked for you. It is a feather in your cap.'

Bendy could hardly control himself. His *brothers*. His brothers, who were mixed up with knaves and pirates. Perhaps if his father knew, he might change his mind. The temptation to come out with it was almost too much for him, but he shut his mouth tight. He mustn't say a word yet; he mustn't. He must see Peterkin first.

His father looked at him curiously. 'You are tired, boy. Of course, you were up before dawn. Perhaps I should not have told you, but I thought you would like to know that you were well thought of. Go home now; ask Mother Collin for some broth and go to bed.'

Thankful to turn away, Bendy said, 'Yes, sir,' and went. He made straight for the paternosterer's shop.

Peterkin's grandmother was sitting at the door. As soon as she heard Bendy's voice her old face broke into smiles. ''Tis you, young master; praise be to God. Peterkin has paid the rent and brought home good food. He says that it is all thanks to you. Every bead I string is a prayer that our good Lord and His blessed Mother may reward you.'

Bendy gulped. He didn't want thanks. What he wanted was to see Peterkin quickly. She shook her head. Peterkin was out, she told him. He'd had a sleep and gone back to the river. She doubted if he would be in till nearly morning.

So there was nothing to be done. Bendy crossed disconsolately to the Crowing Cock. He might as well take his father's advice and go to bed.

Luckily the place was quiet. Work in the scribes' room ended early on Saturdays, and he climbed the stairs without seeing anyone. At the bottom of his ladder he stopped and looked up. The trap door was open. That was odd; Matthew was particular about its being kept closed.

The square of light gave him a glimpse of rafters and one wall of stacked paper. There was a shadow across it, and the shadow moved. He heard a rustle and then a creak. There was somebody up there.

Carefully he began to ascend the ladder. He knew exactly where to put each hand and each foot and he made no sound until his head was through the opening.

Kneeling in front of Bendy's wooden chest was Humphrey. The lid was open and in his hand was a roll of paper – the King Arthur stories.

For a couple of seconds they stared at one another, both too taken aback to move. Then with the ease of long practice Bendy vaulted into the loft. Humphrey dropped the roll into the chest and banged down the lid. But before he could get to his feet Bendy was upon him. He seized Humphrey by the shoulders and shook him – the little rat! Angry as he was, there was more in his fury than fear for his manuscript. Humphrey was gnawing like a fat little maggot at the basis of his life. He hated Humphrey, and into his rage went payment of old scores with something on account for the future.

Humphrey made no attempt to fight back. He blubbered 'Stop! stop!' like a howling cry-baby. When Bendy's arms ached he dragged him across the floor, pushed him on to the ladder, and then, as a parting shot, dealt him a sound box on the ear.

Humphrey clutched at the rungs; he held on for a moment. Then, with a series of bumps that seemed to shake the house, he fell into the scribes' room and lay there in a heap.

Bendy stared down at him. For one awful instant he wondered if he'd killed him. There were voices below. He heard Cornelius crying, 'How now? How now? What's amiss?' Footsteps clattered up the stairs. To Bendy's utter relief Humphrey began to cry; first a snivel, then a moan, and finally a good full-throated roar of pain and rage.

'– he fell down the ladder'

Cornelius's head was the first to appear. As Matthew followed, Bendy drew back. Humphrey was bellowing so that the brothers could scarcely make themselves heard. They consulted loudly.

'What has happened? What ails the boy?'

'I know not; it seems as though he fell down the ladder.'

'The ladder – what was he doing on the ladder?'

'The trap is open,' said Cornelius. 'He asked me a short time since where Bendy was, and I told him "at the water sports". Maybe he went up to make sure. He might have broken his neck.'

'None with a broken neck could make that noise,' said Matthew tersely. 'Boy, hold your peace; let me see where you are hurt.'

Humphrey's sobs eased a little; he stammered something about Bendy. Cornelius broke in consolingly. 'There, there; we know you were looking for Bendy. All is well now; lie still. – Suppose we move him, brother?'

'Yes,' said Matthew. 'Carry him to my bed. Can you manage? He's weighty, mark you.'

There were sounds of scuffling feet and of fresh cries from Humphrey, of Cornelius breathing heavily and Matthew issuing directions.

When they had gone downstairs Bendy turned back into the loft. It was plain that there was trouble coming, but he was so angry that he did not really care. It was probably the box on the ear that sent Humphrey flying, but serve the little beast right. If this was the sort of thing to be expected in the future, the sooner it was over the better. They could send him to Newgate if they liked; under Matthew's rule the Crowing Cock was no better than a prison.

He went on blustering to himself until suddenly he thought of his precious roll. It was safely in the chest, but he undid it to see that none of it was missing. Then he tiptoed across to the corner of the loft, loosened a package of paper from the stack, and lodged the roll on the rafters behind it. Nobody would find it there.

That done he went to the window and stood looking at the dark attic opposite. If only Peterkin would come in. Then, maybe, he could hit back at Matthew and the tables would be turned completely. He pictured to himself how Matthew would crumple up and *beg* him to keep silent. He sighed deeply; if *only* he dared! But it was too dangerous. It would be like setting fire to a house; there was no knowing where it would end.

He sat down on his bed, listening for every sound. The waiting went on so long that he began to tell himself that Humphrey had decided that it was wiser not to mention him. But presently he heard footsteps coming up to the scribes' room. He shivered.

'Benedict; come down!' It was Matthew's voice.

There was no use putting it off, so he crossed to the open trap. His half-brother stood at the foot of the ladder looking up. In all his life he had never seen Matthew so angry. His eyes and mouth were like slits in his white face. His right hand was behind his back. Bendy knew what that meant. He had a stick.

Trying to conceal his trembling, Bendy clambered down. Matthew waited without a word. Then he took a step back, laid the stick on the scribes' desk, and looked at Bendy as though his eyes would bore holes in the boy's head.

'You tried to kill Humphrey. If he dies the common hangman will deal with you.'

If he dies. Bendy went cold from head to foot. He could get out no more than a whisper. 'He fell down the ladder. He just *fell.*'

'Fell!' repeated Matthew; '*fell!* You threw him down. It was a fall to break his neck. You hate him; you set on him savagely but two days since. The poor child has gone in terror of you. And now that he is to be your brother and share with you, you have murder in your heart.'

Appalled, Bendy shook his head. All his defences had suddenly crumbled, for he knew that it was partly true. He *did* hate Humphrey and he had hit him in a rage, not caring *what* he did. He stood almost numb while Matthew went grimly on about the duty of beating the devil's spirit out of him. He only quickened his breathing when Matthew picked up the stick.

Suddenly there was another footstep on the stairs. Matthew looked round impatiently as his father appeared from below. John Goodrich was flushed and panting.

'What's all this?' he demanded. 'Cornelius told me to come quickly. What are you doing with that stick? What's amiss?'

'This young hound set out to kill Humphrey. 'Twas all but wilful murder.'

'*Murder?* Is the boy dead?'

'Not dead, but battered and as like as not to die.'

'Have you called the doctor and the priest?'

'I sent for the chirugeon.'

'If the boy is in danger send for the priest. What are you thinking of?' He swung round to the stairs and called down, 'Cornelius, the priest; fetch him at once.'

Cornelius' voice came back, smooth and consoling. ''Tis all well, sir; the chirugeon is here. He says there are no bones broken. The boy is but bruised and frightened.'

'*So!*' John Goodrich turned back to the room and looked from his eldest son to his youngest, then to the eldest again. 'And now, if you please, I will know what it is all about.'

'Benedict picked a quarrel with Humphrey and threw him down from the loft to break his neck.'

'*Threw* him down?' He looked at Bendy. 'What have you to say?'

Bendy was almost in tears. 'I did not mean to throw him, sir. I hit him and he fell.'

'Had you been fighting?'

Matthew broke in again. 'Fighting is too good a word. He set upon the child. I tell you he had murder in his heart.'

'The punishment for murder is not beating. Give me that stick.'

'Sir, he must be beaten. He is a danger with his violence.'

'Beating is my prerogative. And you cannot beat him now; you are hot with anger and by God's law you may not beat in anger.'

Reluctantly Matthew put the stick into the outstretched hand. John Goodrich heaved a sigh. 'I hurried up the stairs. By your leave I will have a stool.'

Suddenly aware that his father was deathly white, Bendy sprang forward. But Matthew was before him. At the same moment Cornelius arrived at the top of the stairs, a little puffed and smiling nervously.

'The chirugeon has gone. He is sending some unguent for the bruises. The boy is quiet now; his mother is with him.'

'God be praised,' said John Goodrich simply. 'We may all draw our breath more easily. Matthew, if we are to learn what has befallen in this house, I think it would be well if you sat down too.'

Sighing as though it cost him much, Matthew sat down on one of the scribes' benches. Cornelius lowered himself on to another. Bendy alone remained standing. John Goodrich looked at the two grown men. What more could they tell him of what had happened? But it seemed that they had little to add. The house was quiet, they said, when they heard a cry and a heavy crash. They had rushed up to find Humphrey in a heap on the floor.

'And where was Benedict?'

Cornelius looked a little uneasy. 'We did not see him.'

'Then how did you know that it was his doing?'

'Humphrey said so – as soon as he could speak.'

'*Humphrey* said so? Methinks it is time that we heard what Benedict has to say. Speak the truth now, boy; seek not to save yourself by holding something back. You were with me at Paul's but half an hour before. I would hear all that has happened since you left me.'

Bendy saw his brothers glance at each other; why had he gone to his father at Paul's? – their look said it as plain as any words. He pulled himself together and described how he had come straight home, stopping only to speak to the old blind woman. His father cut him short.

'That is well enough. But when you got here, what then?'

'I came upstairs, sir. There was no one about. But I heard a noise in the loft and went up quietly. Humphrey was there.'

'Why should that anger you? What was he doing?'

Bendy hesitated. There was no avoiding it. 'He was searching through my coffer.'

'Searching? For what?'

Help came in the nick of time, and from an unexpected quarter. 'Sir, this is all trash,' Matthew interposed. 'I can tell you why Humphrey was in the loft, and why Benedict attacked him. I had told him that it should be his in the future. It was but natural that he should go to it.'

His father looked at him with raised brows. 'This may shed a new light,' he said. 'It was your purpose to take the loft from Benedict. Where, then, did you propose that he should sleep?'

Matthew actually appeared confused. 'So long as he can behave himself there is room for them both. But I took it for granted, sir, that he will soon be apprenticed. Surely you do not intend him to idle his days for ever. 'Tis high time he was set to work.'

Bendy marvelled at his father's calmness. He spoke slowly and deliberately:

'Thank you, Matthew; I appreciate your thought for the boy. As a matter of fact I have been thinking very much the same. He is to be apprenticed at once. Only today I received an offer for him.'

Matthew watched uneasily through narrowed eyes. 'That is good news,' he said, attempting a smile. 'Where are you placing him? I think you spoke about a notary?'

'No, he is not to go to a notary. I fear you may not be pleased. Master Caxton has asked me for him. The indentures are to be signed without delay.'

For a moment there was a stunned silence. Then Matthew sprang up, the bench crashing behind him.

'The devil take your Caxton and all his works,' he cried. 'Before Heaven, you must be out of your mind, that you contrive such treachery. The boy can begone and good riddance; may he never set foot here again. He has besotted you from the day that he was born. 'Pon my soul, it would be best if you followed him. You will eat but bitter bread at the Crowing Cock.'

Shocked and appalled, Bendy looked at his father sitting as though he were carved in stone. As Matthew stopped for breath, Cornelius broke out, crying that never had faithful sons been so shockingly rewarded.

John Goodrich waited for him to finish. 'My faithful sons have my house, my goods, my business, and the goodwill that the City bears me,' he said coldly. 'I cannot see that they have cause to complain.'

At that they broke out afresh, both brothers storming at their father simultaneously, so that neither could be heard. He stood up.

'Hold your peace!' he cried, banging on the desk with his fist. 'Not another word until your blood cools. Supper is overdue. In a Miserere-while I shall say Grace downstairs; *in a Miserere-while, mark you*. You have my meaning? Then in

God's name act upon it, all of you.' He swung round to Bendy. 'Benedict, go to your loft and stay there. Your guilt is not purged because your brothers forget their duty.'

His father's eye upon him, Bendy climbed the ladder and closed the trap. With a sinking heart he heard the ladder taken away. He was a prisoner.

His mind was in a whirl. The only clear thing for the moment was his father's bidding to say a Miserere. He steadied himself enough to begin the first verse, familiar from repeating it every day at Vespers: '*Miserere mei, Deus; secundum magnam misericordiam tuam.*' – 'Have mercy upon me, O God, according to thy great mercy' – But he couldn't keep it up. By the time that he reached '– cleanse me from my sin' his thoughts were beginning to take shape again. And the first of them all was that he was to go to Westminster.

He could hardly believe it. Only a short while ago his father had called it impossible. Matthew's venom had changed everything. It was like a miracle, only of course it couldn't be a miracle because it had come from his hitting Humphrey when he was blind with rage. His conscience was not easy about that, and God did not permit miracles for things that were wrong. He sighed. It was a pity about that last blow. Not that he re-

A taperstick

gretted punishing the thieving little rat, but he wished that he had stopped short before the end.

Gradually the light faded. He sat on his bed thinking about Westminster. When would he go? Would Matthew try to stop him? A panic seized him lest even now Matthew might persuade his father. What was going on downstairs? What would happen when they let him out? Would he, after all, come in for a beating?

He did not know how long he had sat there when he heard the ladder being replaced. A voice bade him lift the trap. It was his father.

John Goodrich carried a lighted taper, which he handed up to Bendy to put into a taperstick as he scrambled up into the loft. He looked about him curiously.

'I have not been up here for some time,' he remarked. 'Surely that is not all paper? *All* of it?'

Bendy said, 'Yes, sir,' cautiously. At another time it would have been a good opening to talk about Caxton and the *Madalena*, but not now.

His father grunted. 'How can they hope to use all that? Well, I suppose it is not our business. I have more pressing matters to say to you. Let me make sure that I have a tinder box and I will dowse this light. It can be said as well in the dark.'

Bendy stifled a sigh of relief. His father's face was grave but it had lost the look of cold anger. And, after all, he couldn't be beaten in the dark.

His father read his thought. 'You can ease your mind; I am not going to beat you for this night's work. By Heaven's grace Humphrey is recovering and I think you have suffered punishment already. *I* suffered, I can promise you, when they hazarded that he might die. God help you, boy, have you considered what it could have meant?'

Bendy was silent. He *had* considered; his panic downstairs

was proof of it. But he could not yet give in without a struggle. He muttered something about Humphrey deserving it.

John Goodrich caught him up. 'Yes, yes; you were provoked, I know. But that does not excuse your violence. There is no gainsaying that twice in three days you have attacked him savagely. You suffer yourself to be possessed by rage. Because I do not beat you, think not that you are conscience free.' He sighed deeply. 'Maybe it is because you have lacked a mother. When a boy is young it is a mother who teaches him to be

The Charterhouse

temperate, and I wake up at this late hour to find you hot and mettlesome.'

Bendy gulped, glad that the darkness hid him. But his father went steadily on:

'Now you are to go to Westminster, and that troubles me too. As it turns out, you have profited by your ill deeds. But it is certain that I dare not leave you here. If you were goaded beyond bearing, what might be the end of it? So I must give in, and you, my son, must strive to hold yourself in leash. You dote upon your tales of chivalry. Remember that the new-made knight keeps vigil before the altar with his sword; he spends the hours praying that he may wield it worthily and not for the lust of killing. Before you go to Westminster face yourself, boy, and when you have seen your fault go and be shriven, that you may shun it for the future. We confess our sins not only to be absolved but to know our peril and gain grace to guard against it.'

Bendy said, 'Yes, sir,' hoarsely. He needed no more telling; the truth had sunk in. He knew now that he had set on Humphrey because he hated the brat. It was all moonshine to pretend that he was punishing him; he had *enjoyed* it. He wanted to say this to his father, but no words would come.

John Goodrich kept silent for a moment or two. When he spoke again it was in a different tone.

'I saw the Chancellor in Paul's before I came home,' he volunteered. 'I told him that, with my leave, you had been serving Master Caxton today. So he will not be surprised to hear that you are to go to Westminster.'

All Bendy's misery fell from him like a cloak. 'When do I go, sir?'

'As soon as may be, I promise you. Tomorrow is Sunday. Doubtless you will have duties at Paul's. When you are at home remember to keep your tongue quiet and avoid trouble. Now you must go to bed.'

He produced the tinder box and kindled a flame. Bendy, suddenly dazzled, saw his father's face in sharp light and shade. It looked so old and weary that his conscience smote him in good earnest.

'Sir,' he cried, 'what will *you* do when Matthew is wed and I am gone?'

'Not languish here, I promise you,' said John Goodrich decisively. 'I have no mind to cling as a burden to the Crowing Cock. The monks at the Charterhouse will find me a cell. 'Tis high time that I turned my thoughts to something other than this world.'

Bendy caught his breath with such obvious dismay that his father laughed.

'Cheer up, my son. You are not bidden to my requiem. There is nothing strange in a man of my years lodging in a monastery. There will be others to bear me company. I shall pay to be housed and fed, and go to my table at Paul's as usual. 'Tis a pleasant walk from the Charterhouse. And I doubt not that you will see me often enough at Westminster.'

When his father had gone Bendy got into bed and lay staring into the dark. Thoughts were racing through his brain too quickly to rest on any of them. Gradually they merged into each other and he closed his eyes. When he opened them again the moon was up. One slanting beam reached into the room and lighted the far corner. He stared at it. Beyond that stack of paper lay his Malory stories. Anyway, *they* were safe. No one should have them. They would go with him to Westminster.

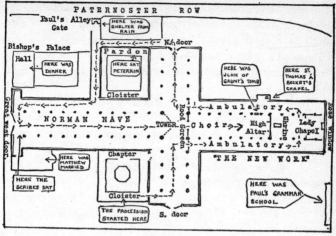

'Paul's'

CHAPTER 10

Meet Me in the Cloister

THE bells of London on a Sunday morning would not let him sleep late, however much he wanted to. So, bearing his father's warning in mind, Bendy rose, dressed, and slipped out of the house without meeting anyone.

He went straight to Paul's, where he served an early Mass and earned his breakfast. There were plenty of other Grammar School boys about, all talking about the water sports. Some of them asked where he had been since Friday forenoon, and he saw no reason against telling them – omitting, of course, the part about the paper. Dinner with the Sheriff was something to boast of, and he followed it up with the information that he was leaving very soon to be apprenticed to the great Master

Caxton, who had actually *asked* his father for him. He was enjoying himself immensely when he caught sight of the tousled head of Will Soper lurking at the edge of the crowd. He stopped abruptly. A pest on the fellow; what did he want? He wished he had not announced so publicly exactly where he was going.

The boys nearer to him were still asking questions when the Falcon, his form master, came striding from the cloister out into the yard where they stood. There was a worried frown upon his face.

'The fellow who was to be thurifer in the procession has just been sick,' he announced. 'I dare not trust him with the incense. Which of you can do it? Benedict, you've done it before, haven't you? Come and vest. Hurry now! The Bishop is almost ready.'

Bendy followed him obediently. To be thurifer was to walk ahead of the Bishop, swinging the hanging lamp of incense. He *had* done it before, but never in the great Sunday procession when the Bishop of London and all the clergy and the choir and the Guilds, with their banners, paced slowly behind the great ceremonial cross right round the Cathedral, blessing all the altars, blessing the people, blessing everyone and everything, and ending with a solemn progress up the length of the nave, under the rood screen and into the sanctuary for the High Mass. It was always a scene of imposing splendour. The citizens of London loved it and filled Paul's to overflowing every week. Bendy saw it suddenly as a grand climax to his life there. He had often walked in the procession as a choir-boy, or as an acolyte carrying one candle among other candles. But now, as censer-bearer, he would have a place of his own; there was only one. He would walk alone, heralding the Bishop.

The procession was forming up by the Chapter House, with the Falcon as master of ceremonies fussing and scolding and pushing the clergy into their places as readily as he pushed the choir-boys. At a sign the cross-bearer moved out into the south transept; the choirmaster followed with the choir, suddenly well behaved; then came all the Guilds, the acolytes, the clerks, and the canons of the Cathedral. Finally the Falcon nodded to the Bishop's chaplain and to Bendy who waited behind him. As they left the cloister Bendy, looking back,

It was fun swinging the censer

caught a refreshing glimpse of the Lord Bishop of London stooping meekly for his mitre to be popped on to his head.

It was fun swinging the censer and he swung it with a right good will, delighted with the clouds of blue fragrant vapour that filled the air. The Bishop's chaplain began to cough; people ranged along the side were blessed through a blue haze; one of the priests holding the edge of the Bishop's cope sneezed violently; the Falcon hurried alongside and hissed. It dawned on Bendy that he was overdoing it, and he slowed the censer down till it was swinging only enough for a tiny spiral of smoke to rise from it. A pity! He had enjoyed the blaze.

The procession turned into the ambulatory and threaded its way slowly round behind the high altar, pausing at each one of the chapels as it went. The sun pouring through the painted glass made the great rose window blaze like a thousand sparkling jewels. The white cottas of the choir and the acolytes

The Bishop's crozier

turned blue or red or green as they passed through the streams of light.

But by the time they had finished the round of the eastern end, Bendy's arm was aching unbearably. He had not imagined that to swing a censer could be such hard work, and with dismay he realized that it was not, by a long chalk, finished yet. They turned into the north transept and actually left the church to pace round the Pardon Cloister, the little cloister surrounding a tiny grave where Caxton had stopped to look upward that first evening during the storm. Pardon Cloister was a sombre place. It had gruesome pictures of the Dance of Death painted along the walls. But today in the sunshine it was quite cheerful, with people in bright clothes standing about to see the Bishop pass.

All of a sudden Bendy saw Peterkin waiting in the shadow

of a pillar. He dared not turn his head to look direct at him, but Peterkin made no bones about it. He pointed to himself, then to Bendy, and then to the spot where he stood. His meaning was clear. Bendy was to meet him there.

At the great west door the procession re-formed; there was still the progress up the Norman nave, and after that the High Mass. When it was all over Bendy was so weary that he wished he could go home. But the Crowing Cock was practically closed to him. Luckily there was Sunday dinner in the Bishop's hall for everyone who had taken part in the procession. At any rate he was certain that he would not go hungry.

The moment that he was free he made his way round to the Pardon Cloister. Peterkin was sitting on the wall waiting for him.

'Gammer said you wanted me,' he began as soon as Bendy was within earshot. 'What's afoot?'

'I'm going to Westminster to be prentice to Caxton,' said Bendy, watching the effect.

Peterkin gave a long whistle. '*That* will stir the pigeons in the dovecot. How has it come?'

Bendy grinned. His spirits were rising. Looking back upon it, yesterday, with the visit to Master Tate, the arrival of the pirate, and the fuss about Humphrey at the end, was a great adventure. He sat down beside Peterkin to enjoy telling it.

But as Peterkin listened he began to frown. 'This is getting pretty near the bone. I've heard of your John Stern. He's a freebooter, running his own ship. *They* know him, but he's a stout fellow, and so long as he doesn't fall foul of them, they give him a wide berth. But if they got wind of *this* it would be a sorry matter.'

Bendy felt a little thrill of excitement. 'He mentioned Mucking,' he said, proud to be in the know. 'It's a creek somewhere by Ipswich.'

'By Ipswich? Stuff and nonsense! Mucking's on the Thames,

hid deep in the marshes. True that it comes under Ipswich Customs, but it is right on the farthest edge of their control. It's just below Tilbury, where London Customs end. That's why *they* favour it. If a vessel is spotted lying at Mucking Creek none of the London Customs craft can touch her. And her master is away again with his pockets well lined before the fellows from Ipswich get there.'

'Then the *Madalena* and the load of Unicorn –?'

'Oh the *Madalena* was there, sure enough. She's gone by now. She had an easy cargo: spices and paper. Before long the spices will be in Tom Twist's pack on their way to half the towns in England. None cares what happens to the paper. 'Twas only carried as ballast for the spices. Your fool brothers paid for it, and there it lies.'

Bendy was shaken. 'Peterkin, I can't know all this and say nothing. Think of my father if Matthew's share in it came out.'

'Don't be a fool,' said Peterkin crisply. 'Go to Westminster and forget it. You've done with the Crowing Cock and so, by your telling, has your father. What good would you do? Revenge yourself on your brothers? That might be a good jest but it would serve your father ill. And as for me and my old Gammer – I swear to you, Bendy, that if they thought that *I'd* let the cat out of the bag they'd spit me like a chicken, and it would be your fault.'

Bendy heaved a deep sigh. 'I wish I'd never heard of the *Madalena*,' he said. 'I'm Caxton's apprentice now, and there's the paper to be thought of – Caxton's paper.'

'Fret not yourself about *that*,' said Peterkin cheerfully. 'That part is my business.'

At that moment a bell began to jangle. The sound came from the direction of the Bishop's palace. Bendy jumped to his feet.

'That's dinner,' he cried. 'I'll see you tonight, or may be tomorrow.'

Peterkin shook his head. 'I won't be there tonight, and to-morrow you'll be gone. Holy saints! I almost forgot. Your father sent a message. You were in the procession and he couldn't speak to you.'

'What message?' Bendy was suddenly alert.

'He bids you haste home directly dinner's done. You have to be ready to set forth in the morning.'

Bendy almost ran out of the cloister. Things were happening so fast that he could hardly collect his wits. Dinner in the Bishop's hall was a great event, and yet he went through it almost as if he were in a dream. The Bishop dined in state on a Sunday with great lords and the important men of the City as his guests. Today the guest of honour was a handsome gentle-man in black and silver with scarlet sleeves and scarlet hose. Somebody said that it was my Lord Rivers, the Queen's brother. Bendy took a good look at him. Lord Rivers was famous as a gallant knight. He had challenged all the knights of Burgundy in the tourney at Smithfield and beaten every one.

As he was gazing at the lord Rivers he suddenly spotted Master Tate in his sheriff's robe also seated at the Bishop's table. It was exciting to recall that only yesterday *he* had dined as a guest at Master Tate's table. He could not resist saying so to the boy seated next to him, a Song School brat who had walked with the choir in the procession. Obviously the boy did not believe him. He looked at Bendy wide-eyed over the bone that he was picking and then stuck out his tongue as he tossed the sucked bone to the dogs. Bendy turned his back, wishing that he had held his peace. If only Master Tate would recognize him! But there was no hope of it, for Master Tate was right up on the dais, while Bendy was at the lowest table, only just inside the door.

When the choristers in the gallery had sung the final Grace and the Lord Bishop withdrew, Bendy hurried home. His father was on the lookout for him, and told him that he had sent a note to Westminster by special messenger soon after dawn and received the answer just before High Mass. He showed Bendy the letter. It was of two lines only, written in Caxton's own hand.

'I rejoice that you have changed your mind. Tarry not. Let the boy come without delay.'

The rest of the day was more like a dream than ever. There was so much to do that he hardly knew where to begin. His

father settled that point for him by sending him forthwith to take leave of his brothers. But Matthew was still so angry that he would not speak to him, and Cornelius only nodded nervously and told him to be a good boy. Thankful that it was over, he crept up to the loft and started to pack his things into a poke.

There was no difficulty about what to take, for he was determined to leave nothing behind. The roll of Malory's stories went in at the very bottom, with his printed Prymer next to them; he would be able to *use* that at Westminster. His clothes took little room; he had so few. His only change of hose was the pair that had got him into trouble with Matthew on the day of the storm. They were still thick with muck, so he took them down to the pump, trusting that on a Sunday afternoon there would be no one about. He had but just started on the job when, to his dismay, the Widow Pratt came into the yard. She seemed to bear him no grudge, for she took the hose out of his hands, saying that they needed a good scouring and she would see to them. Bendy felt slightly ashamed. He asked, a little sheepishly, how Humphrey was, trying to screw himself up to say that he was sorry. She did not give him a chance, but answered only that Humphrey was mending nicely and went straight into the house, taking his hose with her. Bendy watched her go, wondering for the first time if things at the Crowing Cock in the future would be quite so bad as he had pictured them. It also reminded him of his father's admonition that before he went to Westminster he should go and be shriven.

So the last business of the day was to visit Paul's. He had to beg the Chancellor to approve his going, but luckily the Chancellor was too busy to receive a Grammar-School boy off to be apprenticed, and the Falcon, whom he saw instead, was quite friendly and wished him well in English, instead of the usual Latin. The few boys he met were so frankly envious that his spirits rose. By the time it was all finished it was getting dark and there was Compline in the Cathedral. He took his place for the last time, watching the shadows from the candles flicker where the sun had streamed this morning. He glowed with pride as he remembered this morning. Westminster might have kings crowned there and kings buried there; but when it came to a procession, those monks in their black habits would never compete with Paul's.

He stopped to wave for the last time

CHAPTER II

The Printing House

BENDY set out early the next morning to walk to Westminster, carrying his poke upon his back. His father decreed
that it was more fitting for a new apprentice to arrive on foot
rather than to be rowed, like a young lord, on the river.

He felt little regret at leaving the Crowing Cock. The only
bad moment was parting from his father, who walked with
him as far as Ludgate to speed him on his way. But John Goodrich would allow no repining. He gave his son a pat on the
back, told him to obey his master, and then hurried him off
down Ludgate Hill as if the Watch were after him.

Bendy's heart-ache did not last long. At the bridge over the

Fleet River he stopped to wave for the last time. Then, as his father turned back into the City, he gave a hitch to his poke and started off along Fleet Street.

He reached Westminster, footsore but cheerful, before the sun was really high in the heavens. But as he crossed the Abbey Close, towards the Almonry, he felt a wave of shyness sweep over him. There was nobody about, so he came to a standstill in the opening of the postern and looked ahead down the narrow paved lane. It was strange to think that he was not a visitor any longer. He was here for good.

The place seemed deserted, though even from this distance he could hear the creaking of the press in the printing loft above the Almonry gate. He plucked up his courage, pulled his tunic straight, and walked almost tiptoe to the door of the Red Pale. It stood open. Should he knock or should he go straight in?

He peeped round the side of the house, along the edge of the Long Ditch, then, as no one was about, crossed the path and looked into the old stable opposite, from which the stairs went up to the printing loft. He saw instantly a pile of paper in canvas covers standing just inside the stable door. He stared at it. The bales were just like those he had brought with Peterkin. Surely it was new. The first lot had all been sorted and put away.

Suddenly he heard a patter of footsteps. He turned as Elizabeth appeared in the doorway.

'You've come!' she exclaimed in a fierce whisper. 'My father said you'd be here soon, so I did my spinning upstairs by the window. Peterkin brought more paper. It came this morning. Where does he get it from? Do you know?'

Peterkin had not wasted any time. Bendy had a sore feeling that he ought to have been told. But he did not want to be questioned by this sharp little miss. Her quick eyes saw too much. She did not even wait for him to answer.

'Wynken de Worde says it is Unicorn, like the paper that was lost. He wants to find out. But my father told him to leave well alone. What does he mean?'

He frowned. The child was going to be a pest. But deliverance came quickly. He heard a scurry behind him, a squeal from Elizabeth, and a torrent of scolding in a foreign tongue. By the time he emerged from the stable she had vanished in the grip of the old Flemish nurse.

Almost immediately Mistress Caxton appeared at the house door. Had he walked all the way from London? she inquired, with her friendly smile. If he would go to the kitchen he could have a draught of ale and she would send word to his master that he had come.

She led him indoors herself and left him in the charge of a buxom cook-maid, who filled an ale-mug and put in front of him a slice of delicious manchet bread, made with white flour and milk and egg. He was too shy to speak, so he looked round the kitchen. It was bigger than the Crowing Cock's; it had a huge fireplace, with two great pot-hooks and a row of spits standing in front like a five-barred gate. The shutters were folded back so that the window was all open to the air, and on the sill stood a wooden erection with a pulley and a bucket, obviously intended for drawing up water from the Long Ditch.

He had barely finished his bread and ale when Dick Pynson came into the room, stooping under the low centre beam.

'The m-master sent me to f-fetch you,' he said, grinning in spite of his stutter. 'You'd best come and put your things up first. You're to sleep with the rest of us in the l-loft.'

The very sound of it made Bendy feel at home, though, compared with the Crowing Cock, the loft was a large one, with no stacks of paper to take up the space. There was room for a big bed and two small ones under the sloping roof.

'Wynken has a bed to himself, and so do I, because I'm so

l-long,' announced Dick Pynson cheerfully. 'You can sleep in
the big bed with the two l-lads, or you can have a p-pallet on
the floor by the window. Choose as you will.'

Without hesitation Bendy chose the pallet. The window was
at floor level and looked out at the roofs and pinnacles of the
Abbey. He left his poke to mark the place and followed Dick
Pynson down to the printing house.

It was an exciting moment to come into the workshop not as
a visitor but as *part of it*. He had never been there before when
printing was in full swing. There was a solemn air, with everybody standing at their appointed places, like a ceremony in
church. Wynken de Worde stood at one side of the press
bench and Caxton at the other. The two young lads ran to and
fro with inking pads and fresh ink. Wynken de Worde inked
the type with a skilful rolling motion, a pad in each hand –
right hand, left hand, something like playing a big drum. Then
came the business of wiping off superfluous ink and cleaning
the edges, while Caxton, with spotless hands, laid the paper
into the frame, folded the frame over the type, and slid the
whole forme along the bench and into the open jaws of the
press.

At that point everybody seemed to pause for breath while
Dick Pynson stepped forward and with his long arms worked
the lever that turned the wooden screw. The heavy plate
rumbled down, groaned a little as it squeezed the paper on to
the type, and slowly rumbled up again. There was a moment
of suspense as Caxton pulled out the forme and lifted the
printed sheet. He held it in the air to examine it critically; then
he nodded and hung it over a clothes line to dry. There was a
general sense of relief, and everybody turned about to start all
over again.

Caxton suddenly became aware of Bendy, standing engrossed beside him. 'Why, here's the new apprentice,' he
cried. 'Welcome him, all of you, and teach him our ways.

Printing was in full swing

Heaven preserve you, boy, you can't work in those clothes. Some shabby hose and an old shirt are good enough for printer's ink. Lend him an apron, somebody. Stay a minute, though; there's paper to be unpacked. Your friend Peterkin brought it this morning. I believe that it is Unicorn. That is strange, isn't it?' He looked direct at Bendy, his eyes twinkling. ''Tis a pity that the paper cannot print itself with what it knows. Maybe we should have a story as strange as the voyages of Jason with the golden fleece.' He burst out laughing at his own fancy, then pushed Bendy gently towards the stairs. 'Get you down there and examine it. See that it is all of a kind. I believe you are versed in paper.'

With mixed feelings Bendy cut open the first bale. This, he had no doubt, was the very paper that Caxton had ordered from Flanders; Tom Twist and his pirates had seized it; Matthew had paid for it; Peterkin had rescued it; and here was he, Bendy, who knew the story, handling it as casually as though he had never heard of it.

In the meanwhile he sorted it carefully. The paper *was* all Unicorn, and the sheets were all the same size. But they varied in colour and texture, some white, some deep cream, some a rough finish, others almost smooth. He laid them out neatly in separate piles along a bench, and had nearly finished the second bale when Caxton came down the stair.

''Pon my soul, I have done well to pick a scrivener's son,' he exclaimed. 'I don't have to teach you to match paper. Too many books are marred by ill-assorted sheets. Come now; stop for dinner. By the way, I have to go this afternoon to the shop – my first workshop, you know, next to the Chapter House of the Abbey. Copland is in charge of it – my best journeyman after Wynken de Worde. I shall need an apprentice to wait on me, and since you are already spruced up it may as well be you.' He laughed at Bendy's obvious delight. 'Get you to the kitchen now and wash your hands. Mistress

Caxton is over-nice about such matters. Poor lady, she has need to be – or all her stuff would be besmirched with printer's ink.'

Dinner was served in the hall room, with Master Caxton at one end of the table and his lady wife at the other. Elizabeth sat next to her mother, and Wynken de Worde, Dick Pynson, and Bendy completed the party. The other two lads were servants, not apprentices, and so dined in the kitchen.

Bendy was overcome with shyness and devoted himself to his food, but everyone else talked freely, as one family. Dinner was almost finished when Mistress Caxton suddenly clapped her hands.

'Husband, a thousand pardons; I had almost forgot. A message came for you from the shop, and I durst not disturb your printing. Will Copland sent word that a clerk from the King's Exchequer had called about that ship in which you had interest – the *Madalena*; was that the name?'

Bendy paused with a morsel of pudding half-way to his mouth. Caxton tut-tutted irritably.

'The *Madalena*, forsooth. Have they woken at last? What has roused them at this late hour, I wonder.'

'That's not all,' said his wife. 'Copland said that my Lord Rivers had been to the shop. He desires two more copies of the *Dictes and Sayings* that you printed for him. And Copland says that the boy Walter has gone home with a belly-ache, so he is alone.'

Caxton actually laughed. 'Poor Will! he's as fussy as a woman – your pardon, wife! Lord Rivers shall have his *Dictes and Sayings* this afternoon.'

Lord Rivers? Bendy looked up. That was strange; the same Lord Rivers as at the Bishop's table; the lord so famous for his tilting in the lists.

'What are the *Dictes and Sayings*?' Elizabeth asked suddenly. Her father threw up his hands in mock horror. '*The Dictes*

and Sayings of the Philosophers, the very first book to be printed
in England, that my Lord Rivers presented to the King and
made my name thereby; and my own child asks me "What
are the *Dictes and Sayings*?"!' He turned to Bendy. 'Are you
feeling strong, boy? There is much to carry to the shop. The
Dictes and Sayings are big books; they are folios, a hundred and
fifty pages apiece, and leather bound. Can you manage them,
do you think? Into the bargain I have to take the *Chronicle of
England*, but that is in loose sheets, and I will carry it.'

Elizabeth led the procession

Elizabeth piped up again. 'Pray, sir, let me come too. I can
carry a lot.'

Her mother shushed her, but her father looked at her with
an indulgent twinkle. 'Carry a lot, can you? Well, maybe
there is something to go which is about your measure – if your
mother will permit you, of course.'

Mistress Caxton spread her hands hopelessly. 'Sir, if you
will spoil the child it must be as you say.'

The nearest way to the shop was through the Abbey church.
Elizabeth led the procession, carrying three small books with
an air of great importance, and Bendy, laden with a pile of

volumes, brought up in the rear, walking behind his master as a good apprentice should. They went in at the west door, under the scaffolding. Bendy had never been inside before, and he would have liked to look round, but the books in his arms were so heavy that the only impression he got was of tall, slender pillars, like trees in a beechwood spreading out their branches in the vaulted roof. He followed Caxton along a dark aisle behind the screen of the choir, which was the monks' enclosure. When they reached the opening through which they could see the high altar, Caxton signed to him to put the books down, and they all knelt for a minute to say a prayer.

While they were kneeling a monk emerged from the choir stalls. He was stout and elderly and wore the black Benedictine habit. But Bendy suspected at once that he was no ordinary monk, for a gold cross hung from a chain round his neck. As the monk passed close to them he saw Caxton get up, then drop again on one knee and kiss his ring. Elizabeth, kneeling next to Bendy, whispered something. He couldn't hear her, but he knew what she said. That was the Lord Abbot.

The Lord Abbot clearly had something to say to Caxton. They spoke for a minute in low tones, then the Abbot led the way to a small door which opened into the cloister. As they went out Caxton turned and made a sign for Bendy to wait for him.

No sooner had he gone than Elizabeth scrambled to her feet.

'Come to St Edward's Shrine,' she invited. 'It's behind the high altar and you can ask three graces as it's your first visit.'

Bendy hung back. Graces or no graces Caxton had bade them wait. Seeing that he wouldn't come she pattered across to a small chapel at the corner of the transept and beckoned him again.

'St Benedict,' she announced in a whisper that carried right across the aisle. 'Look! He's your name saint. Come and say a prayer.'

Bendy frowned. He would be glad to honour his name saint, but he wasn't going to be hounded into it. At that moment, to his relief, Caxton came back into the church. He looked pleased.

'My Lord Abbot tells me that the Canons of Warwick have need of new great service books,' he said in a low voice. 'They would like them *printed*, if so be that the price is not too high. That is good news, boy. Where one church starts, others well may follow.'

As he talked Caxton moved across the south transept towards a door at the far corner, with Bendy carrying the books beside him. Elizabeth darted ahead and vanished, leaving the door open behind her.

The light streamed in and for a moment Bendy was dazzled as he stood on the threshold looking out. The door opened on to a cobbled path which cut through between the great church on the one side and the round Chapter House on the other. The sun blazed upon the stonework of chapels, and buttresses and pinnacles in sharp patterns of light and shade, while the tall Chapter House opposite cast a deep pool of shadow. The path itself was fringed with an assortment of little houses, some of them no more than booths, huddled at the foot of the great walls or tucked into the spaces between buttresses.

Caxton looked down at Bendy. 'I forgot for the moment that you had not been here before. This is the path which leads from the Abbey to the Palace. The King comes along it whenever he comes to the church. You can see the gate into Old Palace Yard right at the end of the path; and there stands Westminster Hall – though you glimpse but the end of it; and there are the roofs of the Palace beside it. It is a spot beyond compare. Here is my first printing house – that little place on the right, at the turn of the Chapter House – the second one from this end. Yes, you may well gape! How we did it I don't know. There is scarce room to swing a cat.'

Forgetting the weight of his load, Bendy followed his master out into the path. This was a side of Westminster he had never seen and it took him by surprise. There were banners flying round the Palace with bright streamers fluttering in the breeze. Through the gate at the end of the path he caught a glimpse of some courtiers playing at ball in the sunny Palace yard. Though they looked tiny he could see them clearly as they passed in and out of the shaft of light, their long legs and trunk-short doublets and their flying sleeves, all gay and brightly coloured.

He almost cannoned into Caxton as they stopped at the little shop on the right. It was a tiny place with two or three printed books displayed on the open shutter, just as his father used to show finely written pages in the window of the Crowing Cock.

A little wizened man with high shoulders came hurrying out to meet them.

'God save you, master, I've been out of my wits for your coming. My Lord Rivers wants two more copies of the *Dictes and Sayings*; he'll call again at Vespers time. And have you heard about the clerk from the Exchequer? And about the boy Walter? It is near Vespers time already but the place is still unswept. And, sir, the rats have fouled all the paste so that I can scarce use it.'

Caxton patted the man gently.

'Keep your heart up, Will Copland. I'll stay till after Vespers. Here's Benedict, the new apprentice; he shall fetch paste for you presently from the Almonry. And as for sweeping, *somebody* seems to be busy with a broom.' He looked at Bendy, laughing. There was a noise from within like a young colt kicking against the wainscoting. 'See to it, Bendy. The child will cover herself with dirt.'

Bendy laid down his load and plunged into the shop. He found that it opened into a larger workshop, where the curve of the Chapter-House wall left a wedge of unoccupied ground. All the same it was difficult to imagine how there could ever have been room for the press.

Elizabeth, very important, was banging away with a besom and lifting clouds of dust. She handed it over to Bendy with obvious relief.

'*You* can do it,' she said loftily. '*I* want to see my Lord Rivers.'

Bendy could have smacked her. He wanted to see Lord Rivers too. It was rare to get the chance of being close to a man who was the modern Sir Lancelot – unbeaten in a tourney. Since there was no help for it, he went on sweeping after she had gone. But in a couple of minutes she put her head round the door again whispering, 'Hist! He's come.'

Bendy stood the broom up and edged into the shop behind her. Seated by the counterboard, the gentleman in black and silver was talking pleasantly while Caxton laid before him the copies of the *Dictes and Sayings*.

'The real object of my coming, good Master Caxton, was to tell you how much your book of *Jason and the Golden Fleece* delighted the Prince of Wales, my royal nephew. It was a happy thought of yours to dedicate it to him; it made him feel quite the man! As you know, he is living in my charge at Ludlow Castle, and I would gladly take him another book when I go back. Have you aught that you can suggest?'

Caxton bowed. 'It is an honour to serve the Prince. Perhaps a Cato might please him. Every schoolboy has one; and I have just reprinted it with pictures to give it greater interest. Pictures in print are an entirely new venture.'

Lord Rivers burst out laughing. 'Pictures or no pictures, I swear he would not thank me for a Cato. He is eleven years old and athirst for tales of chivalry. You and I hold the same views on that subject, sir, and you will agree with me that it is well to rear our future King Edward the Fifth with healthy notions of true valour.'

'I rejoice to hear your lordship say so. Shall I suggest the History of the most noble *Godfrey of Bologne*? As you doubtless remember, it tells of the last siege of Jerusalem. I translated it from the French myself, so that every man of good will

Ludlow Castle

should burn within him for the defence of Christendom. His Grace the King himself was my patron for it.'

He lifted the book from the shelf, and Lord Rivers turned the pages, till suddenly the unbound sheets lying on the counterboard caught his eye. '*The Chronicle of England*,' he read out. 'That should be good reading for the Prince.'

'None better, my lord. By the study of history we learn what is to be desired and what is to be avoided in the future.'

'True,' said Lord Rivers, and laid the two books together. 'If so be you can have this bound for me before I ride to Ludlow I will take them both. And as they are for the Prince's use you may claim for them from the King's Privy Purse. Hey! I was going to Vespers. Am I late? Can I creep into the royal pew without disgrace?'

He hurried from the shop, flinging a 'Thanks be for your

good service, sir' over his shoulder. Two young courtiers waiting a few yards away, scurried after him. Caxton turned back from the door and sat down wearily.

'A most gallant and knightly lord,' he remarked. 'But, good Copland, did you note? We may claim payment from the Privy Purse! As easily get water from a stone. Now, can you have the *Chronicle* bound in time for him to take to Ludlow?'

Will Copland hummed and hawed. He was a printer, not a binder, he said. And in any case he hadn't any paste.

'Paste,' cried Caxton. 'I had forgotten. Be off with you, Bendy, and bring it with all speed. I have to go to the Exchequer about the *Madalena*.'

Bendy caught his breath. 'Sir, couldn't I come? If you could wait –'

Caxton snapped at him. 'The Exchequer is no concern of yours. Do what you're bid, and go round the outside of the church – the way I showed you, by Chaucer's house. Vespers is going on within.'

Bendy set off at once, smarting under the first sharp words he had heard from Caxton. He dared not even ask how to reach Chaucer's house, so he followed the path towards the Palace and found a way round the east end of the church without difficulty. Before he was out of sight he looked back at the little shop nestling under the Chapter House, like a little dog in an effigy at its master's feet. There was no sign of Caxton following him. Perhaps if he ran all the way he might even now be back in time to go to the Exchequer.

It took him only about three minutes to reach the Red Pale, and Dick Pynson gave him a jar of paste at once. So far, so good! Surely he would be able to do it. He rushed out of the stable and collided with Tom Twist.

He stopped, almost winded by the shock. Tom Twist stood watching him with a knowing grin. As Bendy gasped out,

The little shop by the Chapter House

'What do you want?' he held out something folded neatly. It was the old pair of hose left at the Crowing Cock.

'Your brother's new lady bade me bring you these, young master. She was looking for a messenger and I told her that I knew the way.'

Bendy took the hose, trying to say 'thank you' civilly. He wished to goodness the fellow would go. It was dangerous to have him here. But Tom Twist seemed in no hurry.

'Things have changed for the better for you, I'm thinking, Master Bendy. You do well to tie yourself to the new ways, despite what anyone may say.'

Bendy looked round anxiously. At any moment somebody might appear. 'I am on an errand,' he declared. 'I've no time. I'll bid you good night. That is your way out, by the Abbey postern.'

Tom Twist laughed. 'I knew the back ways of Westminster before you were born, young man. I will not trouble the Abbey.' He turned as if to go off through the Almonry. Then suddenly he stooped and picked up a crumpled piece of paper. He looked at it, folded it, and slipped it up his sleeve. 'It will be useful to wrap spices,' he said. Then he tossed back a nod and a grin and made off across the Long Ditch. He had vanished into the Almonry before it dawned on Bendy that the paper was a piece of Unicorn from one of Peterkin's bales.

He heaved a deep sigh. Was he never to be free of Tom Twist? He paused only to hide his hose in the stable before he set out again, running harder than ever. He had little hope now that Caxton would still be at the shop, and he was not surprised to find that he, with Elizabeth, had left for the Exchequer office some time ago. He finished the sweeping for Copland and helped to tidy up before he started on his way back to the Almonry. Though Vespers was over, he did not go through the church. He hoped that, by going the long way round, he might meet Caxton and hear what was afoot. But he was disappointed. Caxton was home before him. It was not until supper that he got any news.

Wynken began it by inquiring if there were tidings of the *Madalena*.

Caxton laughed. ''Tis sheer buffoonery,' he said. 'She is gone, of course. She came up the river, was cleared by the Customs, and set sail again. As for her cargo, good Wynken, she should have carried spices and paper; but instead she held some barley grains and *floor rushes*, by your leave!'

'Rushes?' cried Mistress Caxton. 'But rushes can be cut for a song anywhere along the river.'

'Precisely!' agreed her husband. 'And, mark you, they did not even see the funny side of it. But there is more to come. They let her go, but now they seem to have become interested in the *Madalena*, and I know not why. They actually asked *me* questions, as though *I* were the villain.'

'You!' cried his wife. 'What madness is this?'

'Trouble not yourself; with my friends at Court I have nothing to fear, and I did not spare them, I promise you. But why should they trouble about the *Madalena* now? What flea is biting them?'

Wynken leaned forward. 'But the paper, sir? Did they give any hope about the paper? Must we live for ever on the pittance that this boy brings?'

'Not for ever, I trust. The shipmaster, John Stern, sailed this very day. He swears that nothing will stop *him*. And I have other news for you. That young Jack Tate, the sheriff's nephew, who rode home with me the other day – you remember him? He is a young man of parts, if ever I saw one. He purposes building a mill to make paper in England, so that it will not need to be shipped at all.'

Wynken slapped his hands together. 'By George, that is the best tidings yet. Then all our troubles will be over.'

'All *your* troubles, Wynken. 'Twill take time, you know, and I am fast growing a Methuselah.'

'Methuselah forsooth!' scoffed his wife. 'I'll not hear such nonsense. Fill your cup again, sir, and bring it to the parlour, so that the boys can clear the platters.'

Hic jacet dominus Thomas Mallare valens miles ob. xiii mar. mccccl xx de parochia Monkenkirby in Comitatu Warwici cui aie ppiciet deus · Amen ·

CHAPTER 12

The Valiant Soldier

Up in the strange loft Bendy could not get to sleep. The day had been endless and so full of new things that his mind was as active as a bucket of tadpoles. If he tried to follow one memory he lost it among a score of others. But there was one particular thought that came back again and again. What was this new mystery about the *Madalena*? What did the King's officers suspect that Caxton did not know? It nagged at him like a grumbling toothache. Was it about Mucking, and did it involve Tom Twist and Matthew? And as for Tom Twist, what did he want with that piece of Unicorn? Was it going to mean trouble for Peterkin?

He almost groaned aloud. He had hoped that with a new life he would leave these worries behind, but they seemed to have followed him to Westminster.

The loft was full of heavy breathing. Though the floor was hard, he was thankful to have a mattress to himself and to be near the window. Before he came to bed, Mistress Caxton had whispered that she had given him a feather pillow to soften his first night. Now he blessed her for it. He had pushed his treasures underneath it – the little printed prymer, a string of beads that Peterkin's grandmother had pressed into his hand, and, of course, his precious roll of stories. As sleep wouldn't come, he turned on to his front and lay quite comfortably with his hand under the pillow, and gazed out of the window.

One side of the slatted shutter was open and he could see the black shapes of the Abbey against the sky. On the left the great church blotted out most of the stars, but to the right the buildings were lower. He could even make out the pointed roof of the Chapter House in the distance, and he pictured to himself the little shop lying snugly beside it.

He was trying to recognize other landmarks when somewhere in the monastery a light caught his eye. It was only a tiny flicker and it vanished; but another took its place, and then a third and a fourth and a fifth, like a procession of glowworms. What could it be? It took nearly a minute to dawn on him that through a chink in the building he was seeing the tapers of monks passing in single file. They must be on their way to the church for the night office.

He raised his head and tried in vain to catch the sound of chanting. But all that he could hear was the murmur of the mill-race down by the river.

The thought of the monks at their prayers calmed him. It was a reminder that while people slept they were kept in safety by the hand of God. He suddenly rolled on to his side, punched his feather pillow, and slept too.

In the morning there was no time to think of anything. Wynken de Worde took the new apprentice in hand and kept him busy all day. Bendy started by learning to clean type, brushing and picking out dried ink from the little metal letters, which, he discovered, were known as *sorts*. When they were quite clean they had to be put away in compartments of the two sloping cases, capitals into the upper case, and small letters in the lower. It was quite a game to find the proper homes, for they were arranged, not in alphabetical order, but according to which letters were most often used; large compartments for the dozens of *e*'s and *t*'s and *s*'s, but only small ones for the *z*'s and *x*'s and *q*'s.

'You'll get a *c*-clout from Wynken if you mix up the *s*-sorts,' Dick Pynson warned him. 'A compositor setting up

A sort

type has no time to check every letter, and if there's an *s* among the *t*'s, woe betide the sorter.'

Bendy heeded this warning and sorted so well that Wynken actually showed him how to hold the composing stick and try his hand at setting up a line of type. This was a proud moment, and he went to bed well satisfied with himself. It had been a good day with no fresh news to disturb his rest.

The next day was much the same, and so were the days that followed. The *Madalena* was not mentioned again and Tom Twist did not reappear. He had no news of the Crowing Cock until the Sunday when his father came to dinner at the Red Pale. Then he learned that Matthew was actually married. The wedding had taken place the previous day at the little parish church of St Gregory, which was attached to Paul's very much as the parish church of St Margaret was attached to Westminster Abbey. His father had attended the wedding and spoke kindly of his new daughter-in-law. He had already taken up his abode at the Charterhouse and seemed contented enough. He had a 'cell' of his own – a tiny two-roomed house – and took his meals in the Guest Hall, where the half-dozen or so elderly lodgers met to eat and chat round the fire.

The following morning Peterkin brought some more paper. He arrived unannounced, as if it were quite a matter of course. Bendy was sorting when he heard of it from Dick Pynson. He

Try his hand at composing

left his work and raced to catch Peterkin before he could get back to the river. He *must* tell him that Tom Twist had picked up a piece of Unicorn.

Peterkin took the news quietly. He said, 'Aye, I expected it'; and nothing more. He did not even show any excitement about the *Madalena*. All that he would say was that his grand-dam was well and sent her blessing; that Humphrey now had the loft and there was no fun in hanging out of the window any more.

Bendy returned to the printing house relieved, but a little

disappointed. Peterkin was safe and sound, but clearly he was determined to keep his own counsel. But as nothing fresh happened, bit by bit Bendy's misgivings faded. The Crowing Cock, Matthew and Cornelius, and even Tom Twist became less real. Life at the Red Pale was what mattered.

From sorting he went on to inking – a dirty but a satisfying job. Sometimes he was even allowed to work the press, though his arms would not reach as far as Dick Pynson's. On some days, as a change from the printing house, he was at the shop, fetching and carrying for Copland or for Caxton himself. It involved wearing a new apprentice outfit of blue tunic and flat cap, bought for him by Mistress Caxton. He had to be neatly dressed, she said, because of all the fine people who passed up and down. Anybody might stop to look at the printed books; even the King himself.

After the first week, the time flew by, its passage marked only by the Sundays when his father came to the Almonry and Bendy walked back with him to the Charterhouse. This had become a regular weekly event. Mistress Caxton made John Goodrich warmly welcome. Caxton was happy to discuss books with him, and Elizabeth attached herself to him, following him about like a little dog. He appeared to like it; he pinched her ear, gave her sugar-plums, and called her his little sweetheart. Bendy was secretly scornful. He was highly suspicious of Elizabeth's antics. He was certain that she used them simply to get her own way.

One fine Sunday Caxton started a discussion on the question of bindings. He was worried about them, he said. Copland was always claiming that he was a printer, not a binder. A young man, James the Bookbynder, worked in a neighbouring shop by the Chapter House; but he was inexperienced and lacked ideas.

'I never see fine bindings now,' Caxton complained. 'When I was in Bruges I had the run of the Duke of Burgundy's library, one of the finest in Europe. I miss it sadly. The library at the Abbey is full of great books, but they are all manuscripts, writ on parchment. What suits them is unfitted for books on paper.'

'Do you know the library at Greyfriars, in Newgate?' suggested John Goodrich. 'Dick Whittington built it and furnished it with books at his cost – perhaps the greatest of all his bounties to the City.'

Fine bindings

Caxton smote his hands together. Of course, Whittington's library was exactly what he wanted; he was a fool not to have thought of it. Within a matter of minutes it was decided that he would join Bendy and his father in their walk back to the Charterhouse and go on to Greyfriars forthwith. Elizabeth, hearing it, begged to come too. Her father said No, but Master Goodrich was on her side.

'Let her come, sir,' he pleaded. ''Tis a pleasure for an old man to have a little maid.'

Bendy almost laughed aloud. Elizabeth had pulled it off again. But his laughter dried up when he found himself walking all the way with her and her Flemish nurse.

At the top of Holborn Hill, John Goodrich left them. He

was tired, he said; he would go straight home. He did not need an escort. Bendy could go to the library with his master.

So they entered the City by Newgate, through the archway under Newgate Prison with its grey stone walls and its slits of windows. Greyfriars, the domain of the Franciscans, was on the left of Newgate Street and covered a stretch of ground in the angle of London Wall. Before they presented themselves at the Friary, Caxton bade Elizabeth and her nurse wait for them in the famous Greyfriars Church.

'They will not have women, let alone little maids, frisking about in their enclosure,' he said. 'Say your beads; and when you have finished there is plenty in the church for you to see. There are the tombs of no less than three queens, and endless princes and daughters of kings. Notice their shields; the heraldry would keep you busy for a year; and if you are tired of heraldry, look at the ladies' dresses. I'll warrant you'll not tire of that. Only, as you look, fail not to say an Ave for them.'

Bendy followed his master through the court and cloisters of the Friary. He had never been in it before, though it was not far from Paul's, and only just round the corner from the squalid Shambles, where the Holly Bush alehouse stood. The Prior himself led them to the library, and as Master Caxton was obviously above suspicion, he bade them take their time and left them.

Bendy looked round it in wonder. It was very long, more than a hundred feet, with windows on both sides. It was all wainscoted in oak and even the ceiling was wonderfully carved. But what took his fancy were the recesses down each side, screened from each other by bookcases, like little rooms where a student could sit to read or write. Each recess had its window and each its desk and benches, with great books chained to them.

Caxton went from shelf to shelf examining bindings and

considering which leather would wear the best. Bendy would have liked to peep into the books. More than anything he would like to have found some volume which told of the Crusades, or the wars, or other adventures and settle down to it. But before he could even discover where such books were kept Caxton was ready to go.

'We will look at the church,' he said. 'As I told the child, there is much to see – more than we have time for tonight. And we must not fail to light a taper for St Francis.'

The church was lofty and spacious, with soaring arches and large windows. In the choir there were no less than nine great altar tombs, all of them of alabaster, with painted effigies and gilded iron railings to protect them.

'It is odd how all these great lords and ladies determine to be buried in the church of the poor man's saint,' remarked Caxton. 'Look, there is his altar, and there is Elizabeth waiting for us.'

The Chapel of St Francis was bright with tapers flickering on candle-stands. Bendy lit one, said his prayer, and then looked about. There were tombs here also. Beside him was a carved inscription. Half idly he read it. '*Dominus Thomas Mallare valens miles*' – the words shot out at him – 'Thomas Mallare, valiant soldier'. Surely Mallare must be the same as Malory; the tomb of Sir Thomas Malory.

Unable to contain himself he turned round. Elizabeth was next to him. 'Look!' he burst out. 'Here's my knight; Sir Thomas Malory; *my* knight!'

She dashed at it. 'Where? Where?' Then, as he pointed, she turned and pursued her father. 'Sir! Sir! Come and see. Bendy has found his own knight.'

Caxton allowed himself to be dragged back. He peered at the tomb. 'Thomas Mallare? Who is he? I have never heard of him.'

'He wrote my book, sir; the stories of King Arthur.'

Caxton appeared not to notice. He leaned over and read the whole inscription aloud, in English. '"The lord Thomas Mallare valiant soldier died 14 May 1470 of the parish of Monken Kirby in the county of Warwick".'

Bendy's eyes opened wide. 'Was he a *lord*? In my book he says Sir Thomas Malory, *knight*.'

'Possibly he was merely lord of the manor. But what is this book you keep talking of, and why do you think he wrote it?'

'He says so at the end, sir. He calls it "this book of King Arthur and his noble knights of the Round Table", and he begs every one who reads it to pray for him.'

'What language is it writ in? *English*? Are you sure? I have had many lords and gentlemen demanding that I should imprint the history of King Arthur, but though there are many writ in French or Spanish or Italian, and other tongues, there is none to count of in English. Did you say you *have* this book?'

'At the Red Pale, sir; upstairs in my poke.'

'Then let me see it.' He stooped over the tomb again. '*This* Mallare comes of an ancient family. See how simple his arms are – a sure sign. There are two coats: first, *ermine, within a bordure engrailed sable, a chevron gules*; and second, *or, three lions passant sable*, a most knightly coat. He may not be the same Malory as your book; but show it to me when we get home.'

Back at the Almonry, Bendy fairly raced up to the loft and came down with the precious roll. Caxton flattened it out on the table.

'Yes, it certainly seems to be about King Arthur. Many people say, you know, that there was no such person, but there are many evidences of the contrary. You can see his tomb at Glastonbury, and Winchester holds the Round Table; and here, in Westminster, at St Edward's Shrine, there is a wax imprint of his seal, enclosed in a precious stone – a beryl, I think it is. One day we will beg the Lord Abbot to let us see it.' While he talked he was turning over the pages. 'But, boy, this is no scrivener's book. I think it is of the author's own writing. See how it is corrected and altered, words are scored out and writ again at the top, and several lines changed, all done in the same hand. No scrivener works like that. How came you by it?'

Bendy went red to the roots of his hair. He stammered out that he had got it at school.

'At school? Surely it wasn't a lesson?'

'No sir; I – I won it, sir.'

'Has your father seen it, or your brothers?'

Bendy shook his head. It was, he murmured, his own private matter.

Caxton looked at him searchingly; then he smiled. 'Well, I will respect your secret. But I must read it, if you will trust me for tonight.'

Bendy went to bed torn between excitement and uneasiness. In the morning Caxton called him. 'Boy; your treasure is in truth a treasure. It is made from the old histories of King Arthur, most of it translated from the French – a thing I longed to do myself, but I lacked time. I have little doubt that it is indeed the work of the Thomas Malory who lies buried at the Greyfriars. Have you noticed the date? He says that he finished it in the ninth year of the reign of King Edward the Fourth; in other words, in 1470, the very year he died.'

Bendy's joy soared like a lark. But the next words brought him down to earth again.

'But mark you, there is a pitfall. Half the pages are missing. Scarce one of the stories is complete. I would like to print it, but I cannot unless we find the rest. Now – where did you get it? If you tell me, you shall not suffer for it.'

'I won it at dice, sir, at an alehouse. They say I was besotted. If my father knew –'

'He shall not know. I have not wormed it out of you to betray you. Where is this alehouse?'

Bendy told him the whole story, including how Will Soper had tried to buy the manuscript back.

'So they have someone else after it, have they?' mused Caxton. 'I tell you what I will do. I will go to the Prior of the Franciscans at Greyfriars. They buried Malory, so they must know all about him. I will go at once.'

Despite Caxton's promises Bendy was on tenterhooks until he returned. Even then it was not until after dinner that Caxton called him and led him out for a stroll towards the mill, where they would be alone and uninterrupted.

'I have a strange tale for you,' he said. 'I saw the Prior of Greyfriars. He told me that Sir Thomas Malory is buried in the Greyfriars Church because he died just near by, in Newgate Jail. He was a prisoner there for years.'

Bendy caught his breath. '"*Pray for me while I am alive that God may send me good deliverance*",' he quoted.

Caxton nodded. 'Yes, he says it himself, which serves to confirm matters. It is a sorry story. The Prior spoke in all charity, but I fear that the man was a rascal. For many years he had been in and out of prison. While he was in Newgate everything he had went to his jailer to be spent for him in alehouses. Which I should judge accounts for how your roll got into the hands of your friend Soper.'

Bendy's heart sank. *This* was not how he had pictured Sir Thomas Malory. 'Then what of the stories, sir?' he asked. 'Did he say nothing about the book?'

'I am coming to that. I asked him if Malory left any rolls of writing, and apparently there *was* one – carefully writ and sealed. The Prior believes that it was a fair copy of all that he had written in prison, for he wrote unceasingly. After his death a kinsman took the roll, with such few poor possessions as he left, and carried it off into Warwickshire, to Dame Malory, the widow. The kinsman was a brother-in-law – so the Prior believes; he was a gentleman of coat armour named Vincent, of Stoke d'Abernon in Surrey. Malory's only son died before him; he left but a grandson, little more than an infant in arms.'

Bendy was thinking deeply. 'But sir, if he was truly a rascal and in prison all his days, how was he learned enough to write his book? You say that he translated the stories out of French into English.'

'Well done; that is good reasoning. But Malory's life, as the Prior told it, explains that. He was lord of the manor of New-bold Revel, by Monken Kirby in Warwickshire; and he spent his youth at the French wars in the train of the Lord Richard Beauchamp, the great Earl of Warwick, who was of all men the noblest – they called him the Flower of Chivalry. To a gentleman in that position French would have been as natural as English; so, you see, Malory grew up with all the knightly virtues before his eyes. But after Beauchamp died it seems as though he lost himself. There were charges of cattle-raiding and other worse deeds of lawlessness. 'Tis even said that he attempted the murder of the Duke of Buckingham. Then in the Wars of the Roses he linked himself to the new Earl of Warwick, Nevill, known as the Kingmaker, who was son-in-law to Beauchamp but a man of very different mettle. The Kingmaker turned his coat and played the traitor as best it suited him, and seemingly Malory turned with him. At any rate he was once more clapped into jail, into Newgate this time, and there he stayed.'

'But many were imprisoned for turning coat,' cried Bendy hotly.

'True; but when there was a general pardon and the others were set free, Malory was specially excluded. I fear me that there must have been more against him.'

Bendy stuck to his point. 'Sir, he couldn't have been as bad as that if he wrote my book. Look at the way he speaks of chivalry; look at his story of the Holy Grail.'

Caxton smiled. 'Well, at least he has one champion. And I am inclined to agree with you, though the facts look black. But that is not our business. It is his book we want, and how are we to get it? That is what I asked myself when I left Grey-friars. So, after pondering, I went forthwith to the Holly Bush. If we could get the missing pages of your manuscript, there would be no need to look farther.'

'*The Holly Bush!*' Bendy could scarcely believe his ears. Caxton had promised! He stared at his master with such eyes of horror that Caxton felt the need to excuse himself.

'I did not give you away,' he said hastily. 'Nobody knew who I was. I just sat down and called for ale. Certainly it is a vile hole and its host befits it. 'Tis strange to think that a boy from such a place could reach the standard of Paul's Grammar School; but no matter – Over the ale I asked the man Soper if he had ever known Sir Thomas Malory, a cheerful knight who was in Newgate Prison a while ago and told some good stories when he was in his cups. I said that some of the stories were written down and I believed that Malory's friends would give a good price for them. I saw his eye light up; but he thought better of it and swore that he knew naught of any writing. So I came away.'

Bendy heaved a sigh of relief. 'Will Soper wasn't there, sir?' Will Soper, he reflected, might have smelt a rat.

'No one was there save a pedlar fellow who sat down for a drink.'

'A *pedlar*?'

'A pedlar with spices to sell. Truth to tell, I thought of John Stern and his stories of contraband. The Holly Bush is just the sort of place that such rogues would favour. This fellow was off on his travels, Oxford way. He actually offered himself as carrier if I had letters or baggage to dispatch. As though I would trust anything to such a vagabond!'

The pulses in Bendy's head thumped like little hammers.

Tom Twist! Was it really Tom Twist? He did not know whether Caxton had ever seen Tom Twist and he dared not ask. But he was pretty sure that Tom Twist knew Caxton. Tom Twist at the Holly Bush with Soper was something new and menacing.

His wits had so obviously gone a-wool-gathering that Caxton spoke quite sharply. 'Boy, you're not listening. I was saying that of course I could go to Stoke d'Abernon in Surrey and ask for Master Vincent. But that would hardly serve. We know that the fair copy was carried to Warwickshire, to Dame Malory. Someone in these last days has spoken of Warwickshire, and for the life of me I cannot remember who.'

'I know!' cried Bendy. 'It was Master Tate. He said that he came from Warwickshire.'

'Of course; it was Master Tate. Bendy, I see light. I will send word to Robert Tate at once, and ask if he can tell me anything of Sir Thomas Malory and his kin.'

Their way back to the river

CHAPTER 13

By All Means Let Him Go

IT was hard, with so much on his mind, to go back to cleaning and sorting type. For the rest of the day Bendy struggled to pay attention to his work; but time and again he found himself mis-sorting. At last Wynken caught him out and promised him a beating if he did not mend his ways. He was quite glad to be put on to the menial task of sweeping the floor. At least he couldn't go wrong with that.

He was on his way to bed when Caxton called him. 'Master Tate writes that he cannot help us,' he said. 'Though he was born in Warwick he has spent all his life in London. But he sends me a letter to introduce me to Master Hugh Clopton, the mercer, who lives, strangely enough, in the old house I pointed out to you, where I was apprenticed. Master Clopton knows Warwickshire well. He goes back and forth. *He* will be the man for us. Put on your tidy clothes in the morning, boy. We will go and visit him.'

Master Hugh Clopton was tall and broad-shouldered with a big nose, blue eyes, and a way of speech that at first Bendy found hard to understand. He welcomed Caxton warmly, saying that in addition to his general fame, he had heard much of him from Robert Tate.

As soon as the compliments were over, Caxton came quickly to the object of the visit. He was anxious, he said, to get tidings of a family named Malory, of the manor of New-bold Revel, near to Monken Kirby.

Hugh Clopton shook his head. 'I am afraid I know but little. My home is at Stratford-upon-Avon, at the south-west of the county, and Monken Kirby is on the borders of North-ampton, a score and more miles away. I hear that Newbold Revel is in sad decay. The present owner is a fatherless child, ruled by his ancient grand-dam. His grandsire, Sir Thomas Malory, was a legend in the county. He died in Newgate a few years back.'

'I heard so,' said Caxton. 'What was his offence?'

'He was held a traitor, I believe. But when I was a boy the tales of his doings livened every hearth. He was a madcap knight; his sword was never in its sheath; and as for law and order, he laughed at it. The sheriffs seized him, but no prison could hold him. He swam the moat at Coventry and fought his way out of Colchester. 'Tis sad that he should have ended in Newgate. But your pardon, sir; all this is beside the point. I can tell you little of his family or his estate.'

'On the contrary, it is very much to the point. My interest is in a book of stories that he wrote in prison.'

Leaning forward with his elbow on his knee, Caxton ex-plained how this boy, his apprentice – he waved his hand towards Bendy – had been treasuring in his poke a roll of manuscript which turned out to be part of the book of King Arthur, done into English by Malory in Newgate. He made the whole story sound so like a romance in itself, with the finding of Malory's tomb, the visit to the Prior, and the tidings that the fair copy had been sent to Warwickshire, that Hugh Clopton was all attention.

'And you want to imprint this book?' he inquired as Caxton ceased. 'Upon my word I am glad of it. In his youth Malory must have been a valiant fellow. He was dubbed knight on the field of battle by Richard Beauchamp, Earl of Warwick, and no man could look higher. To restore his honour by making known his book would be a deed of true chivalry. Maybe he has been maligned. In those accursed Wars of the Roses, red roses became white and white red almost overnight, and many of the thorns had poison in them. Here in London things are comparatively peaceful; we have a Yorkist king and we are apt to think that the Lancastrian red rose is dead. But War-wickshire was a battleground. Burnt-out manors abound and there are still outlaws hiding in the woods.'

'To restore his honour – a deed of chivalry.' Bendy glowed. As the tongues of his elders clacked about the governance of the realm and such matters, he conjured up pictures of a knight setting out to storm a beleaguered castle and rescue Sir Thomas Malory, who lay rotting in the dungeons.

But he pricked up his ears as Hugh Clopton changed his tone. 'To return to your questions about Malory, why not journey to Warwickshire yourself, good Master Caxton? As it happens, I am riding to Stratford next week for a few days' visit. I am building myself a house there, and refurbishing the Guild Chapel, and planning a stone bridge over Avon, and half a score other enterprises which my brother calls hare-brained. He is married and has the manor house at Clopton, close beside Stratford. If you would come with me I warrant that he would

welcome you with open arms. From Stratford to Newbold
Revel you could ride in a day. We should be back in less than a
fortnight. What say you?'

'It is tempting,' said Caxton thoughtfully. 'I have an ink-
ling that there are others with an eye on Malory's book, and it
would be well to act without delay. And another thought
strikes me: are you by chance near Warwick? The Canons
of St Mary's have approached me about printed service
books.'

'Warwick is but eight miles from Stratford, in the direction
of Newbold Revel. Let that decide you, sir. You will travel at
better speed for being with someone who knows the road.
Bring a servant if you wish, but trouble not yourself about
horses. I can provide them. I am known at all the inns along the
way.'

Caxton glanced at Bendy. 'My apprentice could serve me
well enough,' he said with a twinkle. 'You see, sir, it would be
almost dastardly to leave him out. The manuscript of the book
is *his*, so far as we have got it, and it was he who found
Malory's tomb.'

'Then by all means let him come. Now, today is Tuesday.
How would next Monday suit you?'

Before they took their leave Hugh Clopton led them all
over the old, rambling house, and Caxton obviously revelled
in telling endless stories of his apprentice days. In the ordinary
way Bendy would have enjoyed them; but now he was in a
dream, and only woke up on their way back to the river when
Caxton told him that he must get his father's permission before
he could embark on such a journey.

'Doubtless we shall see him on Sunday, and as I have also
invited Master Clopton to dinner, they will meet then,' Caxton declared. 'But that will be too late to ask his sanction. You
had better go to Paul's tomorrow, boy; I will give you a note
to take to him.'

Surely his father must consent! Bendy told himself over and over again that he could not possibly refuse. Nevertheless it was with a beating heart that, the next morning, he pushed open the familiar door into Paul's from the Pardon Cloister.

John Goodrich was writing at his table. His eyes opened wide at the sight of his youngest son.

'Why, Bendy, what brings you at this hour? Nothing amiss, I hope.'

Bendy put Caxton's letter into his hand and watched his face while he read it. He looked first astonished and then pleased.

'This is great good fortune for you,' he said. 'In fact it is quite a feather in your cap. Into Warwickshire? Stratford-upon-Avon? Monken Kirby? Newbold Revel? I have never heard of any of them. It is a great way; surely two or three days in the saddle.' He looked up and smiled at Bendy. 'Of course you have my leave to go. I will write and say so.'

He picked up his pen. Bendy stood looking round at all the usual bustle of Paul's nave. Suddenly his heart sank like a stone. Coming towards them was Matthew.

Master Goodrich, bent over his writing, did not notice his eldest son. But Matthew saw Bendy at once. He halted; then he favoured him with the suspicion of a nod, came up to his father's table, and bowed. Bendy was astonished. It was a long while since he had seen Matthew so polite.

John Goodrich looked up. 'Good morrow to you,' he said a little stiffly. 'I trust your wife is well.'

'Excellently well, sir. She sends her duty to you. It is from her that I bear a message. She begs that you will dine with us next Sunday. But you are busy, sir. I can wait.'

'Take a stool. I have almost done,' said his father. 'Bendy has come for leave to go a-journeying.'

He pushed Caxton's note across the table and went on writing. Matthew looked at the letter, and drew back as if it were unclean. But his curiosity got the better of him. As he read it he frowned. The frown became a scowl. He swore under his breath. John Goodrich looked up.

'What frets you?' he inquired. 'It seems to me a feather in the boy's cap that his master should want to take him.'

Matthew was reading the letter through again. As he laid it down he made a visible effort to pull himself together. 'That may be. But Warwickshire is a powerful long way. In my view it is better for a prentice to stick to his task.'

'I am content to leave that to his master's judgement,' said

To sand the wet ink

his father, sanding the wet ink. He looked at Matthew and relaxed into a little smile. 'It is good of you and your wife to invite me to dinner on Sunday. I am sorry that I cannot come. As you have seen in the letter, I am dining at Westminster to meet Master Hugh Clopton.'

Bendy returned to the Almonry dazzled with joy. All his troubles seemed to have been wiped out at one fell swoop. His father consented to the journey; he had seen Matthew; and apparently there was no trouble likely to arise about the *Madalena*, after all. Caxton had lost interest in it, and the inquiries from the Exchequer office seemed to have died away.

Into the bargain he found when he got back to the Red Pale that during his absence Peterkin had arrived with another load of paper. At first that was annoying; he would have liked to see Peterkin, and pour out all the excitement about Warwickshire. But at any rate Peterkin was safe and sound, and that was yet one more anxiety safely removed.

The rest of the week flew by. Mistress Caxton herself saw to his clothes. His father sent him a fine warm cloak and, what was more, an order to go to Cordwainer Street and be fitted for a pair of real riding-boots, the first he had ever possessed.

Cloak and riding boots

By Saturday evening everything was ready, and he went off to St Margaret's to be shriven; such a journey was a hazard, and a hazard must be faced in a state of grace. When he got back he found the Red Pale in a turmoil. There were lights everywhere, people running in and out, and Elizabeth seated on the lowest stair was weeping bitterly. Bendy was appalled. What had happened?

''Tis my mother,' cried Elizabeth. 'She has fallen down the stairs from top to bottom. The chirugeon is here and they have sent for the priest. Oh, Bendy, will she die?'

Not daring to go farther, Bendy crept up to the printing house, where everyone was hushed and awaiting news. Time passed; the room grew quite dark. Only Wynken continued to work, picking out type by the feel of it.

Suddenly Caxton appeared. 'Praise be to God, the chirugeon says she will not die,' he reported. 'But her leg is broken. He has set it in a splint – Heaven knows with how much pain. I am to call you all to supper.' He turned to Bendy. 'This is the end of our journey, boy. Clearly I cannot think of leaving home.'

All Bendy's hopes came down with a run. Throughout the meal, and the next morning too, he had all he could do to hide his disappointment. Almost the worst moment came when his father and Hugh Clopton arrived for dinner and had to be told that all the plans were unavailing.

'I need hardly tell you that it is a bitter blow,' said Caxton, refilling the wine-cups for his guests. 'My wife would have me go and leave her, but I should not know a moment's peace. The pity is that I have set my heart upon getting Malory's book and I have a shrewd suspicion that there are others with an eye upon it too.'

'I would go for you to Newbold Revel,' said Hugh Clopton. 'But I have too little knowledge of what you want. Why not let the boy come with me? It seems that he knows all about it. I could ride over with him, or at the worst I would send a servant to escort him.'

Bendy could scarcely believe his ears. Caxton reflected for a moment. He smiled. 'That is exceeding generous of you, sir. I must say that I am loth to risk losing that book. So far as I am concerned I should be happy for him to go with you. But it must be for Master Goodrich to decide.'

Bendy looked at his father with beseeching eyes. John Goodrich glanced from one to another. 'I too must thank you, sir; but I would not make a nursemaid of you; the boy is very young. And I must confess myself a little mystified. What is this book, and who is the Malory that you seek?'

Catching his breath, Bendy turned to Caxton. Would he remember that it was a secret? But his master did not fail him. He gave a glowing description of the King Arthur stories, and of the finding of Malory's tomb, without raising any question about where they had come from in the first place. John Goodrich was much impressed.

'It is an honour that you should trust the boy with such a task,' he said. 'But I still feel that he is over young. If he had another with him, for instance –'

'A good thought,' said Hugh Clopton. 'Have you not got another lad who could bear him company, Master Caxton? So far as I am concerned two would be no more trouble than one – so long as they are sober lads.'

Caxton fingered his chin. 'I might send Dick Pynson, he is my eldest apprentice and a reliable fellow. The only objection is he has so great a stutter that none can grasp what he says.'

John Goodrich laughed. 'Then let Bendy do the talking. I'll warrant that he is never backward with his tongue! If *my* consent is needed, good sirs, by all means let them go. Your kindness puts me for ever in your debt.'

The arms of Clopton

Clopton's bridge

CHAPTER 14

A Small Town on the Avon

BENDY and Dick Pynson left Westminster before dawn the
next morning. They were to meet Hugh Clopton's party at
Tyburn – a dismal trysting place, cried Mistress Caxton when
she heard of it. But Caxton laughed her fears away. They were
to go westward, by the Oxford road, and there was no sense in
riding into London in order to ride out of it again. They
would be saddle-sore enough in any case before the day was
done. He himself was up betimes to see they ate a good breakfast, to give them last-minute instructions, and to wave them
off from the Cock in Tothill Street, where the horses had been
stabled for the night.

As they rode side by side on the road across the marshes,
which spread out from the Tyburn brook, they were both
almost speechless with excitement. Dick, in any case, had
hardly been able to get out an intelligible word from the
moment that Bendy rushed to fetch him at Caxton's bidding

yesterday. His joy at the news that he too was to go on the journey was without bounds, but it was abundantly clear that Bendy would, in truth, have to be the spokesman. That suited Bendy nicely. The Malory business was entirely in his charge; but so that Dick's nose should not be too much out of joint, Caxton entrusted him with the letters to the Canons of St Mary's, Warwick, about the printed service books; and also gave him a letter to be delivered to Master Thomas Hunt, a stationer in Oxford, who had set up a press with a German printer named Theodoric Rood to print books for Oxford scholars, mostly in Latin.

The sun was barely up by the time they reached Tyburn, and the famous Tyburn elms behind the gallows stood grey and motionless in the misty dawn. Hugh Clopton and his party had not yet arrived. Bendy turned to face Londonwards, the way they would come, so that his back was towards the hangman's wooden stage. Though he would be shamed to say so, he wished, with Mistress Caxton, that they had started from elsewhere.

They did not have long to wait before they heard the clip-clop of approaching horses. There were three; Hugh Clopton in front, followed by a manservant with a spare horse on a leading-rein. Hugh Clopton was in great spirits. He hailed Bendy and Dick Pynson as soon as he came in sight and called them to ride with him, one on either side.

'I am no Londoner,' he declared, noisily drinking in the country air. 'I am always happiest when my face is turned t'wards Stratford, even though it will take three days to get there.'

'Where shall we lie tonight, sir?' Bendy ventured.

'At Henley, I hope; Henley on the Thames – not to be confused with Henley-in-Arden, which is nigh to Stratford. It is a good stretch for the first day and there are comfortable beds at the White Hart.'

Bendy began to enjoy himself. At first he had been a little uneasy on his horse. He rode only on the rare occasions when he went with his father to visit kinsfolk at St Albans, and even then it was seldom that he had a horse to himself. But now Caxton had seen to it that he had a quiet cob, not too big for him; indeed, he felt very small beside Hugh Clopton's broad bulk mounted on a great weight-carrying grey, and long, lanky Dick astride a tall brown horse.

The sun was still hot for late August. They passed a few villages, each with thatched cottages clustered round a church, and the long roof of a manor house peeping through the trees. But there was little shade and the way ran through open fields, part stubble and part pasture. At midday, when they dismounted to eat a meal at an inn, he began to realize what Caxton had meant by 'saddle-sore', and by the time that they crossed Henley bridge and clattered into the yard of the White Hart, both he and Dick were so stiff they had practically to be lifted from their horses. Hugh Clopton laughed, not too unkindly, and ordered a tub to be filled with hot water for them. Into this they plunged in turn, and, eased by it, stretched out luxuriously on a second bed in his own bedchamber.

It was an effort to stir themselves in the morning, but they were climbing the long hill out of Henley towards Oxford before the sun was getting high.

'I was a fool not to watch the calendar,' Hugh Clopton said. 'The innkeeper has just reminded me that it is the first of September and the opening of St Giles's Fair, the greatest junketing of the year in Oxford. Had I remembered I would have avoided it like the plague.'

'I have a l-l-letter to d-deliver to Master H-Hunt,' stammered Dick apologetically.

'Yes, and fair or no fair, you had best deliver it today, in case I should decide to come back by another route. I have been thinking that it might be well to make your call at

Newbold Revel on our return journey. We could go that way round without difficulty and then take the road from Coventry to London without touching Oxford. It would save my precious time.'

There was plenty in this to keep Bendy's mind busy as they left the road and turned on to bridle-paths through the woods. He admitted to himself that he would have preferred to go to Newbold Revel with Dick alone and have the sole glory of finding Malory's home and bringing back the book. But on the other hand there might be a better chance of success if Hugh Clopton was with them. As for St Giles's Fair, it would be fun to see it; it was almost as famous as St Bartholomew's Fair in London. But would Tom Twist be there? It was sure to attract pedlars from far and wide and Tom Twist had told Caxton at the Holly Bush that he was going Oxford way.

Hugh Clopton seemed to know every track through the beech-woods. They rode single file among the trees, the horses' hoofs thudding softly on the deep cushion of leaves. Bendy had never been in such woods before. Sunshine and shadow flickered across his face and across the backs of the two riders ahead, so that sometimes they were there and sometimes he was all alone. He almost held his breath with the enchantment of it. It made him think of his King Arthur stories, and how Sir Lancelot rode questing through a forest and met four knights under an oak tree. It came into his head that he was on a quest too; his quest was to restore Sir Thomas Malory. Hugh Clopton himself had called it a deed of true chivalry.

After a while they left the wood and came out on a road crowded with people all pouring in the one direction. They ate at a wayside alehouse while they were still some miles from Oxford; they would never be served in an Oxford tavern, Hugh Clopton declared. For the same reason they had best go on to Woodstock for the night. It was an hour's ride beyond Oxford, and he was well known at the Bull. It was also decided that when they had crossed the bridge by the new Magdalen College, Dick should go into the city, with the manservant for escort, and find the printing house of Thomas Hunt, while Hugh Clopton, with Bendy and the spare horse, rode round the outside of the walls to St Giles's fair-ground.

'We will meet in the porch of St Giles's Church. You cannot miss it, Dick; any babe would direct you there today. The horses can be watered at the pond by the church, and we will spend an hour at the Fair. Let it never be said that I brought two lads to Oxford on St Giles's Day and did not allow them so much as a whiff of gingerbread.'

Dick Pynson went off, determined to finish his job as soon as possible. The others followed the crowd, all heading for the Fair. They could only move at walking pace, for which Bendy was thankful. Saddle-sore was too weak a term for what he was suffering by now. He looked forward to dismounting.

But being on foot proved to be as bad, if not worse than being in the saddle. He limped behind Hugh Clopton into the fair-ground, determined to put as good a face on it as possible.

It was a vast place. Tents and booths covered an area as long as Cheap itself and twice as wide. The two sides of the fair-ground were given up to every form of buffoonery – side-shows, as Hugh Clopton called them: there were swings and see-saws, tumblers and jugglers and puppet-shows and even a giant stride. Every showman was yelling to drown his neighbour with the help of horns and drums and hurdy-gurdys.

In the ordinary way Bendy would have loved it, but now the very thought of a swing was agony. Hugh Clopton moved to the centre walks, where the respectable merchants had their stalls. He met old friends among the mercers and the Cotswold wool men, while Bendy followed sedately with one eye cocked for the first glimpse of Tom Twist. He saw no sign of him, but that proved nothing; in those crowds it would be possible to miss one's own shadow. Anyhow he was quite glad when the hour was over and they went back to the horses again.

The next day he was less stiff, but as though to make up for it, the rain came down in torrents. He got a certain satisfaction out of rolling up his new riding-boots till they covered his thighs, and spreading his cloak over himself and his horse almost like a tent. He could scarcely see out at all, but only grip with his knees, set his teeth, and keep one eye on the tail of Hugh Clopton's horse ahead of him. This sort of thing, he reflected a little bitterly, was never mentioned in stories of chivalry.

Except for a pause for dinner they plodded along blindly all day. It was evening, and he was not sure whether he was awake or asleep, when he was roused by a cry from Hugh Clopton. 'See! The Avon!'

He pushed back his hood to find that the rain had stopped. In front of them was a long wooden bridge, built on piles. Round it swirled and foamed a wide, flooding river.

'There is Stratford on the other side.' Hugh Clopton pointed, excited as a boy. 'We must wait, though; there is somebody coming over. In such weather it is not safe to put too much strain upon the timbers.'

They crossed at last, a lengthy process, with Hugh Clopton standing guard to see that not more than one was on each stretch of the bridge. It was almost dark before they trotted through the little town, and candles glimmered in the windows. Bendy wished to goodness that they could stop, but on they went for what seemed an interminable time, along a muddy track beneath dripping branches, apparently far from any dwelling.

At last he saw a light ahead. They walked the horses up a grassy slope and halted outside a large house barely visible in the darkness. The light that they had seen was pouring from an open door. People came running out. He heard Hugh Clopton say, 'Yes, we are weary, brother; and I've two lads here at their last gasp. I beg you let them eat something and then go straight to bed.'

From the moment that Bendy laid his head upon a luxurious goose-feather pillow he knew no more until he woke at the sound of a bell. He and Dick were lying on a mattress on the floor. He was just settling to sleep again when, from within the curtains of a big bed, Hugh Clopton's voice hailed them.

'Get up, you lazy loons. That was the bell for Mass. The chapel here is newly licensed to my brother by the Pope himself, and he's so proud of it that we shall be in hot water if we lie a-bed.'

Clopton, seen by daylight, was an ancient manor house. The rafters of the great hall, where they gathered after Mass, were blackened with smoke, and pieces of old-fashioned armour hung on the rough timbered walls. Master Thomas Clopton had the same long nose and the same blue eyes as his younger brother, but he was a smaller man with a leathery, weather-beaten face. While they drank their morning ale and ate thick slabs of bread and cheese, the men stood by the fire and discussed the news from London. After a while Master Thomas Clopton joined the boys, who were staring at the armour.

After answering his inquiries about their night's rest, Bendy ventured to ask, 'Is this *your* armour, sir? Your own, that you wear, I mean?'

Master Clopton laughed. 'That breastplate? Why, I should be lost in it. It was my father's. He was a big man, like my brother Hugh. The Stratford smith altered an old suit to fit me when I fought at Tewkesbury. There it hangs, on the end wall.'

'*You* fought at Tewkesbury?'

'Why, yes; the Wars of the Roses raged in these parts, and by the time of Tewkesbury all the county squires were out. We Cloptons followed the White Rose, the Yorkist side, luckily for us. The Red Rose paid heavily. Those who could, quickly forgot their colour and slipped back home. 'Twas a bloody time.'

Bendy turned from the armour, 'Sir, did Sir Thomas Malory fight at Tewkesbury?'

Master Clopton looked astonished. 'What know you of Sir Thomas Malory?'

'He wrote a book, sir, and I go to seek it.'

'A book, did he? I should not have guessed it. It seemed that he lived by the sword.'

'Who lived by the sword?' inquired Hugh Clopton, joining them. 'Stay! I know. Sir Thomas Malory. This lad has a letter addressed to Dame Malory from his master.'

'From his master? Is he not your apprentice?'

'Nay, not mine; Caxton's; William Caxton of Westminster, the printer; the same that was once Governor of the English House at Bruges. He was to have come himself on this journey, but his wife was ailing, so he entrusted the boys to me. They have business to do for him with the Canons of Warwick, and this letter to be delivered to Dame Malory. I plan to go round that way on our journey back to London.'

Master Clopton indulged in a subdued little chuckle. 'It will take the Recording Angel to tell you which way to go. She has been dead nigh on two years, God rest her.'

Bendy gasped, and even Hugh Clopton looked taken aback. 'Dead? Who reigns at Newbold Revel, then?'

'The grandson, Nicholas. He must be about fifteen by now, though he's still under the rule of a great-uncle, a man named Vincent.'

'– of Stoke d'Abernon in Surrey,' said Bendy softly.

'Yes, I believe Stoke d'Abernon is one of his manors; but actually he is of Barnake, just over the border of Northamptonshire; he married Malory's sister.'

'All this is about some book writ by Sir Thomas Malory in

The Chapel of the Merchants' Guild

Newgate,' explained Hugh Clopton. 'Doubtless the boy will tell you. But hark you, brother; I must go to Stratford this morning. Will you come too? I have to see about the new work in the chapel of the Merchants' Guild, and I am impatient to find out how my new house goes.'

The four of them started out across a park set with great trees. The sun was shining, the turf firm and springy, and sheep grazed everywhere. It was all so different from their dripping arrival last night that Bendy wished they could spend the morning walking.

But it was only a mile to Stratford, and soon they were back on cobbled streets. It was market day, and the place was so full of country people, with their pigs and poultry and fruit and cheeses, that round the market cross, where five ways met, it was difficult to walk at all. Into the bargain every few yards somebody stopped Hugh Clopton to shake him by the hand. After a while Master Thomas Clopton joined the two boys, explaining with a laugh that a visit from his brother was an event in the town. The people idolized him; he did so much for them. His money had set the Town Guild upon its feet; he'd refurbished the almshouses and the Grammar School; and the Guild Chapel was actually being rebuilt at his expense.

'Come on, and I'll show you. If we await his leisure we'll wait all day.'

He led them along what was obviously a main street. It was wide and clean, and though most of the houses were small by London standards, they all had glass in the windows – a sure sign of prosperity. The end of the street was half cut off by a church shrouded in scaffolding. It had a tower at one end, and so far as Bendy could see, it looked like an ample parish church rather than the chapel of a guild in a small country town.

'See how fine it is,' said Master Clopton, with brotherly pride. ''Tis all in the latest fashion. Look at those new great windows. What the glass for them will cost him I dare not think. And inside there are to be pictures painted on all the walls.' He suddenly swung round and pointed across the road. 'And that is his new great house. Upon my word, we at Clopton will look like paupers beside him.'

At the corner opposite the church stood another net-work of scaffold. This time it was a house, taller than any in the street, built with upright timber of the straightest oak, without a kink anywhere – the sort of timber that only a wealthy man could command. The spaces were filled in with rosy-red brick, the many gables were tiled, and there were windows, still awaiting glass, facing down both streets.

While they were gazing, Hugh Clopton himself arrived.

'Your pardon, brother,' he cried. 'They would not let me go. Ah! I notice they're getting the roof on the chapel; but, God forgive me, I must see the house first.'

The next hour was spent ranging from cellar to roof, up one stairs and down another, exclaiming at the stone fireplaces with the Clopton arms, at the linen-fold wainscoting in the parlour, the carved roof beams in the hall, the painted walls in the great chamber. Hugh Clopton excitedly pointed out each new device for comfort or convenience. Bendy suddenly thought of the ancient stone mansion in Old Jewry. Small wonder that he wanted everything up to date.

When they emerged from the house, Master Thomas Clopton declared that he must not stay to go over the Guild chapel. The bailiff was awaiting him for orders about the tithes of corn from the harvest. The others could follow at their leisure. Bendy offered to go back with him. It was polite, and, truth to tell, he was more interested in Master Clopton's talk than in the new chapel.

They threaded their way back through the market, leaving Hugh Clopton and Dick behind. Bendy took his place apprentice-wise at Master Clopton's heels, and Master Clopton accepted this display of good manners as long as they were in the town; but when the houses were left behind he waited for Bendy to catch up.

'Tell me more of this book of Sir Thomas Malory's,' he said. 'I never knew him well. I was but young when he was well on in years. But I liked him in spite of his wild repute.'

'Wild repute' indeed! But Bendy swallowed his indignation and told, in a carefully edited version, how he had lighted upon the stories, though they were not complete, and how Caxton was burning to set them up in print if only they could get hold of the finished copy. Soon he was telling some of the actual stories, and telling them with all his might, just to prove that the man who wrote them could not have been anything but a noble knight wrongfully accused. Master Clopton was delighted.

'I like to hear of it,' he said. 'Mind you, there are old folk with long memories who delight to talk of the devil-may-care Sir Thomas, to this day. But tell me, how came you to be apprenticed to this Master Caxton? Surely it must be an honour much sought after.'

Bendy, enraptured, explained that his father was a scrivener, one of the privileged few with a table in St Paul's.

'Ah! An interesting craft. We have a scrivener here in the town, mostly for letters and deeds. Occasionally he copies a book, for a special order, but he finds it difficult to get paper. There is but one pedlar that carries it; he brings it direct from the ship.'

Bendy pounced on this. He was just about to ask questions about the pedlar, when Hugh Clopton's voice hailed them from behind.

'Hey! Our long legs can catch up on you. You've been a mighty time on the way.'

'The boy has been entertaining me with his tales of Malory's book. Upon my soul, brother, I hope that he succeeds in laying hands on it. It will go far to restore the old knight's honour.'

'That is what I say too. But it means we must bestir ourselves; my time is limited. Let me see; tomorrow the Guild meets; that is the object of my coming; and the next day, Saturday, I will spend at the new house. We could be off on Monday, I think. We will ride by Warwick to the Malorys, and then straight back to London.'

Master Thomas protested that they were making too short a stay, but Bendy was well content. The object of *his* journey was Newbold Revel.

The next morning Hugh Clopton went off to the Guild meeting, leaving the two boys to go out with his brother for a day's sport, roaming with hawk and spaniel round the fringes of woodland which Master Clopton said were part of the ancient forest of Arden. It was an unrivalled treat, and they returned to Clopton in the evening mists to find Master Hugh there ahead of them.

'Have you heard about the bridge?' he inquired of his brother. 'It cracked last night, in the torrent from Wednesday's rains. They are busy repairing it, but obviously it is fast crumbling. The building of a new bridge must be set afoot at once, and if I am to sponsor it I cannot leave Stratford till the plans are laid. You two lads will have to go to Newbold Revel without me, and come back here when you have done.'

'Think you that it is wise?' Master Thomas demurred. 'They can scarce go there and back in the day, and the way skirts Dunsmore Heath. That is Red Rose country and a nest of outlaws.'

'Two boys without baggage would not be worth the robbing,' said his brother lightly. 'The outlaws, poor devils, are victims of those accursed wars, not common cut-throats.'

'Still, they are bed-fellows to be avoided. Where do you suggest that the boys should sleep if night overtakes them?'

'Doubtless the Malorys will offer them lodging, but even if they don't there is Combe, a stone's throw from Newbold Revel, and Stoneleigh, nearer this way. Both are Cistercian Abbeys with guest houses. Listen, the two of you: if you are not invited to lie at Newbold Revel, go straight to one or the other, Combe or Stoneleigh, beg a night's lodging – pay for it of course – and return here the next day.'

'Why should they return here at all?' suggested Master Thomas. 'Let them go to Coventry. It would take them but about half an hour from Newbold Revel, and we can give them a letter to Master Mascal, the warden of the Mercers Guild of Coventry. He would certainly lodge them safely and send them with the next party of merchants riding to London. In a cloth town like Coventry there is constant coming and going, and they would get home sooner than if they came all the way back to Stratford.'

Hugh Clopton was obviously relieved. He described it as an excellent plan and said that they could start, as arranged, on Monday morning. But by Monday morning he had decided that he would ride with them as far as Warwick. That would not take too much of his precious time, he could make them known to the Canons of St Mary's, and then put them safely upon the right road for Monken Kirby and Newbold Revel.

They left Clopton early, quite reluctant to say good-bye to their kind host. The morning mist had not yet left the fields by the river when Hugh Clopton pointed to the tall tower of St Mary's crowning the hill above the clustered grey walls of Warwick.

'I will take Dick to see the Dean,' he said. 'Bendy can await us in the church. It is a fine one and full of great tombs to look at when his prayers run dry.'

Bendy grinned. He did not in the least mind being left. The Warwick service books were Dick's pigeon. His turn would come later.

For all that, it did seem that they took a long while just to deliver a letter. He said his prayers and then started to look round the church, as Hugh Clopton had suggested. He wandered from one tomb to another, looking at armour and shields. The biggest was in the choir, facing the high altar. On the strength of having served so often in the sanctuary at Paul's, he went to have a look at it. It was another fine altar-tomb of a knight and his lady; his feet rested upon a bear and hers upon a lamb. He wondered why; perhaps they were family badges.

Suddenly he noticed a small door in the wall of the choir. It led down some steps and it was light at the bottom. He was tired of waiting. On the spur of the moment, he decided to explore.

The steps were narrow and very steep. Half-way down was a tiny chapel, beautifully carved. But he did not stop; he wanted to see what lay beyond.

On the lowest step he stood absolutely still. He was in another chapel, a large one. From the figures over the altar he judged that it was the Lady Chapel. But the first thing that struck him was *light*, like the lightest of clouds. It was built of

stone and alabaster, white as snow, with tracery as airy and
delicate as a cascade of icicles. The stone was carved everywhere with leaves and flowers and saints and angels, so fragile
that they looked as though they would fly away. It seemed to
belong to the magic world of King Arthur and Merlin and the
Holy Grail. For as well as whiteness the place was full of
colour. The great wide windows glowed with painted glass;
the roof was encrusted with gold and studded with bright
coats of arms.

In the middle of all this stood one solitary tomb, a high
carved tomb, with little bronze figures all round it, and a great
gilded knight in armour lying in state on the top of it. It looked

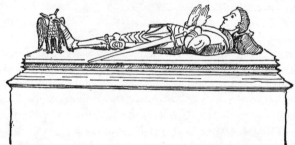

A carved tomb with a knight on it

new, as though it were just made. It was so tall that he could
not see over the top, so he fetched a faldstool that someone had
been kneeling on.

The knight looked slim and young, and, in spite of the gild-
ing, almost alive. His head was bare and his hair beautifully
combed. Bendy noticed the veins in his hands, and then the
hands themselves. They were not folded, as usual, but thrown
back with the fingers open, as though in astonishment. His
head was *raised* from the pillow, as a man raises his head when
he hears his name called suddenly. The eyes were open;
following them Bendy saw that they were fixed upon the

figure carved at the top of the great window, the figure of Almighty God surmounting lines of angels and archangels.

He was so engrossed that he did not see Hugh Clopton appear down the little stairs, his tall figure bent almost in half.

'Ah, here you are, boy. Dick has gone to the horses and I came to look for you. So you have found the new Lady Chapel. All Warwickshire is proud of it.'

Bendy indicated the knight. 'Who is he?'

'The Lord Richard Beauchamp, Earl of Warwick. You

The arms of Beauchamp

must have heard of him. He was so noble a knight that Henry the Fifth left him as Governor to his son, the infant king. The whole chapel is to his memory.'

Bendy gazed all the more. Richard Beauchamp, the great Earl of Warwick! Caxton's words came rushing back. '"They called him the flower of chivalry."'

'Quite right. The *flower of chivalry* or the *father of courtesy*; either befitted him. It was he who knighted your Sir Thomas Malory.'

Bendy let out a long sigh. Quite suddenly everything became clear. He had been *right* when he thought of King Arthur and the Holy Grail in this chapel. This was Sir Thomas Malory's master; his liege lord. This was the knight who stood to Malory for King Arthur and Lancelot and Galahad. When, as an old man, Malory lay in jail, this had all come back to him. Whatever he had done in the meanwhile, it was this that he remembered; and this was why he wrote his stories.

He got down from the faldstool and put it back in its place. He was ready to go. At that moment only one thing mattered. *He must get that book.*

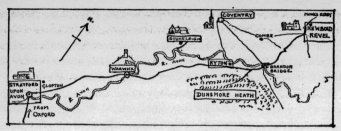

The way to Newbold Revel

CHAPTER 15

Newbold Revel

AFTER a good meal at a tavern Dick and Bendy rode out of Warwick by the east gate. Hugh Clopton paid for the meal and sent them off with many instructions. Dick carried the letter for Master Mascal, head of the Mercers Guild in Coventry, which would assure them of hospitality and of an early passage back to London. The horses came from Clopton, but Master Mascal would provide them with others and send these back to their owner. Their money was divided between them: Dick's hidden in his boot, Bendy's in the large pouch strapped to his belt. If they did not stay the night at Newbold Revel, they were to trust themselves to no one except the monks, or the mercers at Coventry. Finally when they reached London they were to make his excuses to Master Caxton that he had not ridden with them all the way.

They were both in high spirits. Dick was beside himself because he had got an order from the Dean not only for a great Missal, but also for a *Legenda* to match – the companion book which contained lessons from the Scriptures and from the lives of the saints for reading on their proper feast days. They were to be folios – the largest book possible – and they were to have the rubrics in red, which was quite new for print.

Bendy was just as excited. He could hardly wait for Dick to finish before he broke in with his own story about the tomb of Richard Beauchamp, who was Malory's liege lord. Now that they were actually on their way to Newbold Revel, Dick suddenly became interested, and as they jogged along Bendy began to tell stories about King Arthur from the book. Dick

Water-bottle

was all ears. Time passed unnoticed till, as the sun was at its highest, Bendy said with a sigh, 'Phew! I am thirsty. Have you water in your water-bottle?'

Dick stretched for the water-bottle tied to his saddle. Bendy took a mouthful; but he quickly spat it out, and Dick confessed ruefully that he had not renewed it since he knew not when. But now that they knew they had no water, they were both instantly consumed by thirst. They rode on, hoping to see some dwelling where there was a well; but just there the country seemed uninhabited. At last Dick spotted some willow trees a short way from the road. Willows meant water, so they walked the horses across a stretch of marshy land only to find a pond fouled by cattle.

'It's fed by a stream from the hill,' Dick pointed out. 'If we follow the stream up we're bound to find a place where it is clean.'

The hill was wooded and the ground rough, and as they climbed they seemed to be getting deep into a wild forest region. Bendy was just about to say they should turn back, when Dick cried, 'Look! A house. They must have water there.'

The house was no more than a tiny thatched cottage, standing in a sunny clearing. Cocks and hens scratched about among dead leaves and a couple of pigs rootled in the undergrowth. But there were bright flowers in a patch by the house, and an old straggling rose tree smothered the roof with small white roses.

Dick threw his rein to Bendy. 'Hold the horses and I'll g-go and ask a drink for b-both of us.'

Bendy watched him go to the door and stick his head inside. He seemed to find no one, for he strolled round the outside and came to a stop, staring up at the roof. Then Bendy noticed that the climbing rose seemed to be mysteriously alive. Somebody was hacking at it savagely. Suddenly Dick beckoned. Bendy hitched the horses to a tree and ran.

Just round the corner there was a rough ladder propped against the wall, and at the foot of it stood a little old woman, bent and gnarled, like an ancient witch. Her face and hands were bleeding, her clothes hung in tatters, and she babbled like one possessed.

'She's trying to cut down the rose; she wants us to help,' whispered Dick. 'Have a care, Bendy. Maybe she's bedevilled.'

The old woman went on gabbling and sobbing. Bendy half turned to go, then some words struck home.

'No,' he cried. 'It *is* the rose! She says if it stays there they'll come back and burn the place down. Don't you see? It is a *white* rose, and they said that this was Red-Rose country.'

Protesting that it was but n-nonsense, Dick soon followed

Bendy's lead. Together they tugged and hacked with the old woman's chopper till the branches lay on the ground and not a petal remained to show its colour. The old woman blessed them ceaselessly, and though they could understand hardly a word she said, she gave them each a mug of goat's milk.

'I still think she was crazed,' said Dick as they mounted again. 'Who would care, red rose or white, what grew upon a hovel like that?'

'Crazed by something that happened in the wars,' Bendy

Pointed a skinny finger

reflected grimly. 'They say that London knew nothing of it. Hey! Let's get on. We've wasted time enough.'

They made their way back to the road, leaving the wild region behind them. It was quite a relief when they came to a village again. They asked the name, and were told that it was Ryton-in-Dunsmore. Newbold Revel was nigh to the township of Monken Kirby, six or seven miles farther on.

The lanes turned and twisted crazily. At last Dick said crossly they must have covered another ten miles at least. He stopped again at the next cross-roads to inquire from a bow-legged old man who was picking faggot wood from the hedge and piling it on to a shaggy pony. He looked such a witless creature that

Bendy doubted if it was any use asking him. But he understood them easily enough and pointed a skinny finger to an overgrown track which left the road a little way ahead of them. That, he said, was the demesne of Newbold Revel. If they followed their noses down it, they would come to the house.

With a grin Dick held back for Bendy to lead the way. 'After you, fellow,' he said. 'I had a fair field at Warwick. This is for you.'

They rode along the track for a furlong or two more, and Bendy was just about to call over his shoulder that the old fool had misled them, when they rounded a clump of bushes and saw the manor house standing in a wide stretch of rich grass and trees.

It was certainly an ancient place, half castle and half farm. A battered old tower leaned up against a buttressed hall, while at the other end a two-storeyed wing was propped on beams as though it would fall down. It faced a courtyard surrounded by a stone curtain wall with ramshackle byres and barns shored up against it.

With thumping heart Bendy approached the pallisade of timbers that served as a gatehouse. There was no one to stop him, so, followed by Dick, he rode through.

In the courtyard two boys were grooming a horse, both dressed peasant-wise in coarse shirts girded by leather belts. One of them straightened himself and came forward.

'God save you. What's your will?' His air was certainly not that of a peasant.

Bendy dismounted. 'By your leave, I have a letter addressed to Dame Elizabeth Malory; but I am told that she is dead and that I should tell my business to her grandson.'

'I am her grandson. I am Nicholas Malory.'

Bendy eyed him. He liked the look of him. It would be a good thing to get him on to his side. 'My business concerns a book of King Arthur and his knights writ by your grandsire,' he said quickly. 'My master is the worshipful Master William Caxton, the printer, of the Abbey at Westminster. He has seen your grandsire's book and he asks leave to imprint it. He was coming himself to beg to be entrusted with the manuscript, but his lady wife is ill, so he sent me with a letter in his stead.' He had rehearsed it so often that it came out with a run.

Two boys were grooming a horse

Nicholas Malory looked at him blankly. 'What is *imprint*?' he asked.

It was Bendy's turn to be taken aback. It had not occurred to him that there was anyone who did not know what printing was. As he hesitated Dick butted in, stammering that a printing press could make many copies of a book instead of just one.

'But why should you want to make many copies of my grandsire's book?'

'So that everyone may read it,' Bendy cried. 'Master Caxton is all afire for noble stories of chivalry. He has printed the *Recuyell of Troy* and the *Canterbury Tales* and the *Chronicle of England* and many more; but your grandsire's stories of King

Arthur are the best of all.' He took a quick breath. 'I *found* the book; I know it by heart.'

'How could you have found it? It is in the money coffer, all in a roll, tied up and sealed, pages and pages in tiny script.'

Bendy's eyes brightened. So it *was* there! 'I got mine at school – Paul's School in London. Master Caxton says that it is but a small part – maybe a part that was thrown out when your grandsire died in Newgate.'

Nicholas Malory scowled. 'Say not Newgate to me. My grand-dam said that I must never hear it without challenge.'

Bendy could have bitten his tongue out. 'I ask your pardon. My master says that the stories are of such spirit that all who read them will know that Sir Thomas Malory was a noble knight and held wrongfully.' As the boy's face lightened, he went on. 'Today I saw the tomb of the Lord Richard Beauchamp, your grandsire's liege, and I swear that I know how your grandsire came to write of King Arthur and his noble knights.'

'You saw the tomb? My grand-dam took me there. She told me how he had dubbed my grandsire knight, and how my grandsire near worshipped him. It was for his sake that my grandsire followed the next Earl of Warwick, who was a Nevill and not of Beauchamp blood, and I must never forget it. It was when Nevill changed his coat that my grandsire was called a false traitor.'

'No traitor ever wrote his book,' cried Bendy. 'It is the best book that ever was made, save Holy Writ, of course; and the part about the Holy Grail is almost like Holy Writ. So is the last part, the death of Arthur, and the end of the sword Excalibur.'

Nicholas broke in eagerly. '"*Then Sir Bedevere departed and went to the sword and lightly took it up and went to the waterside; and there he bound the girdle about the hilts and then he threw the sword as far into the water as he might; –*"'

Bendy took it up. '– "*and there came an arm and an hand above the water and met it and caught it and so shook it thrice and brandished and then vanished away with the sword in the water*".'

'That's it.' Nicholas clapped his hands. 'And, do you know the part about the great tourney at Winchester on Lady Day, when Sir Lancelot came into the field with Sir Lavaine as if it had been thunder – ?'

They both began at once to cap each other's quotations from the book, till Nicholas Malory cried, 'Come you in; I'll get the manuscript. Come to the hall.'

Bendy needed no second telling. They were half-way across the courtyard when in the doorway of the hall an old man appeared. At the sight of him Bendy slowed down. This was no countryman like Nicholas; his silky-white hair was combed smoothly down almost to shoulder length, and his snowy beard clipped to a sharp point. Though his gown of deep blue cloth was old and faded, it was edged with fur, and soft leather boots were folded round his ankles. He stepped out into the evening sunshine.

'How now, nephew,' he said courteously. 'You have friends, I see. Be so good as to present them.'

Nicholas fumbled for words, and could not find the right ones; he looked at Bendy, hopelessly confused. Bendy stepped forward. He had no doubt that this was Master Vincent, who had actually brought the manuscript from Newgate. So he began his speech again, exactly as before. 'By your leave, sir, I carry a letter –' and so on to the end.

'A letter for Dame Elizabeth? Give it to me.'

He waited while Bendy dived into his pouch. Then, without reference to his nephew, he unfolded the sheet and held it up before him, first near, then farther away, as though he could not read the writing.

'Pish!' he said impatiently. 'My spectacles are within doors. Tell me what it says.'

Bendy began, nervously, to read the letter aloud. Caxton wrote in terms of the greatest courtesy to the most right good lady, the Dame Elizabeth Malory, to set forth his praise of the stories of King Arthur and his noble knights, made into English by the worshipful Sir Thomas Malory, though he had seen those stories only in some small part. And how because the noble order of chivalry had been in these late days forgotten, he desired heartily that men might read and learn the deeds by which knights came to honour. And how the Prior of Greyfriars had made known to him that all the stories so writ by Sir Thomas Malory were now in one roll in her safe keeping. And how, therefore, he prayed that she would entrust the roll to his messenger, who was his sworn apprentice, that the book might be imprinted by him at his printing house within the Abbey of Westminster, where he had imprinted books for the most excellent King Edward the Fourth, and many noble gentlemen; to the truth of which the most worshipful Master Hugh Clopton of Stratford-upon-Avon, or the Prior of Greyfriars, would bear witness.

Bendy was breathless by the time he came to the end. Master Vincent listened carefully, but, to Bendy's disappointment, he made no comment. Instead he asked searching questions about how two boys came to be riding without escort so far from home. Did they know the country? Where did they sleep?

Bendy explained how they had ridden with Master Hugh Clopton and that he had been delayed in Stratford because of the bridge; that he had told them if need be to go to the Abbey at Stoneleigh, or the Abbey at Combe, and that they carried a letter to Master Mascal, the mercer, at Coventry, who was to put them in the charge of a party riding to London.

'I see,' said Master Vincent gravely. 'But, tell me, this *other* messenger who came; is he also from this printing house?'

Bendy's heart missed a beat. 'Another messenger?'

'A pedlar with spices to sell. He produced authority, but I did not read it.' He suddenly glared at Bendy. 'The riddle for me is whence comes this interest in Sir Thomas Malory? He has been dead a dozen years and all that time his writings have rested here. Now the scribes are after him like vultures. What does it mean?'

For a moment Bendy was silenced. His main thought was that Tom Twist had *not* got the book. But Dick broke in, forgetting his stammer in his anger.

'Our master is no vulture. I'd have you know that he was Governor of the English House at Bruges and emissary of our lord the King to the Duke of Burgundy.'

'Indeed? Well-favoured in the Yorkist camp, eh? All the more strange that he should busy himself with one who died a prisoner for the Red Rose.'

'Good uncle,' Nicholas Malory broke in, 'it is not a matter of Red Rose or of White. This fellow here knows the book as I do; he can repeat it parrot-wise. He says his master cares only for chivalry, and that was my grandsire's purpose. My grand-dam told me so.'

'Hold your peace, fool! There has been trouble enough in this family, thanks to your grandsire's ideas of chivalry, and I'll allow no more.'

'Sir, I am his grandson and his heir. I have the right to say –'

'You young blockhead, you have no rights at all. You are not of age. Till then I shall follow my own judgement.' He turned back to Bendy. 'If I have seemed to lack courtesy to your master, boy, I regret it. By all telling he is a man of honour. But I am resolved that neither he nor any other shall have the manuscript from my hands.'

He turned to go back into the hall and then thought better of it.

'You say that you are to lodge at Stoneleigh or Combe – or did you say Coventry? Combe is the nearest. Nicholas, bid the wenches bring cake and ale. They must have something before they go.'

He chatted to them quite pleasantly as they took the mugs that the maid-servant brought. Dick did justice to the food, but Bendy could hardly swallow the ale, and the cake he left untouched. Nicholas Malory stood kicking at a grass tuft, all the fight gone out of him. He let them go with hardly as much as a God speed.

'A lily-livered puppy,' Dick raged on the way back to the road. 'He said the book was his, but one peck from the old cock and he had his tail between his legs.'

Bendy took no notice. He was sick with misery. He had failed to get the manuscript, and at this moment it was not even a comfort that Tom Twist had not got it either.

After one look at Bendy's face Dick took charge. 'We'll go to Combe tonight,' he decided, 'and on to Coventry in the morning.' Near the cross-roads the same old man was still pottering about gathering sticks. Dick called out, 'Which way to Combe Abbey?' The old man pointed to the road on the right, leading to flat green water-meadows. The sun was down and a sea of white mist lay across the valley. They had covered some distance and shapes were growing indistinct in the dusk when Dick cried, 'Listen!'

Bendy halted. He heard the muffled drumming of hoofs on the grass-grown track. The moon was just rising, an orange ball, out of the mist. Bendy's heart thumped as a horse came at a canter, its rider bent over its neck, and Nicholas Malory pulled up beside him.

'Take this and go quickly,' he gasped. He held out to Bendy a roll of paper tied tightly and sealed. 'I took it from the coffer. Begone as fast as you can. Keep away from Combe or Coventry or Stratford or anywhere near by that you have mentioned.

If my uncle misses it he'll fetch the Justices and they'll follow you.'

'What will happen to you?' cried Bendy.

'For all he says, I do but give what is my own. I must go back at once. If he misses me he may search the coffer; if not it might be long before he opens it.' He wheeled his horse. 'God be with you. Make good speed.'

Before Bendy could even thank him he had gone; the sound of hoofs grew fainter and fainter.

Dick let out a deep breath. 'Phew! There's nothing d-dull about this business, I yield you that. *Now* what do we do? It seems all ways are closed to us.'

Bendy pressed the precious roll into the bottom of his pouch. 'We'll go straight to London,' he said. 'We mustn't waste a moment.'

'Not *now*,' snapped Dick. 'The horses couldn't do it even if we could. We must lodge somewhere. I've no mind to sleep in the saddle.'

A thought struck Bendy. 'We'll go to the old dame with the white roses. She'll shelter us for the night.'

Dick grumbled, but admitted that it was a good idea. No one would ever find them there. 'How d-do we get there?' he demanded. 'The nearest village was called Ryton-in-Duns-more, but it all looks alike in this light.'

'We must get back to the cross-roads and go back the way we came. But hurry; it's too near to Newbold Revel for my liking.'

At the cross-roads they stopped again. The way on the left led to Newbold Revel, but they argued in whispers about which of the other two roads was the right one.

Suddenly a voice from the shadows said, 'Be 'e lost *again*, my masters? Where would 'e go this time?'

Bendy peered. It was the old man with his pony and his faggots. 'To Ryton-in-Dunsmore; which way?'

The old man stepped into the moonlight, his bow-legs throwing a shadow like a gigantic frog. 'A tidy step. But do 'e listen well to what I tell 'e. You take *that* road,' he pointed, 'until 'e cross Avon at Bretford Bridge – a stone bridge; 'e can't miss it. A furlong or two beyond that, the road forks; there be three great oaks in the middle. Follow your shield arm' – he waved a shaky left fist in the air – 'your *shield* arm, mark you, not your sword arm. That's all.'

Bendy fumbled to find a penny. As they moved away they heard the old man's voice behind them. 'Your shield arm, mark it well. By the three oaks, follow your shield arm.'

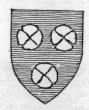

The arms of Vincent

'Follow your shield arm'

CHAPTER 16

Open to the Sky

As the moon got up the mist vanished and the way became quite light. At first they rode in silence, with ears alert for any hint of pursuit. But the countryside seemed deserted. Only once did they fancy that they heard the sound of a trotting horse, but it died away and they decided that it must have been going in another direction.

Presently they began to talk, planning how to get to London, and how to send a message to Stratford, because they still had the horses and the Cloptons would be anxious when news failed to arrive from Coventry. They discussed Newbold Revel and wondered how Nicholas would fare if his action was discovered; and then Dick wanted to know about the pedlar who had tried to get the manuscript. In the end Bendy told him the whole story of Tom Twist and Will Soper and the Holly Bush; how he had won the stories at dicing and how, that way, the whole business had begun. There was so much to tell that they had reached the bridge over the Avon before it was finished, and soon afterwards came to the fork in the road by the three great oaks, just as the old man had said.

'Follow your sh-shield arm,' Dick imitated the cracked old voice.

They turned the horses' heads towards the left and started to go gently uphill.

Bendy was still intent upon his story when Dick said suddenly, 'How shall we know where we turned off the road for the cottage?'

'Easy,' said Bendy. 'We have to go through the village, and then there is a marsh with a group of willows.'

'Yes,' Dick agreed. 'But where is the village? I don't remember coming through all these trees.'

Bendy looked round. It was true. They seemed to be in a wood, with the moon half lost. Moreover the track was now so narrow that they could no longer ride abreast.

'We *must* be right,' he said doubtfully. 'We turned to our shield arm. What shall we do? Go on or turn back?'

'We can't turn here; it's too dark. Go on until we reach the next patch of moonlight.'

They moved forward cautiously, for they could see no path and the horses were deep in dead leaves.

Suddenly there was a crackling of branches and a thundering of hoofs. In sudden panic Bendy cast a glance over his shoulder. Something reared up at his back. A blow from behind caught him; he felt himself falling. As he hit the ground there were shouts and the whinny of a frightened horse. Then everything went black.

When he came to he was in pitch darkness and almost stifled. At first it seemed to be a nightmare in which the bed heaved and bumped under him. He felt sick and every inch of him ached. Then bit by bit he realized that the heaving and the bumping was the movement of a plodding horse. His arms were lashed to his side, his ankles tied; he was smothered in something dark and musty, and he was lying across somebody's saddle. The worst pain of all was in his head; but he realized that, pain or no pain, he must not struggle. He must lie still.

Though his arms were bound he could move his fingers. Fumbling he touched a hard edge. It was a cut strap. He knew instantly; his pouch was gone.

His first thought was old Vincent at Newbold Revel; he had fetched the Justices and pursued them. But the Justices wouldn't attack like this. He tried to remember what the Cloptons had said about outlaws. A name came back to him. *Dunsmore*. 'Dunsmore Heath – a nest of outlaws.' He felt sicker than ever. What fools they had been. The old woman's cottage was at Ryton-in-*Dunsmore*!

A wave of terror swept over him. Then he thought again of the book. Outlaws wouldn't want *that*. It must have been the money they were after. If only he could keep quiet he might yet get the book back. He fixed his mind on Malory. *He* had escaped from two prisons.

They were moving at a walking pace on soft ground. Bendy let himself go limp, wondering how much longer he could endure the bumping and the stifling blackness. Then suddenly the horse's hoofs clinked upon paving. They stopped. Close to him someone gave a short whistle.

In a few seconds a bright light appeared. It flared straight into his eyes, almost blinding him, and yet he was still smothered. It dawned on him that the cloth over his head was riddled with moth holes and somebody was holding aloft a lighted lantern.

'I got 'un,' said a gruff voice close beside him. 'Old Bowlegs sent 'un into the woods true enough.'

'Both on 'em?'

'T'other got away. But this 'un had what we were after.'

'He's alive?'

The deep voice grunted. 'Live enough, and kicks like a mule. I had to clout the wits out of 'un. What's to be done with 'un now, know you?'

'If he's well tied up, tip 'un in the straw. He'll keep till we get orders.'

Bendy felt himself heaved across a broad shoulder. He

A lighted lantern

gripped himself, determined not to cry out. His captor carried him a few steps, then dropped him, not too roughly, on to a soft mound.

'He'll do,' said the deep voice. 'Come on, neighbour; we'd best kindle a fire.'

The light faded. Bendy was in complete darkness, apparently lying on a pile of mouldy straw that smelled of burnt rags and rats. He rolled on to his side to save himself from suffocating, and thrust forward with the point of his chin. The old rotten cloth which seemed to be tied over his head and shoulders broke away enough for him to breathe. If he could have got a hand to it he could have torn it, but he was too tightly bound. It was best to save his strength and await what happened next. He lay aching from head to foot. All the horrors that he had heard about the Wars of the Roses came crowding into his mind. He tried to pray, Paters and Aves, one after the other, familiar prayers that came without effort, like a life-line to hold on to.

Suddenly through his moth-holes he could see a light again. It was streaming out through a doorway in a black wall. Apparently the doorway led into a stone-flagged hall. He could hear echoing footsteps as the two men made their fire.

'Hold the torch to it, neighbour; the wood's damp,' said the gruff voice. ''Tis well there's a bit of roof left.'

'A bit of roof left.' Bendy's mind flew back to the talk about burned-out manors. What were they doing here? Was it a meeting-place?

The fire was crackling merrily when he heard the sound of horses in the distance, and then the clatter of footsteps entering the hall. There seemed to be a crowd – half a dozen at least, to judge from the voices – all talking at once in a blurred country sing-song. He could hardly make out a word, till one voice cut through the hum. It was a shrill voice, with a piercing twang, a voice used to making itself heard among crowds.

'Give way, you fellows. Yield me a place by the fire. I've been afoot all day.'

It was a Cockney voice. Bendy held his breath. He knew it all too well. It was Tom Twist.

The chatter went on again, with scarcely a word intelligible. The thumping of Bendy's heart almost suffocated him. What should he do? Tom Twist at one with the outlaws? What would they do to *him*?

Suddenly there was a clapping of hands and a call for quiet. Tom Twist's voice rang out again. It sounded as if he were master of the meeting. 'What news have you for me, good neighbours? A ship for Brittany will call at Mucking Creek at the new moon, and tidings must go out with her. I am bidden to give account of what the muster roll for the Red Rose would be in this region. I'll hear you one by one, and put it down as peppercorns in my list of spices.'

Mucking Creek and the Red Rose! This was something new with a vengeance. Henry Tudor in Brittany was getting his news by way of Mucking Creek.

'Come, speak up! There's naught to fear. I've carried spices to half a dozen counties and I tell you the Red Rose buds are ripe to burst. The Yorkist King is ailing and his son but a child. Now, I have some names here and I must know if they are to be counted on and the number of followers each could bring. First, Master Bennet Medley of Whitnash; who knows Master Medley? You do, old Clutterbuck? Is he a likely fellow?'

As he listened to the long list of squires and yeomen, Bendy felt utterly bewildered. None of this had any connexion with the book. Why had he been brought here? It could not be mere chance, because the old man had deliberately sent them astray.

At last the questioning died down. Somebody fed the fire so that its light poured afresh through the open door. The voices again became a jumble.

'By the way,' Tom Twist spoke up again, 'I asked some of you to keep watch for a party visiting Newbold Revel. They were going there to seek a roll of writing. Now I covet that roll, and if we keep track of them I may contrive to get it. Has anyone seen them yet?'

A gruff voice answered; Bendy knew it at once. 'Aye, master; they came. We took the roll without much ado. Here it is, at your pleasure.'

'The roll? You've got it?' Tom Twist cried out. 'Upon my soul that was sharp work. How in Heaven's name did you manage it?'

Bendy's captor chuckled. 'We set old Bowlegs to watch; he's as bright as a robin's eye. When they came they were only a couple of lads, so he directed them this way and sent word to us. The rest was easy.'

Bendy bit his lip in anguish. They had been completely fooled. Tom Twist was roaring with laughter. 'Stab me! That's the best jest of all. What I get for that roll I'll share with you and Bowlegs, I swear I will.'

But there were murmurs among the men. One of them spoke up angrily. ''Tis perilous to have matters set out in writing. I thought it was understood that nothing should be writ which might get us hanged.'

'Clutterbuck, you old dunderhead, there's no meat for hanging in this. 'Tis but a bit of my private peddling; a roll of tales, writ in Newgate Jail by Sir Thomas Malory, who was well known round here.'

A chorus arose: 'Writ in jail? Old Sir Thomas? Did you ever? Old Tom Malory.'

But the man called Clutterbuck was not to be put off. 'What tales? I mind me that Malory turned his coat a time or two.' The rest followed him like sheep. 'Aye; turned his coat. What's this writing? We ought to know.'

Tom Twist's voice was sharper than ever. 'Clutterbuck, you'd not trust God's own angel. Well, it's a long story, but you'd best hear it. Throw some wood on the fire. You'll get a laugh out of it, anyway.'

The fire crackled; there were sounds of shifting places and Tom Twist began again. 'To start with, I sell paper to a bunch of scriveners in London, in Paternoster Row. They are two brothers and they do a trade in writing tales that I carry round the fairs. The paper that I sell to them comes into Mucking Creek; the spice-ships carry it as ballast. It earns a pretty penny for the Red Rose.'

Bendy held himself rigid. He must be dreaming. He

couldn't really be lying bound hand and foot and listening to a lot of outlaws talking about his own brothers. But Tom Twist went plodding on.

'Now these two brothers are both crack-brained in one quarter. They are red hot against the new-fangled way of making books by printing; maybe you've heard of it, maybe not; no matter. 'Tis a threat to all scriveners. Now these two vent their spleen against a fellow who has set up to print in Westminster, a fellow named Caxton. He prints stories like the *Canterbury Tales* which they consider their own preserve. They'd have his blood if they could get it, but as they don't know a cook's knife from a bodkin they've devised a scheme to starve him of paper. None can make books without paper.'

There were chuckles round the fire, as though the story had caught its hearers' fancy.

'Now, all paper is shipped and comes up the river; and for months they've paid hands down for every shipload to be waylaid and held off from Westminster. They filled their house to bursting and, perforce, they've rented a barn at Mucking to hold it. But here's the best joke of all. A lad working for a waterman well known to us begged a load or two for a customer of his own. I let him have it and asked no questions, even if I cracked a guess where it went. This Caxton is a pleasant fellow. I sell spices to his lady. . . . And if the paper *is* twice sold – well, the Red Rose needs the money. Shipmasters must be paid.'

There was laughter. But Clutterbuck broke in again. 'What has all this to do with the roll of writing? Be you fobbing us off, master?' Once more there were background murmurs: 'Fobbing us off?' 'Be he fobbing us off?'

'Nay, nay,' cried Tom Twist. 'No one could fob *you* off, Clutterbuck. The roll is no more than a parcel of Malory's tales and I'm just about coming to that. Malory used to write them in Newgate; his jailer got hold of them and sold them.

'*It's a long story but you'd best hear it*'

They drifted piecemeal round the alehouses, and one day a fat lout of a boy who worked for my crack-brained pair picked up a handful somewhere and carried them home. Though they were but odds and ends his mother bade him to take them to his master, the scrivener, who, it chanced, was courting her. The scrivener declared they were just what he wanted for his little books, and he offered the boy a pretty penny to find the rest. But before the boy could pull it off Caxton got wind of the tales and decided to print them. He learned that there was a complete copy at Newbold Revel, so he packed off a messenger to get it. My friend the scrivener went well-nigh mad. He sent for me and promised me the earth if I could get to Newbold Revel first and keep the fair copy out of Caxton's hands. If needs be they would destroy it rather than it should reach the printing house.'

Destroy it! Bendy gasped so loudly that he feared they must have heard him. But Tom Twist was still talking. 'So *that* is your roll of writing. Now, Clutterbuck, are you satisfied?'

Chatter broke out again; it sounded good-humoured enough. Suddenly Bendy heard the gruff voice of his captor.

'What's to be done with the boy, master?'

'Boy? What boy?'

'The boy that carried the roll.'

'Saints on high, you didn't bring the boy too? Where is he?'

'Outside, master; trussed up like a chicken. Shall I fetch him in?'

Bendy bit his lip till the blood ran. If they knew he'd heard everything he'd never get out alive.

'Fetch him in? Great Heavens, no! He's a lad I'm acquainted with. He'd know me at first glance.'

The man laughed grimly. 'I vow he'd not know his own mother after the way I clouted him. He lies like a log.'

'Then let him lie. – But stay; weren't there *two* boys?'

'Aye, master. The other got away.'

'*Got away*? You stand there and tell me he got away? You fool! You dolt! Don't you see he'll be fetching help. They'll find us here. Devil take you, man; you've put us all in peril.' His voice rose shrilly. 'Haste, all of you; rake out the fire; tread out the embers; there's no time to lose. We must away!'

The clatter grew to a stampede. Above it Bendy heard Clutterbuck shout, 'There's a well out yonder; drop him in'; and then Tom Twist's voice cutting through: 'Nay, you fool. They'd find him and spur the Justices. Cut his bonds and leave him. When he comes round he'll not know how he got here.'

Bendy lay flat on his front, hardly able to breathe for the thumping of his heart. He heard footsteps approaching. With the greatest effort of his life he forced himself to lie still. The footsteps stopped beside him. He felt what he judged to be a knife slipped through his cords. It cut upwards and outwards. He was conscious of the slackening, at his ankles and round his body and arms. As though for a parting shot a toe prodded him. It was not harsh, but it was more than he could endure. He let out a groan, and then held himself taut for what would come next. But the gruff voice only grunted, as if to itself, ''Tis well; he lives.'

At the other side of the house, horses trod the ground as their riders mounted. The owner of the gruff voice hurried away. The horses started off; sounds grew fainter, until they faded into nothing.

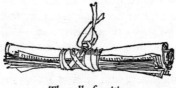

The roll of writing

The Gatehouse at Stoneleigh

CHAPTER 17

The Black Abbot

FOR a time Bendy lay still. Though he was free, every movement was agony. Then he began to loosen himself, inch by
inch. The cloth, when he got his head clear of it, proved to be
a tattered cloak, riddled with moth. The air seemed cold and
fresh, in spite of the reek of mouldy straw. The only sound was
an owl hooting in the distance. He could see stars overhead but
nothing more. It would be hopeless to try to find his way in
the dark. He settled farther into the straw and dragged the
smelly cloak over him. His aching limbs were bearable if he
did not move.

When he woke, stiff and cold, it was broad daylight. He
looked up at the sky through a criss-cross of charred and
blackened beams, wondering for one moment of panic where

he was. As memory returned he raised himself on his elbow, wincing at the pain in his head. It was too tender to touch, but his fingers exploring found the hair matted with dried blood. But, head or no head, his one thought was to get away quickly, in case *they* came back.

The place was undoubtedly a ruin. Even the straw was part of the torn-down thatch. Struggling to his feet, he ventured through the doorway, across the blackened remains of the hall, with embers still scattered on the hearth, and out into a weed-grown courtyard where at least the sun shone.

The house stood like a grim skeleton in a clearing of the woods. Thankful to get away, he stumbled across the rough ground and plunged in among the trees. Once out of sight he sat down, resting against a young oak, and tried to think things out.

What he had heard was almost past believing – Tom Twist a go-between for the Red Rose, and Mucking Creek not only the haunt of pirates and smugglers but the place where ships picked up messages for Henry Tudor in Brittany. Caxton's paper, hidden there, was paid for by Matthew, and the money went to the cost of all this treachery.

As for the Malory stories, it was actually *Matthew* who was after them. That made everything seem crazier than ever. But it explained Will Soper's bargaining and Humphrey's thieving, the dirty little cur. Humphrey had shown part of the stories to Matthew, and he knew that Bendy had the rest. If he and Will Soper didn't get them before Matthew learned where they were, their profit would be gone.

When Matthew once saw the stories he wanted them for his scribes. That was natural; they were as good as the *Canterbury Tales*. So when he got wind of it that Caxton was on the track of a complete copy he must have gone all but mad; Tom Twist had said so. Bendy could picture it all; Matthew sending Tom Twist off, post haste, to Newbold Revel, and even vowing to *destroy* the manuscript rather than let Caxton get it. The worst was that Matthew's spite was capable of anything and *Tom Twist had the roll.*

Bendy struggled to his feet. Somehow he must get to London. There were only two people to whom he dare tell this story: to his father or to Caxton.

But how was he to get there? It was three days' ride; he had no horse, no money, and his legs would never carry him. He supposed that he ought to try to get back to Stratford, but he shrank from it. The whole story would have to come out, and Heaven alone knew what the consequences might be. But first of all he must find food and shelter; if not he might die here out in the woods. Which way should he go? The sun was not yet noon-high, so he judged which must be south-east. As well start in the direction of London as any other way.

He moved very slowly, following the tracks of woodland creatures and helping himself from tree to tree. Then all at once he found a tiny path; it led downhill, and presently came out into a narrow bridle road, winding through the woods. A road must lead somewhere, and horses had passed along it recently. Could it be Dick, bringing help? Or even the outlaws again? But the world was beginning to spin round him. Outlaws or no outlaws he could go no farther. He dropped on to a grassy bank and lay still.

He did not know how long it was before he was roused by voices. He looked up terrified and saw two monks with two or three horses. The older one, in a white habit, leaned over him.

'He's coming round. Poor lad, he's had a powerful crack across the pate.'

'His belt is cut; he's been robbed,' said the younger, who wore a brown cloak.

''Tis those ruffians of Dunsmore again. Have you the flask, brother? Dip a sop in wine.'

Leaning against the old monk's knee, Bendy took one dripping morsel of bread and then another. It revived him, and when they questioned him he was able to say that he was a Londoner; he had been set on in the woods and had lain out all night.

'We must take him to Stoneleigh,' said the white monk. 'You are well-blessed, my son, that we came this way. I am the cellarer of Stoneleigh Abbey. We have been over to one of our granges for the weighing of the corn. Look to the horses, brother; we can put him on to a pack-saddle if you arrange the bags of grain.'

The bread and wine had put fresh life into him, but though he was safely propped among the bags of grain, the cellarer insisted that the young monk must walk beside him. So, in procession, they moved slowly along the bridle-path, out of the woods, and down into the peaceful valley.

Now that he could think again, Bendy was consumed with worry. First and foremost, had Dick really got away, and if so where was he? And how was he to answer when he was questioned? It would be easy to tell the whole story; but if he did, not only might there be trouble about the Justices and the manuscript, but Tom Twist and the outlaws would be hunted down, and the truth about Mucking Creek would come out before he could tell his father. Come what may, he must keep it dark until he reached London.

In the end he decided to say that he was one of two apprentices on an errand for their master. They were returning to London when they were attacked and robbed. The other boy escaped and was probably half-way home by now. If the monks would let him rest for a day he too would find some means of getting home. If they pressed him with more questions he could pretend that since the knock on the head he could remember nothing.

With so much thinking his head began to ache again in real earnest and by the time they reached the Abbey gate he was

The sop of wine revived him

truly unable to answer questions. The great doors were opened
to them and the guest master came, at the father cellarer's
summons, from the guest house adjoining the gateway. Bendy
was led, pack-horse and all, across a stretch of scythed grass,
past the cloisters and the Abbey church, to the infirmary,
where another white monk gently cut away his hair and
washed the wound in his head.

'It is not mortal,' he told the guest master as he bound it up with linen. 'Put him to bed with a hot posset to make him sleep; he should be better in the morning.'

At the guest house Bendy found himself not in a dormitory with the other travellers, but in a little cell all to himself, where besides a bed and a small coffer, there was a prayer desk and a carving of Christ on the Cross, to remind him how he had been preserved in all his perils.

The posset did its work. It was broad daylight when he woke. The guest master, plump and smiling, stood by his bed.

'No need to ask if you have slept, my son. You are better? That is well. Now try to tell me what befell you. How came you to be alone in those woods?'

It was what Bendy had dreaded. He answered as briefly as he dared and shook his head for the rest. The guest master did not press him. He went away and soon afterwards the infirmarian appeared and examined his head. He said that it was healing nicely and Bendy should get up.

But before he had put more than a toe out of bed, the guest master returned, bringing with him Bendy's friend the father cellarer, with a huge bunch of keys dangling from his girdle.

The two monks in their white habits stood on either side of the bed and questioned him, kindly enough, but with a quiet persistence. He stuck to his story about riding on his master's service with just one fellow apprentice; but it was impossible to avoid giving his master's name. He was almost aggrieved when he saw that *Master William Caxton* meant nothing to them. So when they inquired his master's trade he said quite indignantly that he was a mercer and one-time Governor of the English House at Bruges. To his dismay they obviously did not believe him. After all, was it likely that a mercer of that standing would entrust his business to a couple of apprentices? Without another word they left him, and as the door closed he heard the quest master say, "'Tis fishy. Clearly the boy knows more than he will tell.'

Bendy dragged himself out of bed. His head was throbbing and he was almost in despair. Would he after all have to tell everything?

He was only just dressed when two lay brothers, in brown habits, came to fetch him. He was, they said, to appear before the Abbot. They gave him time to wash himself at a stone trough and then conducted him, one on each side, across the

A cell at the guest house

sunlit grass to the main building of the monastery. Bendy's heart was thumping. He had a vision of standing up to be questioned in a great hall, and it was an enormous relief to find himself taken to the Abbot's parlour, a small room, very plain, but with some bright logs burning in the fireplace.

The Abbot of Stoneleigh, a thin, shrewd-faced man with scanty white hair, looked no different from any of his monks, except for the wooden cross hanging from his neck and the ring which Bendy remembered to kiss. There was a second monk sitting by the fire; out of the corner of his eye Bendy caught a glimpse of a black habit, not a white one.

The Abbot inquired courteously if Bendy had slept in comfort, as if he were some important guest. 'We are troubled about you, my son,' he said. 'The good fathers who questioned you feel that you are concealing something. Now, it is no part of our hospitality to pry into your business; but you are young, you have been struck down, and we must do our best for you. What are you hiding? The wilds of Dunsmore give shelter to gangs of outlaws who pester the countryside. To know what happened to you might help to lay them by the heels.' He paused and looked at Bendy searchingly. 'Why do you not speak? Are you in some trouble? Do you fear their vengeance? Or is it that you are, though maybe quite innocent, one of their number yourself? Be not afraid, my son; we will protect you.'

Bendy bit his lip. The Abbot's gentleness shook him. But as he hesitated the Abbot changed his tone. He began sternly to rap out questions. Where did he live? Who was his father? Where did he get his schooling? *Paul's?* He put a quick poser or two, and as Bendy gave the correct answers he tried another line.

'You say your master is a mercer. What is his name?'

'His name is William Caxton.'

'Caxton? The printer?' As Bendy nodded, the next shot came like a bolt from a crossbow. 'Then on what errand did Caxton send you here?'

All at once Bendy saw daylight. Why hadn't he thought of it before? 'We were sent to the Canons at Warwick. They want printed service books.'

The Abbot was taken aback. Suddenly a voice from near the fire said quietly, 'That is true, Father Abbot. *I* passed the word to Caxton.'

Bendy swung round open-mouthed. The monk in the black habit also wore a cross. He recognized him in a flash. It was the monk he had seen with Caxton; the Lord Abbot of Westminster.

It was easy now; everything had changed. His answers were accepted at once and, to his great relief, nobody questioned why he had kept it all so dark. After a few minutes' talk about the new service books, and Caxton, and the art of printing, the white abbot turned to him with a smile.

'Well, my son, your patron saint, St Benedict, has looked after you to some purpose, even sending a Benedictine Abbot to speak for you. If the Benedictines of Coventry had not suffered a case of small-pox the Lord Abbot of Westminster would have lodged there instead of here. Now even your way home is made easy, if of his goodness he will let you be of his party.'

The Abbot of Westminster laughed. 'You make it sound as though St Benedict enticed the small-pox so that this young man might profit by it. As for travelling with us, that goes without saying. With your leave we will ride early tomorrow morning.'

Bendy was lost in wonder. Everything had fitted so neatly for him, just like the links in a chain, starting with the chance that brought the father cellarer riding through that particular wood at that particular moment. It could not be chance, of course; it was a little private miracle, a set of links made specially for him. He needed no urging to make him offer his thanks to God, to St Benedict, to his own guardian angel, and anyone else who might have had a hand in the matter.

He was still marvelling the next morning when he found

Links in a chain

himself on a baggage horse beside a young lay brother from Westminster on another baggage horse, with the Lord Abbot and two of his monks riding ahead of them. The first night they lodged with the black canons at Wroxton Abbey, the second at the great Benedictine Abbey of Abingdon, and for the third, which was Saturday, they reached Hurley Priory, on the banks of the Thames, not far from Henley, where Bendy had lain in an agony of stiffness on that first night of the journey. Hurley Priory was a cell of Westminster itself, the Abbey's daughter house, where the Lord Abbot was received as father. They were to rest there over the Sunday while the Abbot held a Chapter and received his tenants from the Priory lands.

Bendy was thankful for the delay. As the time drew near when he would have to tell his story he dreaded it more and more. Where would it lead? What would happen to Tom Twist and the outlaws? – to Matthew and Cornelius? – to *Peterkin*? He was really tempted to hold his tongue. But there was the manuscript; Nicholas Malory had trusted him with it; it was his *quest*. Whatever happened Matthew must not be allowed to destroy it.

The Lord Abbot's house at Westminster

CHAPTER 18

Challenge to the Crowing Cock

THEY reached the Lord Abbot's house at Westminster at about vespers time, and after offering his thanks and getting a blessing in return, Bendy crossed the Close towards the Almonry. It seemed more like two years than just a fortnight since he and Dick had ridden away.

He had taken off his bandage and covered his scars only with his cap; but his head still ached and his knees felt like jelly. He paused in the opening of the postern, just as he had done the day he came to live there. Ahead of him lay the Almonry passage with the familiar printing loft over the gate.

Then, weary as he was, he laughed aloud. Outside the house stood Elizabeth, her distaff under her arm, idly swinging her spindle. She must have heard him for she looked round. Her eyes grew big; but instead of coming to meet him she darted indoors and he heard her shrill voice crying, 'He's here; he's here. He's not dead; he's *here*.'

Bendy followed her. The house seemed dark and full of people. He saw Caxton's face, and Mistress Caxton's, and Wynken's, and Dick's – yes, *Dick*. He stumbled forward and suddenly found himself in his father's arms.

The evening and the night vanished in a dream. He woke early in the morning to the sound of bells. He had been roused by bells day after day: Stoneleigh, Wroxton, Abingdon, Hurley. But these bells were familiar. Slowly it dawned on him that he was back in Westminster.

He opened his eyes and found himself in a strange bed with curtains drawn round it. All at once it came back to him. He had been put into the guest chamber to share his father's bed.

Beside him his father was still asleep. Thankful for time to think, Bendy lay still, recalling bit by bit all that they had told him last night.

Dick, apparently, had arrived only two days before, bringing the news that Bendy was lost. He had made his way back to Stratford and fetched the Cloptons to search the woods of Dunsmore, but though they found an empty ruin and a tattered blood-stained cloak, there was nothing to show that Bendy had been there. When Bendy told his own story, how he had been rescued by the monks of Stoneleigh, and brought home by the Abbot of Westminster, his father, eased from worry, was almost angry. Why, in Heaven's name, had Bendy not sent word to Stratford? Had he no thought for anyone but himself? But Mistress Caxton, her stiff leg propped on cushions, would allow no upbraiding.

'Look at the boy's head. How could he possibly think when his skull was all but broken. He should be in bed. Master Goodrich, by your leave he must go in the guest-chamber with you and I will send up something to make him sleep.'

As he lay staring at the daylight through the chink in the bed curtain, two thoughts separated themselves and stood out clearly. First, no one had so much as mentioned Malory's manuscript. Did they realize that it was gone? Secondly, he must speak to his father alone, and what time could be better than now?

Without waiting for his courage to ebb, he sat up so suddenly that the bed-ropes groaned. John Goodrich opened his eyes.

'Awake already, Bendy? Have you slept your pains away?'

Bendy leaned over him. 'Sir, there is much to tell you. Will you hear me now?'

His father sat up at once, and drew his bed gown round his shoulders. 'I am all ears,' he said. 'Go slowly, that I may miss nothing.'

It was hard to know where to begin. Bendy decided that Newbold Revel was the best point, and he described vividly how Master Vincent refused to let them have the roll, and how Nicholas Malory rode after them. Gradually it became easier. His father listened so keenly that he spared nothing; how he had been knocked senseless and cast upon the mouldy straw; how the outlaws had arrived and lighted their fire and talked. At the mention of Tom Twist his father cried, 'Nonsense; you must have dreamed it.' But from then on he was silent, so silent that Bendy needed all his courage to go on at all. Mucking Creek; the *Madalena*; the hired barn full of paper; the money for the Red Rose; the Malory stories and the order to Tom Twist to seize the manuscript at any cost lest it should reach Caxton; he kept nothing back. When he had finished he clutched his hands together under the bed-clothes, not daring to look round.

Suddenly John Goodrich cried aloud, 'Before God, it can't be true!' He rounded on Bendy, pouring out question after question with hardly a pause. He went right back to the beginning, to the first time that Bendy had heard of Mucking Creek, the day that Caxton first came to the Crowing Cock. Everything came out, including the dicing at the alehouse, and even the merest details that Bendy had almost forgotten. It was as though his father were piecing it all together for himself.

At the end he looked at Bendy, his face ashen white, but his eyes blazing. 'You young *fool*!' he cried. 'You suspected all this, and yet you kept it from me. If you had told me I could have nipped it in the bud.'

'Sir, I dared not. You would not have believed me.'

John Goodrich went suddenly quiet. 'True. I should not have believed you. And so it has reached this pass, and the infamy of it all will kill me, I think.'

Bendy could hear the pounding of his own heart. Another knocking merged with it. The door opened and Caxton's voice said, outside the bed-curtains. 'We heard talking and knew you were awake. My wife asks how you both fare this morning?' As no one answered he peeped through the curtains and saw John Goodrich's face. 'Are you ill, sir?' he exclaimed.

'Not ill, but sick at heart,' said the old man brokenly. 'I would rather have been dead than hear the story I have just heard. Would to God that I could disbelieve it, but, alas! it groans with truth. If you can spare the time I would be thankful to tell you at once. My conscience will not rest until you know it.'

Caxton drew the curtains back. 'My friend, if it eases you tell me,' he said gently. 'Otherwise hold your peace. I am prepared to trust your conscience even if you are not.'

John Goodrich sighed. 'Sit down, sir. The boy shall tell you, just as he has told me.'

Bendy's heart sank. Must he go through it all again? But it was easier this time. As soon as the story reached the point of the meeting of the outlaws, his father took it up. Unable to lie still, the old man struggled from the bed, and with his bed-gown wrapped round him, paced up and down the room, pouring it all out. Bendy watched, the sheet pulled up to his chin, with the sensation that he was in the midst of a storm too big for him.

At last his father came to an end and sat down exhausted.

Caxton turned to Bendy. 'Put on your clothes and fetch wine,' he whispered urgently.

Bendy obeyed. When he came back, having dealt as best he could with Mistress Caxton's inquiries, the two men were talking quietly.

'If you are so determined we will *all* go to the Crowing Cock,' Caxton was saying; though believe me, sir, I would spare you if you would allow it. I admit that the thought of getting the load of Unicorn fills me with content, and of course, there is also the Malory manuscript. I would not willingly forego that. After all, it nearly cost this boy his life.'

The journey by wherry was a gloomy one. John Goodrich sat stern and silent, and Bendy was equally miserable. It was all very well to talk about getting the Malory manuscript; but it seemed as if they had failed to grasp that Matthew threatened to destroy it. Surely by taking Caxton to the Crowing Cock they were putting it into the deadliest peril.

Caxton tried to cheer them up by chatting to Bendy about things that had happened while he was away. The *Chronicle of England* was finished and Wynken was setting up the type for the *Polychronicon* – a book of natural history, penned by a monk of Chester more than a hundred years ago, to which Caxton himself had written a new chapter to bring it up to date. More exciting news was that the shipmaster, John Stern, had actually arrived with a load of paper – welcome enough, though Wynken grumbled that it was only *Lilies of France*, poor stuff compared with the Unicorn that Peterkin brought.

At the mention of Peterkin, Bendy looked up and caught

Caxton's eye upon him. Clearly they were thinking the same thought.

'Your friend Peterkin has been in my mind,' Caxton said. 'He has served us well and we cannot leave him to be ensnared by these rogues. What say you to bringing him to Westminster? I could arrange for him to be apprentice at the horse ferry, and doubtless Mistress Caxton would find a refuge for his

Lilies of France

grandmother where he could visit her – with the nuns at Kilburn, for instance.'

Bendy's eyes lit up. Caxton thought of everything! His master watched his face.

'You think well of the scheme, eh? Then take time by the forelock. See him, or his grand-dam, when we are in Paternoster Row. Bid them come to the Almonry at once. The sooner the safer; that is my advice.'

With a beating heart Bendy followed the two men up the hill. Everything hung on what might happen in the next half hour. As they rounded the corner from Ave Maria Lane, his eye flew first to the bead-maker's shop. If only Peterkin's grandmother were in her usual place and he could speak to her. But even from this distance he could see that the doorway was empty. At the same instant Caxton stretched out a hand and halted them.

'Look ahead!' he said softly.

Bendy held his breath. Emerging from the yard of the Crowing Cock was Tom Twist with his white horse. Would he turn and see them? But he did not even look round. He gave the old horse a slap across the rump and trudged off in the direction of Cheap.

Caxton glanced at Bendy. 'That, I take it, was your friend the pedlar,' he observed. 'Maybe we have come in the very nick of time.'

The shutters of the Crowing Cock were open, but the workshop appeared to be empty. To Bendy's surprise his father knocked at the door. A new boy came, whom Bendy had not seen before, and John Goodrich told him to call his master. In a few seconds Matthew appeared, obviously surprised to see his father. He glanced at Caxton and stiffened, but he said no word, and Bendy, watching like a hawk, remembered that he and Caxton had never actually met face to face.

'I have grave matters to discuss with you,' said his father with his old air of authority. 'By your leave we will go up to the parlour. Summon Cornelius. What I have to say cannot be said without him.'

Matthew frowned, his eyes shifting distrustfully. But he stood back while his father led the way upstairs. Waiting his turn at the bottom, Bendy glanced through to the kitchen and caught a glimpse of a pot simmering over a bright fire; he was instantly reminded of that afternoon when he had come in wet and old Mother Collin had been stirring the broth – the afternoon when he first heard of the *Madalena*.

They found Cornelius already upstairs, working at his writing table. John Goodrich waited until they were all there. Then he turned deliberately to Caxton and said with a cold formality, 'Sir, I ask leave to present to you my two elder sons, the Masters Matthew and Cornelius Goodrich. My sons, I beg you to pay your respects to the most worshipful Master William Caxton, late Governor of the English House at Bruges.'

Cornelius, very white, sheepishly made a little bow, but Matthew stood rigid, looking only at his father.

'Sir,' he said, 'my duty is yours to command. But your guest and I have naught in common. I pray you hold me excused.'

He turned away, but before he could take a step Caxton said

A pot simmering over a bright fire

quietly, 'You are mistaken, sir; we have much in common; as, for example, the roll of manuscript from Newbold Revel writ by Sir Thomas Malory.'

Taken aback by the swiftness of the challenge, Matthew hesitated. 'I – I know not what you mean.'

'Then I beg you give it thought. Your messenger *stole* the manuscript from mine last week in Warwickshire, and, if I

233

mistake not, he has delivered it to you but a few minutes since.'

It was a shot in the dark, but it hit the mark. Cornelius, behind them, gasped audibly. Matthew glanced round at him and jerked his head. Bendy saw it. Was it a signal? He remembered the bright fire and swiftly planted himself at the top of the stairs. If they wanted to burn the roll they would have to fight their way past him.

Matthew steadied himself. He addressed Caxton. 'Sir, all that is no concern of mine. If I send my man on a mission and he succeeds where yours fails, that is no matter for dispute.'

'Then your man *did* succeed. Maybe you are unaware that he was refused at Newbold Revel. He got the roll by a savage attack upon my messenger, who had been entrusted with it by Malory's heir. He had your orders to keep it out of my hands at any cost; he said so; and the cost I'd have you know is within an ace of murder.'

Matthew looked startled. His eye roved quickly from one to the other of them. Then he recovered himself.

'This is but hollow talk. Since you insist, I admit that I sent my man to fetch the book. But I have as good a right as you; there is no more to say.'

His father could hold himself no longer. 'Your *man*!' he roared. 'Tom Twist your man! A rascally pedlar, a cut-purse, a traitor. Drop that mask, you fool. We know everything – the paper, Mucking Creek, and all the rest of the vile story. All I dare hope now is to save you from the gallows.'

'The gallows? Great heavens, did the fellow die after all?'

John Goodrich gave a grim laugh. 'The fellow? No, he did not die. You are at least spared the guilt of Cain. Did you not know that it was your brother who was set upon by your orders? Boy, take off your cap.'

With sinking heart Bendy obeyed.

Cornelius breathed, 'Holy Saints!' But Matthew's face

showed no emotion. He stared at the scars on Bendy's head, then turned back to Caxton, his lip curling.

'I commend you, sir, that you should use my brother to bait your trap. I had heard that he was to ride with you, but I little guessed for what purpose he would be used.'

'Insolence will not help you,' rapped his father. 'You are floundering in deep water and you know it. I warn you that everything has come out. Tom Twist has given you away. You'll likely be hanged for treason.'

'*Treason?* How treason?'

'Because you are caught deep in the toils of the Red Rose, you fool. Mucking Creek is a hot-bed and the roots spread all over England. Your dirty dealings have sunk you up to the neck.'

Matthew's face was white. 'I have no notion what you are talking of. What has Tom Twist said?'

'He told all your story to beguile a gang of outlaws after they had bound your brother and left him for dead. You had best have it from him. Bendy, come here.'

With his shaking hands knotted behind him, Bendy stood by his father's side and told his story yet once again. It was easier this time, for both his father and Caxton helped him to make everything clear. He was allowed to omit nothing, beginning from the point where Caxton had been obliged to stay at home and had charged him with the business of the manuscript, right down to the story that Twist had told in the ruined house.

'Moonshine!' snapped Matthew hoarsely as Bendy stopped. 'The boy fell on his head and lost his wits.'

'That will be for the Justices to decide,' said his father coldly. 'The King's Customs may turn a blind eye on piracy, but, never fear, the name of Henry Tudor will send them hot-foot to Mucking. Before Heaven, I know not which I would rather, that you were hanged for treason or dishonoured before

the world with this dunghill conspiracy, this scurvy con-
temptible trafficking in paper.'

'We had no thought of treason,' cried Cornelius shakily.
'How could we know about Lancastrian plottings?'

'Your money has gone to serve it. You'll be hard put to
make anyone believe that you paid out your gold to keep
paper mouldering in a shed. God be praised, spite carried to
such lengths is not common among grown men.'

'What I should like to know,' said Caxton in his quiet
voice, 'is why these good masters should have put themselves
to so many pains to do me injury? It must have cost much
thought as well as money. 'Pon my word, 'tis almost sad that
it should have been in vain.'

Matthew turned on him. 'In vain?'

'In spite of it the paper reached me – enough at any rate to
keep the press fed. Did you not grasp that, sir, from Bendy's
story? Twist sold it a second time from your store in the barn.
He had taken your money for it but that did not hinder him.
He sold it knowingly to a waterman, who purveyed it to me.'

Matthew's eyes blazed. ''Tis a lie. Bendy invented it.'

'I assure you he did not. I have had the paper – Unicorn
from the *Madalena*. Twist thought himself clever to have
tricked you. What did he say, Bendy – "the best joke of all"?'

Bendy screwed himself up again. Though he remembered it
clearly enough he realized that he must keep Peterkin out of it,
so he repeated only that 'a waterman begged it for a customer' and then continued word for word until he got to 'the
Red Rose needs the money'.

His father broke in again. 'You see! You have been duped
by this fellow to your own utter ruin.'

Matthew fixed his eye on Bendy. 'If you are lying, boy, you
shall ache for it. What waterman did he sell it to? Tell me his
name.'

Caxton answered for him. 'A swarthy fellow; Black Jack

they call him. He's dumb; his tongue is cut out. No use to question him.'

For a moment everyone was silent. There was no sound except for Matthew growling under his breath. Then suddenly Cornelius cried out, his voice shrill and panic-stricken, 'In God's name, brother, must we be *hanged* for this double-dealing knave?'

Matthew ignored him. He stood staring at Caxton as though thinking intently. His eyes were narrowed and his mouth hard set. He spoke at last. 'You have had *all* the paper?'

'The whole load of Unicorn? Indeed not; the greater part must still be there unless he has sold it in other quarters.'

'Then you will have it. Before Heaven that scoundrel shall not profit from it more.'

Caxton smiled gently. 'That is wise of you, sir. If the barn is empty you may escape notice at Mucking Creek.'

'How will you make him part with it?' quavered Cornelius. 'We dare not anger him, brother.'

'Of course he will part with it. I will see him –'

Caxton interrupted. 'Is that wise? Surely the less dealings you have with him the better. If it is a matter of moving the paper, I know a shipmaster familiar with Mucking Creek. He is hand in glove with everyone on the river; there are no secrets hid from him. Suppose that I sent *him* to fetch the paper and bring it to Westminster. Then you would not be implicated at all.'

Matthew hesitated. 'He would take it to Westminster? Without questions?'

'Of course he would have a written order from you; but given that I warrant that he would fetch it safely – and with no questions.'

There was another long pause. Then Matthew turned to Cornelius. 'Brother, a pen and paper.'

Scarcely able to believe his eyes, Bendy watched while Matthew sat down at the desk, pen in hand. He was now positively eager to get rid of the load of Unicorn. The way that Caxton had worked everything round seemed little short of a miracle. Bendy looked at him, as he stood gravely watching without a sign of triumph on his face. Small wonder that the King had made use of him for state matters.

Then suddenly Bendy remembered Malory. In the excitement he had actually forgotten. Stricken with guilt he moved a step nearer to Caxton. Had Caxton forgotten too? Matthew had been defeated about Mucking Creek, so it was more likely than ever that he would revenge himself by destroying the manuscript.

But the moment that Matthew's quill squeaked over the flourish of his signature, Caxton said quietly, 'I thank you, sir; I will hand this order to John Stern at once. Now there is only one matter which might imperil you.'

Matthew scowled again. 'Imperil? What matter?'

'The matter of the manuscript. If Malory's family call in the Justices it will be traced to Tom Twist, and he, without doubt, will set the blame on you. It would draw attention to all your dealings with Tom Twist. Remember that the roll was entrusted to *me*. Only when it is safely in my hands will you be free from the danger of questioning.'

Matthew sprang up, as if he were about to snatch the order back. But he thought better of it.

'A plague on you,' he cried. 'I'm sick of the whole business. Cornelius, in Heaven's name give him the manuscript.'

Bendy's heart thumped as Cornelius fumbled among the papers on the table. From them he produced a roll tied tightly with ribbon, just as the roll had been when Bendy received it from Nicholas Malory. Caxton accepted it gravely. Then with the shadow of a smile he passed it to Bendy.

'Have a look at it, boy. See that it is the right one.'

With shaking fingers Bendy untied the ribbon. He had

never examined it before, but he was not going to say so. The edges of the paper were bruised and dirty, but the tiny writing was black and clear. He read the first lines aloud: "'*It befell in the days of Uther Pendragon when he was King of all England and so reigned —*'"

'That is well,' said Caxton calmly. 'Do it up and give it to me. *I* will carry it this time.'

Once more there was silence. Nobody moved.

At last John Goodrich let out a long sigh. 'My son, I am weary,' he said. 'Will you not offer us a sup of wine?'

The winecups were filled

For the second time that day Bendy found himself despatched to fetch winecups. Downstairs in the kitchen everything was fresh with new whitewash and instead of the goodwife Collin, Humphrey's mother hovered nervously by the fire. It was plain that she was aware of trouble in the parlour, for she welcomed Bendy's message with obvious relief. Wine must mean the end of quarrelling. As she gave the cups a swift polish and set them on a tray, Bendy swallowed his pride and asked after Humphrey. To his surprise she told him that Humphrey was now working for a notary in the neighbourhood of

Gray's Inn; she added discreetly that a boy was better apprenticed outside his own family. The loft was empty, she said; it was much improved. Perhaps he would like to go up and look at it.

That suited Bendy perfectly. Now that everything was safely settled the only remaining problem was Peterkin. When the winecups had been filled and passed round, he slipped away and climbed the familiar ladder.

One glance at the loft was enough for him. The old sheepskin on the bed was replaced by a patchwork cover. The stacks of paper were hidden by brightly striped hangings. His coffer was still in its old place. He lifted the lid and found it full of neatly folded linen. Everything was spick and span but cold and strange. Disgusted, he turned his back and went to the window.

Peterkin's lattice shutter was closed. He whistled, then waited, almost holding his breath. To his delight he heard a scuffle opposite. Someone fumbled with the shutter and Peterkin himself appeared, his head tousled and his eyes heavy, as if he had just woken from sleep. At the sight of Bendy his whole face lit up.

'Holy smoke! What are you doing here?'

Caxton's Colophon

Bendy almost fell out in his excitement. 'There's lots to tell. Peterkin, you're to come to Westminster.'

'To Westminster? What for? Paper?'

'Nay; to *live*. Caxton's going to apprentice you to the horse-ferry. You're to bring your grand-dam too.'

'To *live*?' Peterkin's eyes were nearly popping out of his head. 'Why, what in Heaven's name has happened?'

'It's too long to tell you now. Things have been going fast. But Caxton said you were to come at once. He said "the sooner the safer", those were his words.'

Peterkin whistled. 'So that's the way of it. You're sure it's for my gammer too?'

'Yes; both of you. And make haste!'

Peterkin grinned and grabbed at the shutter.

'We'll be there before you,' he said.

Postscript

THIS last chapter is not part of the story. It is just a postscript which you can read or not as you like. But I think you may enjoy knowing what is true in the book you have just finished, and what is made up.

Writing a book of this sort is rather like a detective story in reverse. There are clues all the way through it; but they are not put there by the author to help the reader to unravel the plot. The clues in this sort of book are bits of history, and facts about people and about places that really existed. It is the author's job to find them all out, and then to knit them together so that a story comes to life.

When I decided to write about Caxton and the difficulties he must have encountered when he began to print in England, and in particular about his printing of Malory's *Morte d'Arthur*, the clues piled in so thickly that I could hardly pick my way. But if you care to read these next few pages I will try to tell you about it.

Let me start by admitting that the family of scriveners at the Crowing Cock is entirely imaginary; so is Tom Twist, and Peterkin, and Humphrey, and all Bendy's little circle in his life at Paternoster Row. But they *could* have lived very much as they live in the story, for Paternoster Row was the centre of the trades connected with books, and remained so until it was destroyed by bombs in 1941. John Goodrich could have been one of the scribes licensed by the Dean and Chapter; and Bendy could have gone to Paul's School, which was at that time a Choir and Grammar School for boys connected with the Cathedral, though it had not yet been re-formed by

Dean Colet into the school which we know as 'St Paul's' today.

But when we come to Caxton I have kept as closely as possible to all that is known about him. He was brought up as a mercer and became Governor of the Domus Anglorum at Bruges, carried out several diplomatic missions, retired and took up printing at Westminster, just as he himself describes it to Bendy and his father. Whenever I could do so I have put into his mouth his own views in almost his own words, especially on his favourite topic of the decline in the knightly virtues. As he himself tells you, he wrote prologues and epilogues for most of the books that he printed. These make excellent reading, for they are vivid and full of his outbreaks of horror about the new world that was fast replacing the world of chivalry of his youth. To restore the old noble ideals was the object of almost every book that he printed. I wish I could have included more, for he shows himself a warm, wise, and witty person who deserves to be remembered as something more than 'the first English printer'. For his family background, about which nothing is certain, I have used what seems to be the most likely version. I am afraid that I have made Elizabeth a pert little miss; but that is what she may well have been, for an Elizabeth Caxton of Westminster (presumably his daughter) was in trouble with her husband before she was twenty years old.

At this point I want to say how much I owe to the very great kindness of the Keeper of Muniments and Archives at Westminster Abbey, Mr Lawrence Tanner, M.V.O. This busy and distinguished scholar actually found time to take me round the Abbey and show me the place where the first workshop stood, outside the Chapter House, and the probable site of the Red Pale itself, where No. 1 Victoria Street now stands. To crown this he went so far as to put into my hands the printed proofs of his own recent researches before they had even been published, a generosity which it would be hard to cap. On these solid foundations I have built up a story which is *only* a story, but I hope may not be too much 'fiction'.

The main plot is about Caxton's paper. In actual fact he used many different papers, among them those with the water-mark of a Unicorn and of a Hand and Flower, which I have illustrated from the originals. There is no reason to believe that Unicorn was his favourite paper, nor that there was any plot to prevent it reaching him. But there seems little doubt that he met with considerable opposition from scriveners and others whose trade was endangered by the printing press. All paper was imported (though Jack Tate succeeded in producing some excellent paper at his paper mill at Hertford, which was used by Wynken de Worde after Caxton's death); and the piracy and smuggling and the corruption among the Customs men were very much as Robert Tate and shipmaster John Stern described them. (It was in this very year, 1482, when Tate was Sheriff, that Edward IV introduced his *wafters* and *conveyors* to try to mend matters.) Mucking, truly the first creek outside the boundary of the London Customs area, was a likely enough place for smugglers. Of course there is no historical record of any conspiracies with Henry Tudor being carried out through pirates and smugglers. But common sense suggests that there must have been an 'underground movement'. It is unlikely that only three years later Henry Tudor would have landed suddenly and won so decisive a victory at the Battle of Bosworth without plenty of quiet preparation.

When it came to Malory my detective work became really exciting. Like Bendy I started knowing nothing about him except his plea for prayers at the end of his book. The reference books give only the bare outline of the rather wild life of Thomas Malory of Newbold Revel in Warwickshire, who spent many years in Newgate and died a prisoner. But he came to life for me just in the same way as he did for Bendy, and it seemed impossible to believe that the man who wrote as he did of chivalry and the Holy Grail could have been a mere rogue and jail-bird.

Then came the discovery that Malory was buried at Greyfriars, which had not been mentioned by any of the reference books which I had so far consulted. I did not find the grave, as Bendy did, because Greyfriars Church was destroyed by Henry VIII and all the gravestones sold. But I chanced to notice the record of it in the pages of John Stow, who, nearly four hundred years ago, wrote about 'old' London. The next clue was pure coincidence. At the church at Stoke D'Abernon in Surrey (which contains the oldest brass in England) there hangs a family tree of the Vincent family. There again the name Malory jumped out at me, for it shows a marriage between Master Vincent of Stoke D'Abernon and Barnake, near Newbold Revel in Warwickshire, and the sister of Sir Thomas Malory.

From that point coincidences and clues knitted themselves together so tightly that the story took shape almost by itself. Bendy would have to go to Warwickshire. But where could he stay? Who was there, connected with Caxton, who had foothold in Warwickshire? John Stow again provided the answer. Hugh Clopton, a London mercer from Stratford-upon-Avon, lived in the very house in old Jewry where Caxton had been apprenticed. So I, like Bendy, went to Stratford and found plenty of interest; for not only did Clopton build the long stone bridge of fourteen arches and rebuild the lovely Guild Chapel, which both stand to this day, but he also built a great house (alas! no longer standing) which, a century later, became the home of – can you guess? – Yes, of Shakespeare.

From Stratford to Newbold Revel I went through Warwick (a *Legenda*, with Caxton's printer's mark upon it, really *has* been found at St Mary's, Warwick); and in the Beauchamp

Chapel, by the tomb of Richard Beauchamp, Earl of Warwick, I found the answer to the Malory problem, just as Bendy did. This noble knight was Malory's liege lord. Malory followed him in the French wars. When Beauchamp died Malory ran wild. But years later, when he lay in Newgate Jail, it came to him to make amends by writing of King Arthur and his Knights, stories which glow with the virtues of nobleness and chivalry. The rest was ready to hand. Dunsmore heath, a wild region well-fitted for outlaws; Stoneleigh, where only the gatehouse and the guesthouse remain of the original abbey; and Newbold Revel itself, long rebuilt and now a training college for teachers. At the time of Bendy's journey Nicholas Malory would doubtless have been living there, probably with his great uncle Vincent, of Barnake only about five miles away, to keep an eye on him.

These are only the main clues which were knitted into the story. There are so many more that you would get bored if I were to make a list of them. Any of you who have read *Ring Out Bow Bells* will recognize many of the places and of course spot the reference to Dick Whittington, who was mayor when Caxton's *master* was an apprentice. You may also recognize John Stern, the Good Pirate, as Nicholas Fetterlock's uncle in *The Woolpack* (although he, of course, is an imaginary character). I have described old St Paul's, with its tall spire, as fully as I can because it was destroyed in the Great Fire of 1666 and so you can never see it. But I have said less about Westminster Abbey. You can go there for yourselves and I hope as many as possible of you will do so, for you can never come to the end of its beauty and its interest. If you go, try to picture Westminster as it was in Caxton's day. That is difficult because the building of Victoria Street and Westminster Bridge (a *real* bridge this time!) seems to have twisted everything round. But Tothill Street is still there, facing the great west door; Westminster Hall stands as firmly as ever; and there is a street called Long Ditch. The streams and ditches which made West-minster into an island presumably still exist but they have all gone under ground. The Almonry has vanished completely, but if you go and stand just inside Dean's Yard you can dis-tinctly see a gap between the backs of the houses in Great Smith Street, which is, likely enough, the last trace of the Almonry passage.

There are one or two points about Malory's book which I should like to make clear. The first is that though Bendy's adventure took place (if it *did* take place!) in 1482, Caxton did not print the book which he called *Morte d'Arthur* until 1485. He did a great deal of editing. We know this, not only because he tells us so in his epilogue, but also because another copy of Malory's stories has recently been found in the library at Win-chester College. This Winchester Malory is hand-written, in other words a scrivener's copy, and it differs from Caxton's in a great many places. Now I have confessed to you that I *in-vented* this story about the scriveners of the Crowing Cock, so obviously I cannot possibly suggest that Matthew or Cornelius did after all produce the King Arthur manuscript. But there is nothing to prevent *you* from using your imagination about it as much as you like!

The other small point is about Malory's name. I have used the spelling *Malory* throughout the book, which Caxton used, to avoid confusion. But it was sometimes spelt as *Malorye*, or *Malorie*, while he himself wrote *Maleore* and on his tomb it was inscribed as *Mallare*.

Now let me tell you a little bit about some of the pictures. I have drawn many places which still exist and which you can go and see, such as Clopton's bridge and the Guild Chapel, both at Stratford-upon-Avon, the gatehouse at Stoneleigh and, of course, Westminster Abbey. A plate has recently been put up outside the south door of Westminster Abbey church to say that Caxton's first workshop stood near by. Mr Tanner makes it clear that this workshop must have been alongside the Chapter House. Therefore, in the picture on page 148 drawn on the spot a few weeks ago, I have been bold enough to put in, from imagination, a little house built round one of the great buttresses. Of course this is not supposed to be a *likeness* of Caxton's house, but we do know that little buildings of this sort were in use many years ago. If you will turn to another picture (on page 97 this time) you will see how houses were often tucked into every nook and corner of a great church, actually relying on the buttresses for support. This second drawing (page 97) is copied from a photograph of Rouen in France which means that the houses must have been there until

The water mark of Tate's paper

quite recently. Indeed, for all I know they may be there still. I have not been to Rouen but I have actually seen similar ones leaning up against other old French churches.

To turn from Westminster to old St Paul's, nobody seems to have made detailed pictures of it in the days of its glory, so we have to rely on a very few later sketches and drawings. But there are so many facts known about it that clever architects and writers have made it possible for us to imagine it in as much detail as if pictures actually existed. In drawing it I have kept closely to these records and I hope you will get some feeling of its magnificence.

There are one or two drawings, such as Paul's Wharf (page 59) and Ludgate Hill (page 129), which I have 'reconstructed' from the records of John Stow and others (it is Stow who mentions the *pikes* on the bridge, presumably there to stop people from falling into the Fleet River); but the only historical place which is drawn *wholly* from imagination is Newbold Revel. The house has been rebuilt so many times (it is now a fine Georgian mansion) that I felt free to picture Malory's home just as I fancied.

If I had to choose from the whole book one place which I should like you to visit (after Westminster Abbey, of course) it would be the Beauchamp Chapel at Warwick. In the drawing on page 189 I have shown only the figure of Richard Beauchamp, Earl of Warwick, so that you may notice, as Bendy did, how his head and his hands are raised in wonder at the glories that he saw. But I want you to realize that this figure is only a part of the splendid carved tomb which is in its turn only a part of the supremely beautiful chapel. If you ever get the chance, go and look at it. Then you will understand, as Bendy understood, how this noble knight, 'the flower of chivalry', who was Sir Thomas Malory's liege lord, may well have inspired the book of King Arthur and his Knights of the Round Table.

By the way, did you know that you can still go to St Giles's Fair at Oxford on September 1st?

Also by Cynthia Harnett

THE WOOL-PACK

'About the medieval wool trade in Cotswold, it is the best children's book I have seen for years. Beautifully illustrated (by the author) it holds you in suspense all the time. Unreservedly recommended' – *Western Daily Press*

THE GREAT HOUSE

An absorbing story of life as it was in the late seventeenth century. An ancient house has sinister occupants, and Geoffrey is in disgrace for trying to persuade his architect father to save it and build the new house elsewhere.

Some other Puffins

GOLDEN PENNIES
Graeme Farmer

A gripping adventure story set in Australia in 1851. Jack and Lucy go with their parents to Ballarat, where gold has just been discovered, and their story tells of the troubles that surround the whole family. Then things start to improve when Lucy finds three nuggets.

THE BOY WITH THE BRONZE AXE
Kathleen Fidler

An imaginative reconstruction of the way the Bronze Age probably spread to outlying Stone Age settlements.

UNDERGROUND TO CANADA
Barbara C. Smucker

Based on the true history of the Underground Railroad, this story tells of two negro slave girls who make the perilous journey north to freedom in Canada.

BONNIE DUNDEE
Rosemary Sutcliff

The exciting and romantic story of John Claverhouse, Viscount of Dundee, seen through the eyes of his devoted follower, Hugh Herriott.

THE BRONZE BOW
Elizabeth George Speare

Daniel, a Jewish boy, is obsessed by hatred of the Roman invaders who crucified his father, until he hears a preacher named Jesus and begins to wonder whether violence is the right answer. A Newbery Medal winner.

CHILDREN OF THE OREGON TRAIL
A. Rutgers van der Loeff

Stirring adventures of pioneering families heading westwards in their covered wagons.

CUE FOR TREASON
Geoffrey Trease

Peter Browning runs away from home and joins a band of strolling players. He becomes involved with Robert Cecil's secret service and a plot to kill Queen Elizabeth.

SUMMER OF THE ZEPPELIN
Elsie McCutcheon

It's the First World War and, while her father is fighting in France, Elvira lives with her stepmother Rhoda. But she runs away to an abandoned house, where she meets Bill, a German POW.